Outlaws of the Wild West

Pistols at dawn, seduction at sunset!

Meet Hunter Jameson, Castillo Jameson
and Zane Pierce. These notorious outlaws
make men quake in their shoes and
set women's hearts aflutter wherever
their cowboy boots take them!

They pride themselves on their skill in the
saddle and their prowess in the bedroom, but
now these outlaws will be facing their greatest
battle yet as they meet the only women with
the power to tame their wild ways!

First read Hunter's story in

The Innocent and the Outlaw

And look for Cas and Zane's stories,
coming soon!

Author Note

The Wild West is one of my most favourite periods in history. It's an era that was only a little more than a lifetime ago, but was such a time of change and lawlessness that it spawned legends we still know today. I am so happy and excited to revisit that time for this new Outlaws of the Wild West series, and to share with you my first full-length Western romance.

When choosing a setting for my first Western series I immediately thought of the Montana Territory. Aside from its majestic natural beauty, it's a place as tempestuous as any you'd find in the Old West. Home to mining barons, brothel madams, outlaws and average people just trying to get by, it really is the perfect setting for adventure and romance. I chose Helena specifically because at one time it was home to more millionaires per capita than any other city in the world. It epitomised opulence set against a rough backdrop, which is what first intrigued me with this story. I loved the idea of Hunter the rough outlaw juxtaposed with Hunter the wealthy gentleman.

I hope you enjoy getting to know Hunter and Emmy as much as I did. And I hope you'll join me later as I delve into the lives of his brothers. Thank you so much for reading.

THE INNOCENT AND THE OUTLAW

Harper St George

Published in Great Britain 2016
by Mills & Boon, an imprint of HarperCollins*Publishers*
1 London Bridge Street, London, SE1 9GF

© 2016 Harper St. George

ISBN: 978-0-263-91713-0

Our policy is to use papers that are natural, renewable and
recyclable products and made from wood grown in sustainable
forests. The logging and manufacturing processes conform to the
legal environmental regulations of the country of origin.

Printed and bound in Spain
by CPI, Barcelona

Harper St George was raised in rural Alabama and along the tranquil coast of northwest Florida. It was this setting, filled with stories of the old days, that instilled in her a love of history, romance and adventure. At high school she discovered the romance novel, which combined all those elements into one perfect package. She lives in Atlanta, Georgia, with her husband and two young children. Visit her website: harperstgeorge.com.

Books by Harper St George

Mills & Boon Historical Romance

Outlaws of the Wild West

The Innocent and the Outlaw

Viking Warriors

Enslaved by the Viking
One Night with the Viking

Digital Short Stories

His Abductor's Desire
Her Forbidden Gunslinger

Visit the Author Profile page at millsandboon.co.uk.

For my grandfather, who loved all Westerns—
even the romances.

I want to thank my amazing critique partners,
Tara Wyatt and Erin Moore, for holding my hand
through the entire process of writing this book.
I also want to thank my agent, Nicole Resciniti, and
my editor, Kathryn Cheshire, for their excellent advice
and for believing in my writing.

Chapter One

Emmaline Drake knew trouble when it walked through the door. Five years of serving drinks had taught her that only three kinds of strangers ever entered Jake's Saloon in the tiny backwater town of Whiskey Hollow. The first two were drifters and loners who sought the saloon as a refuge from a world that didn't accept them. They kept to themselves and rarely caused trouble. A drink, a meal and conversation with a pretty girl were enough to send them on their way. But then there were men like the three who stood just inside the saloon's swinging, slatted doors. These men were the third type and just looking at them caused a knot of dread to churn tight in her stomach.

These men were outlaws.

If there was anything Emmaline knew, it was how to spot an outlaw. Thanks to her stepfather's profession, she'd had years of experience identifying the variations in that type of man. As a rule they were notoriously badly dressed, though the clothing of this particular group belied that rule. Even with their dusters covered with a layer of dust, the fine cloth and texture of their breeches and coats were apparent and their boots were obviously high quality. But it wasn't the clothing that made the outlaw. It was the eyes. Outlaws had the eyes of predators—full of violence and aggression.

Violence crackled like energy in the eyes of these men.

They paused to boldly survey the room and all conversation died. A quiet wave sucked out the sound as it moved throughout the handful of tables, silencing the patrons and leaving tension in its wake. Even Lucy, Jake's wife, who'd been pounding away on the woefully out of tune piano in the corner, faltered and let her fingers fall still. No one overtly acknowledged the newcomers, unless you counted the sideways glances from behind hunched shoulders as the men in the room took note of them without shifting their positions. The customers were like dogs, bristling at potential intruders.

After taking note of every occupant in the room, they did another pass, no doubt noting the bare wood floors and rough edges of the place. Jake hadn't spent much money on making the place appealing. There was no need when the nearest competition was more than a two days' ride away.

Emmaline stood at the bar, her hands clenched on the scarred and polished wood. She swallowed as she watched them through the narrow, cracked mirror that hung behind it. It was framed in an elaborate plaster that had been gilded at one time, but most of it had long since chipped away, leaving it a mere ghost of its former self. She had thought many times that that was probably an apt description of the town itself. Once it had been a thriving mining community, but when the creek had been picked clean of gold, everyone had moved on.

Gesturing to Jake for three whiskeys, she turned to set eyes on the strangers. They were taller than the mirror had suggested and meaner looking. The quality of their clothing struck her again. Their breeches weren't patched with the leather that sometimes adorned the thighs of the men who spent most of their time in the saddle. They were tailored, not the simple clothing of ranchers and cowhands. Even their coats were a thick wool that would have made her envious if she hadn't been so busy trying not to be afraid.

They were no ordinary outlaws. These weren't the same type of men she'd known in her stepfather's gang. These men exuded power along with danger, a dark intent that said it was no accident that they had found their way to the saloon on that particular night. They were on the hunt and every man in this room had something to hide. It was a combination that could turn deadly with only the slightest provocation.

Each of them was over six feet tall, but the one on the right towered over the others by a few inches. He wasn't the least bit gaunt as often happened with tall men, as if they couldn't possibly eat enough food to support such a build. His powerful frame matched his height and his black eyes blazed with fury as he boldly looked over everyone in the room, sizing each of them up for the threat they might present and then discarding them one by one. It was hard to imagine the man who could pose a threat to him. An angry red scar ripped down his cheek and contributed to his fierce appearance, but he would've had no problems carrying out the look without it.

The middle one, a Spaniard, with his thick black hair and furrowed brow, appeared just as fierce as his partner, but more measured and calm. Less brute power, despite his broad shoulders and thick chest. His vivid green eyes were alight with intelligence and intensity, and he exuded an autocratic air that left her willing to bet anything that he was the leader.

But it was the one on the left who drew her attention and held it. With his physique, he could've been a match for the leader, except that his hair was lighter, that indefinable shade that hovered between rich brown and golden blond. His features were more refined, too, though undeniably masculine, a square chin with the hint of an indentation and a full, sculpted bottom lip. He seemed almost lazily indifferent, except that his eyes carried a calculating intensity that held her momentarily rooted to the floor when he happened to glance her way. A bolt of awareness shot directly to her belly as their eyes met, sending her pulse soaring and making her look away quickly as if she'd been caught doing something sinful.

The giant of a man moved to a table near the door and the other two followed suit, moving with caution, clearly suspicious of everyone else. The dark blond one on the left moved with surprising grace for a man of his strength, like he knew the full power of his body and knew how to control it. Somehow, observing that made her more aware of her own body and exactly how much of her breasts were on display. The realization made her blush.

"Em?" Jake's voice penetrated the strange fog that had come over her.

"Yeah?"

Eyebrows raised, he nodded to the three drinks on the tray beside her.

Always sensible and rarely flustered, she shook off the inexplicable fog that had come over her and grabbed the discolored tin tray with both hands.

"Be careful." Because she knew him well, she could easily discern the grimace lurking behind the caterpillar moustache that obliterated any hint of a mouth. But it was the nervous gesture of his hand running through his graying hair that ratcheted her anxiety up a level. He was always calm, even on that night two years ago when that bank robber had come in and everyone had recognized him from the flyer hanging beside the door. Jake had merely grabbed the short-barreled shotgun he kept behind the bar and offered the man a chance to leave. He had taken it.

Unable to stifle the impulse in time, she turned her head to look at the billboard postings. There were five posters there, but none of the drawings resembled the strangers. Of course, two of them were drawings of men with kerchiefs covering the lower halves of their faces, so there was always the possibility.

"Do you know them?" she whispered and turned her attention back to Jake.

He shook his head, but his eyes shifted to their table again. "No, but I have my suspicions. Go on now. We'll talk later."

How was she supposed to remain composed when he went and said something like that? Now that the men had settled themselves at a table, the conversations resumed and the tension in the room decreased notably. Lucy even resumed her piano playing, but at a more sedate pace. Her own anxiety should have begun to abate, but it hadn't, her stomach refused to stop its churning and she couldn't shake the feeling that something was terribly wrong. That something dangerous and profound was about to happen and she was powerless to stop it, like being stuck on a runaway train that was about to run out of track and she could only hold on and watch as it flew over the edge of a cliff.

With Jake's warning spinning around in her mind, Emmaline tightened her grip on the tray and slowly made her way to the table. She'd long ago become accustomed to the revealing nature of her outfit, but as she approached, she longed for the modest dresses she wore every day on the farm. The costume she wore at the saloon had been one of her mother's gowns from her days in the brothel in Helena. Emmaline and her sisters had modified it by shortening the deep red silk to knee-length and adding two layers of black lace taken from another gown. The bodice had already been obscenely low, so they had only had to add the matching black lace there. It revealed a large amount of her cleavage with its nonexistent sleeves, mere scraps of fabric that dropped low off her shoulders to hang down her upper arms. Her legs at least were covered in sensible black, woolen stockings. She'd started out with her mother's silk ones, but they had worn out years ago. She'd always disliked the costume, but never more so than now as she walked toward a table full of outlaws.

She shivered as she approached the doorway. Though the days were getting warmer, winter had refused to relinquish its grip on the nights. The other customers were drinking and keeping warm at tables near the cast-iron stove that sat further inside, but not the strangers. Apparently they preferred to keep their distance, as if she needed any further proof of their dubious intentions.

As she advanced, the pretty one with light hair—*is that how she was referring to him?*—

turned the full force of his gaze on her. It licked its way up her legs and over her hips, settling on her breasts for a moment before finally making its way to her face. He'd sat back in his chair, one leg stretched out before him, almost lazy in his regard of her. She had worked at the saloon for almost five years, so she was used to the looks men gave her. She even encouraged them in the hopes that those passing through would leave a little extra on the table for her—the locals had nothing extra to leave. But with him…the look was different. It wasn't merely taking in what the dress put on display. His eyes demanded her attention, demanded her response, demanded much more than she was willing to give, while his lips promised more than she could risk imagining. One corner of his mouth turned upward, a suggestive smile that had her blushing again. Holy hell, what was happening to her? Men didn't affect her this way. She didn't allow it, because she knew they couldn't be trusted.

Tearing her gaze away from him, she focused her attention safely on the scarred, wooden tabletop as she sat the tray down and offered her customary greeting. "Welcome, gentlemen. Jake sends his regards."

"Jake?" The pretty one spoke, his voice a deep

rumble that warmed her deep down in ways she refused to acknowledge.

"The owner." Without looking up, she gestured over her shoulder toward the bar where Jake stood watching...she hoped. Then she carefully sat a tumbler with a finger of whiskey in front of each man. On the rare occasions Jake thought it necessary, he'd preemptively send over a free drink to welcome a new customer. If the man felt indebted or grateful to the proprietor, he'd be less likely to leave a mess behind. Sometimes it worked, sometimes it didn't.

The giant picked his up and tossed it back before she'd even finished.

"Rotgut." The hard voice matched its owner.

Glancing up, she met his disapproving look with a challenge in hers. "We don't serve rotgut, sir." She actually didn't know if that was true or not. Men complained that other saloons cut their whiskey, but nobody had ever complained about Jake's. She wouldn't put it past him, though. With the amount of business they'd had lately, it was barely worth her time to make the trip into town for work.

"My friend has expensive tastes." The pretty one pulled a wallet out of a pocket hidden inside his coat. It was a smooth, chocolate-colored leather with no creases, almost brand-new, she'd guess. When he opened it to extract a note, she could see many others nestled inside. The confident way he carried himself, along with his clothing, had left little doubt in her mind as to his wealth, but this only confirmed that she was right to be suspicious. What were they doing in Whiskey Hollow? Bringing trouble, she was certain of it. "A bottle of your finest Kentucky bourbon." His gaze licked over her and one corner of his mouth tipped up as he extended a ten-dollar note to her.

"We only have rye. Overholt?" The question forced her to look at him. She was struck anew by the strong, masculine beauty of his features. High wide cheekbones, strong granite jaw covered with a dusting of honeyed stubble, perfectly formed lips. This one was trouble in more ways than one.

He merely gave a single nod, indicating the substitution would be fine, and lifted an eyebrow when she hadn't taken the money.

Remembering herself, she grabbed the note, deliberately making sure to not touch him, and gave a small smile to the other two. They did not return her smile. "I'll be right back."

Emmaline managed to keep her steps even and measured all the way back to the bar. But when she placed the tray down, her gaze speared

Jake where he stood. "They want a bottle of rye. Come to the back and help me get one."

He looked like he wanted to argue—she knew he kept a few bottles under the bar—but she needed to know what he knew of them. Some instinct warned her that their presence had something to do with her stepfather's absence. He and her older stepbrother, Pete, were over a week late coming home from their latest job, which wasn't entirely uncommon, but no one had heard from them. A hollow feeling in the pit of her stomach said that the job had gone terribly wrong. As much as she disagreed with their lifestyle, it turned her stomach to think of what would happen to her and her younger sisters without them.

"Who are they?" she asked the moment Jake stepped through the door to the tiny storeroom filled with crates of bottled beer and barrels of moonshine. "Does their presence have anything to do with Ship?" Though he was her stepfather, everyone called him Ship, even her younger sisters who were his blood.

"Calm down, Em." He placed a hand on her shoulder. "I don't know anything for sure and getting upset won't help anything. You've heard of the Reyes Brothers? That could be them. That one in the middle, the one that looks like a Spaniard, I think he's their leader."

The Reyes Brothers. A chill prickled her scalp and cold ribbons of fear trailed down her spine. Ship had talked about them the last time he'd been home. Though she hadn't gotten the impression the two had crossed paths, he'd described the successes of the gang with the glee and admiration only someone hoping to rise to those levels could summon. They moved cattle across the border. Lots of cattle. Which was only illegal depending on which side of the border they were on. But to hear Ship tell it, they'd made a fortune guarding mining and land claims and even that wasn't technically illegal, unless it involved killing. She couldn't remember anything else he'd said. The only detail she'd taken to heart from that conversation was that no one crossed them and lived to tell about it.

Had Ship done something stupid like try to steal from them? Had he taken Pete with him?

"That doesn't make sense. They work down near the border. Las Cruces, or was it Santa Fe? Damn, I can't remember. Why would they be here?"

Jake shrugged. "My buddy down off Green River swears he saw the Spaniard there last month buying supplies. He'd know because he spent some time near the border just last year. Says he was in a saloon down in Perez and in walked the Spaniard with a giant, I suppose that one he brought with him tonight. Both better dressed than normal outlaws. He walked in and called out to a fella playing faro. The man charged him with his gun drawn so they shot him. The Spaniard left and the giant followed him out. No one said a word and the poor son of a bitch was carted out the back and his winnings divided amongst those at the table." He ran a hand over the back of his neck and glanced at the closed door leading to the bar. "Seems like if they were in Green River last month they could be here now. It's not that far away."

"Is this the same buddy you have to carry out every time he comes in because he drinks an entire jar of moonshine?" When he gave an irritated sigh, confirming her words, she continued, "That man could be anybody."

"Sure it could, but how often do you see men dressed like that step foot in here?"

Not many passed through here if they could help it, not since all the mines had been bought out and the creek picked clean of gold, and certainly none dressed like those men. They were here for a reason. "Do you think they're looking for Ship? Is he hiding?"

"I don't know, Em. I wish I could say. I haven't heard a word from him. Just go back out there and act as if nothing's wrong. You don't know anything."

Grabbing a bottle of Old Overholt—how anyone could drink it, she didn't know—she gave Jake a quick nod and headed back out. A small part of her had hoped they'd left, but there they sat, deep in discussion about something. Perhaps their next murder.

Jake followed her out and placed three fresh tumblers on her tray. He gave her a nod of encouragement and then she was off to the lion's den. She kept her gaze down the entire walk over, unwilling to lock eyes with the pretty one again. If she could just get through this, then she could prove to the knot in her belly that nothing was wrong, that nothing had happened to Ship and Pete.

Without a word, she sat the tray down on the table and unloaded the bottle and three fresh tumblers, before retrieving the tray and turning to go. It was easy, simple. There was absolutely no reason to believe that these men meant her any harm. The pretty one had actually smiled at her earlier. And she knew that smile. He wanted to do something, but it didn't involve hurting her. Quite the opposite, in fact. Everything was fine.

But then the Spaniard reached out and put a hand on her arm, his long, tapered fingers curling gently around her wrist. "A moment, please." His voice was soft and quiet, commanding respect from the confidence and intensity of the tone rather than the volume. Though his grip was gentle, she could feel the strength he held in check.

She followed the length of his arm up to his face, afraid to hear his next words. But he held silent, waiting for her to meet his gaze. When she did, she was startled to realize his eyes were the exact odd shade of greenish-gold as the pretty one's. They were striking against his darker complexion. Could the two be related?

"Yes?"

"Tell us what you know of Ship Campbell."

Chapter Two

Emmaline froze, focusing very hard on meeting the stranger's eyes to ensure that she wouldn't flinch. Though she had known deep in her bones that he was there looking for Ship, it was still a shock to hear the words. A million thoughts went through her mind at once. What did they want with him? Had they really come all this way to find him? If the strangers were looking for Ship, then it meant that Ship was still alive. But what had he done this time? Dear God, the man was too foolhardy to go off robbing banks. Why hadn't she tried harder to stop him? Lord knows they bumped heads more often than not, but she didn't want him dead. He'd taken her in like she was his own daughter—though that wasn't saying much—and they needed the meager supplies he brought them.

She was staring too long. *Say something!*

Damn Ship and Pete! She was the one in immediate danger just then, not them. Did the men
know who she was? Her instinct said no, since
they hadn't immediately noticed her upon coming into the saloon. All three of them had looked
over the other customers first. That meant they
thought that Ship might be there. Did they know
where he lived? Had they already ridden out to
the farm and found her sisters alone?

Before she could let her fear run wild, she
licked her suddenly parched lips and tried for a
nonchalant tone. "The name sounds familiar, but
I don't believe I know him." Partial truths. That
way the lies sounded more believable. Pete had
told her that once and she'd wondered why it was
something she'd needed to know. Apparently he'd
been preparing her for the day someone came
looking for them. Oh, God, what had they done?

The Spaniard stared at her as if trying to
decide if he believed her. With careful preci-
sion, she removed her gaze from his stare and
looked to the pretty one. He'd moved forward, elbows resting on the table with his hands cupped
around the tumbler he'd just splashed whiskey
into. He stopped swirling the liquid around the
clouded glass to watch her. His gaze was narrowed on her face, trying to catch a tell, anything
that proved she was lying.

And then he smiled. A small, almost imperceptible upturn of his lips on the left side. It was followed by a clarity in his eyes, a softening of the intensity that had been leveled on her as he'd tried to figure her out. That clarity was a knowing that hadn't been there before. That's the moment she suspected that she was a terrible liar.

"Can I get you anything else?" She did her best to level her gaze on the Spaniard. He didn't bat an eye as he stared her down, but knowing that she was quickly losing her grip on her composure, she raised an eyebrow and glanced to her wrist where he still held her. She needed to get away from them.

After a moment, when she would have sworn her heart stopped beating, he let her go. Giving them a tight smile, she somehow managed to keep her walk steady all the way back to the bar. She couldn't tell if they knew that she was Ship's stepdaughter. She couldn't tell if they'd bought her lie. The only thing she knew was that she had to get home to her sisters. The thought of Ginny and Rose home alone, vulnerable to those dangerous men, made a jolt of panic threaten to suck the air from her lungs. At twelve and nine, she hated to leave them home alone anyway, but she had little choice in the matter when they needed food and Ship left them with so little. Sometimes the meal she brought home from Jake's was all she and the girls had. The small garden she managed to tend during the warm months barely kept them supplied with enough vegetables to last through the winter, and the chickens wouldn't lay when the days got shorter. Not that they had many hens left after Pete's last drunken binge when he'd demanded a feast for himself and the men.

Stifling her anger along with the disturbing images of what might happen if the outlaws found her sisters alone, she set her tray on the bar and tightened her hands into fists to stop their shaking. "I have to go home, Jake." Trying to appear casual and in control, she dared not look back over her shoulder at the table.

"What did he say to you?" Jake topped off the beer he was pouring and set it on the bar, careful to not look too interested in what she had to say.

"He asked about Ship. I don't know if they know who I am, but I have to get home and check on my sisters."

He nodded in understanding, but in the very next breath warned her against leaving. "They'll get suspicious if you turn tail and run now."

"Maybe, but what if they sent someone there already? He could be hurting them."

"Yeah, what if?" He wiped at a drop of beer on the unvarnished bar and slanted her a dubious look. "You think you can help them now?"

"I think my revolver could do some damage."

Jake sighed and looked out at the men talking in small groups near the stove, anywhere but at the table with the three strangers. "You shouldn't go alone, Em. I don't like it."

"Me neither, but I have to. I'll wait a few minutes and pretend it's the end of my shift."

He grimaced, but didn't argue. "At least take Bette. She's over at the stable."

Bette was a swaybacked horse that was at least thirty if she was a day. Emmaline figured she had a better chance of making the four-mile trip faster on foot. "Thanks, but you know how I feel about horses. Besides, it's too dark to see the road and I'm afraid I'd break both our legs before I made it home."

"I'll come out after closing and check on you and the kids."

"I'd appreciate that."

He gave her a nod and she made herself look busy until she could slip out the back. She didn't even take the time to change as she would have on a normal night. Instead, she pulled Pete's old coat on over her costume and tucked her winter dress under her arm as she stole out the back door, heart beating wildly, her only thoughts of getting home.

The hastily erected buildings of the town showed their age. Even in the light of the half-moon, it was clear they were nothing more than unpainted clapboard held together by a few nails. The alley she stepped into was a mess of mud and muck left over from the storm that had rolled through almost a week ago. She took in a breath as she stepped off the back stoop and into the bog, grimacing as it sucked at her boots and thankful the trail leading out of town would be an easier walk. Everywhere else had dried out, while the town's roads stubbornly held on to the mud.

Her little part of the world was still cold in early April, particularly at night when the sun disappeared, leaving the valley to languish in the shadow of the mountains. A bitter wind blew in over those peaks and often didn't let up until morning. Sometimes it blew so long, Emmaline feared that it would never let up, that it would just keep blowing until it blew every trace of their lives away. She'd oblige it and leave if she could ever scrape up enough money. But with Ship's schemes, Pete's drinking, and everyday expenses like food and clothing, it didn't look like that day would ever come. Besides, there was only one way to get the kind of money she'd need to take her sisters with her and ensure their safety, but it was so abhorrent, she couldn't consider it.

But then there were the nights that came later into spring and summer. The wind could be gentle and warm, and the moon was clear, lighting stars in the sky for as far as the eye could see. On those nights she loved it here in her quiet part of the world. On those nights she didn't mind the long walk home. On those nights she could actually begin to think that everything would be all right, eventually.

This wasn't one of those nights.

Casting a harsh glance toward the swells in the distance still covered in snow, she took a deep breath and pulled the collar of her coat up to cover her ears. It was going to be a long walk.

She had ended up half running the familiar path home, until she had to slow down a little while later from the stitch in her side. But with a trickle of sweat running down between her shoulder blades, she didn't mind the cold anymore, so she alternated between running and walking.

She was about halfway home when she heard the sound. It might have been horse hooves hitting the dirt, or it could have been her own imagination. Either way, she decided it was time to delve into the long, brown grass instead of staying on the path. It gave her a better chance of hiding, if she had to. No sooner had she thought that, then the sound became clearer. Definitely horse hooves. Stopping for a moment to try to hear over the wind, the sound became sounds and she realized that it was more than one horse. She'd bet her life that three horses were coming her way.

Breaking out into a run, she half ran, half leapt over the knee-high grass that tried to slow her down. But the sounds kept drawing closer and she wasn't getting anywhere fast. Heart in her throat, she decided the only option was to hide. The moon was only half-full, which meant there was enough darkness to keep her hidden if she stayed very still. She chanced a quick look over her shoulder to see a shadow of movement, but it was still far enough away that she was certain they hadn't gotten a clear view of her position.

With no choice left, she darted for a thigh-high copse of brown grass and nestled inside it, all the while praying that it was too early in the season for snakes to be out of their dens. Blood pounding through her veins, she pushed her hand inside her coat to wrap it around the locket that hung down low between her breasts. It had been a gift from her father to her mother, passed on to Emmaline years ago when they'd still lived at the brothel. She didn't know if it had really been from the father she'd never met or not, but she'd always loved it.

Foolishly hoping the tin trinket had powers of protection, but knowing from years of hoping to get away from Ship and his outlaws that it did not, she clutched it tight and waited. Her wide gaze stayed locked on the shadowy figures coming toward her.

From the moment they had ridden into Whiskey Hollow, Hunter Jameson had known they were in the right place. It was the perfect hideaway for scum like Ship Campbell. Decrepit and forlorn, the town was a blight on an otherwise beautiful landscape. Virtually abandoned when the gold had been scavenged and depleted, he couldn't imagine why some had stayed. He was more than happy to leave it behind.

Two weeks and they were no closer to finding Miguel. To make it worse, this mission was a distraction from their real goal, which was to find the men responsible for the death of Castillo's grandfather and to recover his stolen inheritance. A wild-goose chase in the middle of the night wasn't helping matters.

"Dammit, Cas, she doesn't know anything. We need to track down other men who've ridden with Campbell. The girl's a waste of our time." And no matter how attractive she was in the dance-hall dress, and how much his body liked her, she was off-limits. Her disturbing blushes and wide, soft eyes made him think there was more to her than met the eye. More to her than he had time to figure out.

"We'll see what she knows," Cas muttered and scanned the tall grass in the distance, hoping to catch sight of her.

They had caught her trail just north of town, exactly the direction the drunk from Campbell's gang had said Ship lived. He'd then told them that Ship's daughter could be found working at the saloon, but that had been all he'd known.

"I understand your reluctance," Cas assured him, his voice only slightly accented. "But that was the only saloon in town. That drunk described the girl perfectly, down to her dark hair and light eyes. She's Campbell's daughter and she could know something."

"He didn't tell us her name," Hunter argued. "Could be some other girl. Plenty of dark-haired girls in the world."

Cas raised a brow. "Did you see another girl there?" They hadn't seen any other people aside from those in the saloon; if there were any other residents of the tiny town, they were at home hiding. "You know it's her. And you know she was lying as well as I do."

Hunter couldn't dispute that. Her eyes had widened at Ship Campbell's name, and they were too innocent to hide lies. She knew the man they were tracking, but he doubted she knew anything about Cas's younger brother. "She won't be good for anything but slowing us down."

"She'll talk before morning. Won't slow us down for long." This came from Zane.

In the years he'd been riding with his half brother Cas, the brooding Zane, and the rest of the gang, they'd never failed to make someone talk who wasn't so inclined. That was partially what worried him, though they had never been forced to interrogate a woman. There was no doubt in his mind that she knew who Ship Campbell was, but every instinct he possessed said she had no idea about Miguel. She wasn't a criminal like Campbell. Eyes didn't lie and hers were deep, blue pools of undiluted innocence. "She doesn't know anything. I'm sure of it."

"I'll take that bet." Zane chuckled and spurred his horse forward.

"That bastard Campbell has Miguel. I know it, Hunter. I'll do whatever it takes to get him back." Cas picked up his pace and followed Zane.

Hunter spared them both a cutting glance. His black faltered slightly in his step, uneasy with the tension he sensed in his master. Patting his neck and murmuring gently to calm him, Hunter turned his attention back to the trail they were following. The drunk hadn't known any more. If he had, he would've talked before Zane's fist left him unconscious.

Zane was like that sometimes, too powerful for his own good, too caught up in protecting the family to allow anyone to threaten them. He was loyal to a fault. Generally that power and dedication made him excellent at his job. Men would spill what they knew at the sight of him, or at least with very little persuasion. Hunter cringed to think about using intimidation like that with the girl. Especially a girl who refused to talk because she legitimately didn't know anything. She wasn't a criminal. Her innocence wasn't feigned. It was real. Her father might rob banks and outlaws, and ransom Cas's younger brother, but that didn't mean she'd had anything to do with it.

Or was it just simply his attraction that made him want her to be innocent of Campbell's crimes? He wanted her. That much he had known from the second her gaze had connected with his. The attraction had hit him low, like a punch to the gut. And dammit if she hadn't returned his interest. Raking a hand through his hair, he blew out a breath to clear his head. The last thing he wanted was to be involved with a Campbell, so it annoyed him that he found her intriguing.

He suddenly wanted to figure out why. Slapping the reins, he soon outpaced Zane and Castillo, his sharp gaze taking in the grasslands. There were copses of trees in the distance and if she'd made it that far then they might lose her. But some instinct—the same one that wanted her for his own—told him that they were very close.

After a minute or two, a movement caught his eye, but it was too shadowed to distinguish from the scenery. He might have disregarded it as unimportant had the moon not decided to aid in his pursuit and shine a shaft of light down on that particular spot. The ivory of her skin shone like a beacon in the night, as if the gods themselves were gifting her to him.

Smiling, Hunter set a path directly for her, anticipation already warming the pit of his belly.

Chapter Three

~~~~~~~~

Emmaline's heart sank the instant she realized they were riding directly toward her. Panic threatened to overtake her, but she managed to keep a grip on herself. There were only two choices: fight them or run and hide. Neither of those seemed to have a chance in hell of working out in her favor.

If she ran, she could try to make it to the trees to hide, but even as she looked to confirm the distance she knew that she wouldn't make it. It was too far; the very reason she had opted to hide in the grass. Transferring her grip from the locket to the old Smith & Wesson Schofield hidden in the pocket of her coat, she pulled it out. Like her coat, it was a castoff of Pete's, given to her when he'd bought his new Peacemaker. Despite the scoundrels Ship and Pete sometimes brought home, she'd never had cause to shoot a man. She didn't want to shoot one now. She had to get home to her sisters, and on the small chance the strangers didn't already know where she lived, she wouldn't risk leading them to her home.

Her hands shook as she slid bullets into the cylinder, wondering why she'd allowed her fear that it might go off on its own to stop her from keeping the damned thing loaded for emergencies. She counted each one as she did, a simple way to keep her mind focused on the task and not give in to the anxiety that threatened to overtake her. The bullets were cold in her fingers, making her realize that she'd forgotten her gloves back at the saloon. Finally loaded, she ran her thumb over a bit of rust as she pulled back the hammer, her hands shaking. She didn't want to shoot anyone. Maybe if they realized she had a gun, they'd leave her alone.

Closing her eyes to steady herself, she opened them and raised her arms to aim. They must have seen her gun, because they split up, each taking a different direction. She frowned, but it hardly mattered, she just wanted them to leave. Aiming in the direction of the nearest one, making sure her aim was a bit high, she fired.

The shot left her ears ringing and her hands vibrating from the shock, but she'd missed. The rider changed directions, galloping off to her right. Readjusting her aim, she followed him, but he moved too fast for her to get a clear shot. Dammit! Knowing she might not get another chance, she pulled the hammer back anyway, but then the grass rustled very close to her left side. She swung back around to that side, but before she could even get a glimpse of who had approached, she was knocked off balance by a large body. The momentum sent them rolling together through the tall grass until they finally came to a stop. She had managed to keep a grip on the butt of her gun, and pulled her hand up immediately, only to have it slammed back to the grass.

In a blind panic, she fought, but he wrestled the gun from her and threw it away before pinning her wrists to the ground over her head. She bucked to get him off, but he settled the full weight of his torso on her, effectively stopping her fight. His heavy, muscular thighs on either side of hers held her virtually immobile. Only then, when she was trapped, did she look up into the face above her own. Of course it had to be the pretty one staring back at her, his expression fierce and angry.

"You could have killed someone!"

"You could have left me alone." Though she

knew it was useless, she struggled beneath him anyway.

"It was stupid thing to do. You're outnumbered."

"What would *you* have done? Waited patiently for three strange men to come and get you?"

A sliver of moonlight crossed his features, creating hollows below his high cheekbones and showing the anger that lit his eyes. He was livid, but he smirked at her remark. His lips parted a bit to reveal a flash of white teeth, a predator toying with his meal. A shot of fear darted through her belly and it was as exciting as it was terrifying. Or maybe it was the wicked excitement that terrified her. She couldn't bear to acknowledge its existence, much less contemplate it. Jerking her gaze away, she held herself rigid beneath him and asked, "What will happen to me?"

Her question must have settled him, reassured him that she was accepting her fate, because he relaxed above her, his muscles softening just enough so that she felt the weight of him pressing her down even more. It wasn't as unpleasant as it might have been. He'd settled into the ease she remembered from the saloon, tempering his fierce edge just a bit. "That all depends on you, sweetheart. If you cooperate, you'll be fine."

She almost believed him, but then he called

for rope, his voice hard as it rumbled through her. A coil landed in the flattened grass near them. He moved off her then, to grab her upper arm and pull her up to her feet. Only then did she realize how her legs trembled as her knees threatened to buckle. He must have seen, because his voice gentled as he pulled her wrists in front of her to tie them together. "Cooperate and you won't be hurt," he reminded her.

But she couldn't stand there docilely to let herself be bound. Every instinct within her urged her not to let them take her. So she pretended compliance until he gave his focus to the task of tying her wrists and then she elbowed him hard in the ribs and took off. Though he grunted at the impact, she barely got two steps before he pulled her back against his chest. He was tall enough that she fit tucked beneath his chin so that he could look down to finish the task. His arms held her pinned while he fit the noose around her wrists and tightened it before she could do more than yelp in surprise. Pressure built up in her chest, but she fought it down and stared at her bound hands. She'd never before felt so horribly helpless and vulnerable and angry, all at the same time. She'd done nothing to deserve this. Damn Ship and every outlaw she knew!

She pulled at the binding and struggled against

her captor's hold, but then the Spaniard walked up to them, holding her gun loosely in his right hand. It wasn't a threatening pose, but she knew that it could be aimed at her in the blink of an eye, so she stilled her struggles. She fervently hoped that he hadn't been the one she'd shot at. But, then, that would only leave the giant and she really didn't want him angry with her either.

"I'll ask you once more and this time I'd appreciate an honest answer." He paused to allow the importance of those words to sink in, his handsome face solemn and fierce at the same time. "What do you know of Ship Campbell?"

She pressed back into her captor's chest, instinctively trying to distance herself from the gun. She might have imagined it, but his thumb traced lightly over the exposed skin of her wrist. The resulting involuntary shiver it caused unnerved her, so she jerked away, making him grasp her arms tightly. Instead of answering the question, knowing that her voice would only give her away, she shook her head.

The Spaniard sighed and looked down, shaking his own head at her. "Looks like we have an interesting night ahead."

The deep voice at her back rolled through her. "The horses!"

At that, the giant walked out of the darkness

and into her line of sight, holding the leads of all three horses. The dead weight of dread settled in her stomach, but she resolved herself to her fate. If they had followed her, then that meant they didn't know where she lived and more than likely her sisters would be safe. If she could keep that information to herself until tomorrow, then Jake would find them alone at the farm by morning and take them back to the saloon. They'd be safer there with him.

She just had to make it through the night. The thought made her heart pound in her ears. These men wouldn't give up until she told them whatever they wanted to know. They weren't taking her to keep her tied up; they were taking her to force her to talk. She closed her eyes to fight back the treacherous tears that threatened. Whatever happened, she could endure it as long as she knew the children would be spared. She had to; they needed her.

The pretty one moved forward to his horse, a beautiful animal whose coat shimmered black in the moonlight with a pretty white star pattern between his eyes. What sort of outlaw owned such a magnificent creature? With the force of his body propelling her toward the horse whether she wanted to go or not, she didn't have time to ponder the answer to that question. When they reached it, he stopped and looked down at her. She knew because his breath was suddenly very close to her ear, sending a strange tingle shooting through her, making her turn her head away to stop it.

"I can sit you in front of me without tying you down, if you promise to behave."

"Go to the devil." She bit the words out between clenched teeth.

His chuckle was anything but reassuring. Before she could anticipate his movement, he picked her up and sat her awkwardly across the saddle. When she would have kicked out, he grabbed her ankles and wrapped the length of rope hanging from her wrists around them, so that she was literally bound hands to feet. Then he mounted behind her and placed an arm securely around her waist and pulled her back against him.

His breath brushed her ear as he spoke. "We have a ways to go, so use the time to think hard about telling us the truth. No one wants you to get hurt."

She almost scoffed, but held herself in check. Ship had brought home plenty of men like these. Ruthless men who wouldn't hesitate to hurt her if it got them what they wanted. Though Ship had taken care of her and her sisters in his own way, by giving them shelter and the most basic of necessities, their lives with him were far from safe. She lived in constant fear of his enemies finding them at home alone, or even Ship's own men becoming disgruntled and taking their anger out on one of them. It was bound to happen eventually and it looked as if it finally had. She hated to admit it, but if it meant keeping Rose and Ginny safe, she would have already given him and Pete up if she only knew where they were.

The ride to the abandoned miners' shack took a little over two hours. Though she'd held herself stiff for the first hour so that she wouldn't touch him any more than necessary, the girl had eventually relaxed into him. Hunter had to admit that he liked how that felt. He liked her in his arms, warm and soft, her faintly floral scent teasing his nose so that he was imagining far more of her body than he wanted to. Once or twice her ragged coat had fallen open, revealing the creamy flesh that her dress put on display. He'd pulled it closed both times, because it was cold and because he didn't want to dwell on how much he liked looking at her. She was an attractive woman, but still, the way he wanted her was embarrassing. His loyalty to his brothers was more important to him than anything else. But this was asking too much.

It was almost with relief that he pulled up in front of the shack and dismounted. A glance at her face confirmed that the fear she'd been fighting had taken hold. Her eyes were wide with it and her hands trembled as he massaged them to ensure good blood flow. When she met his gaze, he had to look away from the force of it and remind himself that they were doing this for Miguel. Miguel, a stupid kid with a big heart who'd been in the wrong place at the wrong time. He didn't deserve to be taken any more than she did. But there was no telling what that coward Ship Campbell had done to him, so if there was any chance at all that she knew where Miguel was, they had to find out.

Without a word to her, he easily lifted her over his shoulder and walked toward the shack they had staked out before heading into town. The word 'shack' was generous. It was a small, one-roomed affair, just large enough to keep a man out of the elements, with a crudely built hearth and place for a bedroll. If the four of them slept here tonight, they'd almost be shoulder to shoulder.

If Campbell hadn't taken Miguel to retaliate for his pal's death, Hunter would be at home in

Helena by now surrounded by the luxury he'd once taken for granted, yet had come to appreciate in his years of riding with the gang. Their activities necessitated weeks camped outside and meals that were humble at best. The fact that Miguel had been kidnapped just after their last job, thus delaying his trip home, only angered him more.

Zane had already lit the lamp in the single room and was kneeling at the hearth to start a fire when Hunter walked in with her. No one was around to see their smoke, and even if there was, they'd be long gone before anyone came to check it out in the morning. Setting her on her feet, he took the knife from his belt and bent to cut the rope from her ankles and then her wrists. It only took a moment to jerk the old coat off her shoulders and down her arms, before catching her wrists again and tying them—despite her protests—and looping the end of the rope around the low rafter in the ceiling. She gasped when he pulled it tight so that her arms were raised high above her head and only her toes touched the ground. Though she didn't say a word, her eyes were accusatory, making him feel like a bastard for putting fear into them.

He took a step back to get a good look at her in the light. Her dark hair had loosened so that it tumbled in disarray almost down to her waist. Her features were delicate and gentle, pretty in a wholesome way that wouldn't normally hold very much attraction for him. He liked experienced women who expected nothing more than a fun night. But there was something more in her pretty face. A challenge. A secret. Something that made him want to study her longer.

His gaze caught hers and held as her eyes blazed at him, anger beating the hell out of the fear that was also there. It displaced but couldn't completely hide her interest in him, lurking in their depths. Was she even aware that it was there shining out at him? No, she didn't know what she was revealing to him. Her eyes were wide with an openness that was almost naive. It drew him in, even though he knew it couldn't be real. She worked in a saloon. She knew men.

Turning on his heel with a muffled curse, he glared at Zane who was standing, having just finished with the fire. "Don't touch her. She's mine." He'd meant that he would handle the interrogation, but the words felt too right. Too primal. This was a bad idea. Zane flashed him a knowing grin and held his hands up in compliance.

Hunter was fuming as he walked outside and over to where Cas was taking care of the horses.

Without bothering to say a word, he tore into one of his saddlebags to make sure it was the one with the food he'd stashed there earlier in the day. Dried beef, not exactly the supper he'd been hoping for, but it was all they'd get that night and it looked like much of his portion would go to the girl.

"Hunter?" Cas's voice cut through his anger.

"What?"

"Taking her was our only choice. Even if she doesn't know anything, which I still don't believe is true, we need her to exchange for Miguel."

Cinching the leather bag closed, he glared at his brother. "Zane won't talk to her. I'll do the interrogating."

"Hunter—" But whatever he was planning to say, he stopped when he noted the determination on Hunter's face.

"You're my brother, Cas. I joined up with you because what happened with your grandfather— his murder, the money stolen from your family—was horrible. I want to help you restore your family's empire and bring his killers to justice. I vowed to help you do that and I meant it. But the girl isn't part of that." He nodded toward the shack. "She's mine."

Cas took in a deep breath, clearly torn between his need to find Miguel quickly and his respect for his half brother. Finally, he relented. "You have until morning. If she doesn't talk by then, I'll have no choice."

"She will." Hunter smiled, slinging the saddlebag over his shoulder and tucking his bedroll under his arm, before going to confront his captive. She'd talk by morning, because he had no intention of letting Zane—or anyone else—touch her. She was his.

Chapter Four

The moment the pretty one had stepped outside, the giant lowered his hands and took the few steps necessary to cross the room and stand in front of her. Even with her extra height due to the fact that her hands were strung up to the rafters and her weight was supported by her toes, he loomed almost a head taller. She sucked in a deep breath and tried to control the trembling that threatened to begin in her limbs if she even dared to imagine what he might do to her. Just one of his large hands could break her. Bracing herself for the possible blow, she forced herself to look up to meet his stare, refusing to be cowed by him. Hard, black eyes stared back at her, a cold mask that left her longing for the comfort of the pretty one's presence. She had no reason to expect that he would protect her, but he *had* seemed reluctant to hurt her. A scar slashed through one brow and a high cheek-bone making the giant look forbidding and almost barbaric.

"My brother has a weakness for comely women."

Brother? His darker complexion clearly proclaimed his native heritage. There was no way the men were brothers, but she couldn't dwell on that with his next words. "You'd do well to confess your secrets to him."

"And if I don't?" As soon as the words were out, she longed to call them back. She'd become accustomed to verbally sparring with Ship's men, but these men were predators and Ship wasn't around to save her with his influence.

His lips parted in what might have been a smile, but as she stared at his even white teeth she could only imagine it to be the grin of a wolf as it toyed with its prey. "Then you find out if I share his weakness."

The creak of the door opening and the scuff of a boot stepping inside the shack was such a relief that her entire body unclenched as her breath whooshed out. The pretty one stood broad and tall just inside the doorway, his brow furrowed as his sharp, narrowed gaze took them in. A hitch in her chest that she attributed to relief made it difficult to breathe for just a moment.

A part of her wanted him to scold his *brother* for daring to approach her while he was gone, but he just moved forward to set his saddlebag and bedroll on the floor in front of the fire. The giant joined him and they stepped to the door, murmuring in voices too low for her to hear, though she caught the occasional word in Spanish. Then the big man nodded and closed the door behind him as he left. Her gaze went back to the bedroll. It appeared they intended to stay the night in the shack. Would she sleep in the bedroll with him or hang like this all night? With her fingers already starting to fall asleep, both options seemed unsavory.

He shrugged out of his duster and folded it lengthwise before holding it out as if to drop it on a table, but the room was bare of anything save the lamp sitting on a crudely built stool. Noting that, he allowed the coat to drop behind him to the floor before looking back to her. His hands rested at his waist, guiding her attention to the impressive Colts with their pearl inlaid grips holstered at his hips. Searching for other weapons, she made a sweep of his person, her gaze raking down long, powerful legs to the knife tied at his ankle. Its blade was almost a foot long. It made her own tiny knife, hidden in her boot, seem like the pathetic security that it was.

Feeling just slightly more defeated than she had before, she allowed her gaze to rove back up to his hands. They were so large, just one had managed to wrap itself about both of her wrists with ease. In his position, his shirt was stretched taut across the muscles of his chest, revealing just how thick and solid it was. Sometimes the added layers of material from a thick coat and duster made a man seem much larger than he was. Often the men who rode with Ship or the ones who came into the saloon seemed formidable until they divested themselves of their outer wear to reveal a soft middle or a gaunt frame. Not this one. He was trim around the middle and just as muscled as she had imagined he would be. She'd ridden before him on the horse and had felt that strength at her back, but she'd hoped she'd been mistaken. The slender thread of hope that had made her think she might be able to survive long enough in a physical skirmish to reach for his knife or gun broke beneath the truth of his powerful frame. It was hopeless to plan that sort of escape. No, she'd have to come up with another plan quickly. Her sisters must be worrying themselves sick and her heart clenched to hug them against her and reassure them that everything would be all right.

He was watching her, but hadn't yet moved.

"What do you plan to do with me?" she asked because she couldn't keep quiet under the force of his scrutiny any longer.

"That's an interesting question. One with an answer that depends more on you than on me." He smiled. A slight upturn of his mouth on the left side that made her once again note how beautifully sculpted those lips were. It was a ridiculous observation, but there it was and, once noted, it wasn't something that could be unseen. Forcing herself not to look at them, she instead watched how he moved with ease and control as he closed the distance between them. Lazy indifference was the phrase that came to mind. Without a care in the world, almost as if he hadn't strung her up at all and they were about to have a drink back at the saloon. The thought almost made her laugh and she realized that her very real fear must be making her daft.

"You're toying with me."

Genuine amusement flashed in his eyes as he came to a stop before her, too close to be decent, but then the entire situation smacked of indecency. "Regretfully, no." He breathed out the words. "Answer my questions honestly and you'll be fine, sweetheart." His hand rested on her waist as he moved to stand behind her. With her arms strung up, she couldn't turn her head to watch him so she waited as he came to a stop behind her. The sudden silence in the room was only broken by the crackling of the fire and her own breath. He was close, his body heat actually warming her backside, but if it was because he was purposely standing close or if it was just an unfortunate accident of the room's dimensions, she had no idea. Until his fingers touched her ribs. Closing her eyes, she bit her lip to stifle her gasp of surprise and managed not to squirm as he ran his hands down the sides of her hips and then her legs, coming to a stop at her ankle boots. When he began to untie one, she kicked out.

"Don't take my shoes!" If she managed to escape she needed her shoes, but more importantly, she didn't want him to know about the knife.

He ignored her protests and clamped an arm around her legs, effectively turning her into a twitching worm with no limbs. The extra weight pained her wrists, so she stopped fighting and hung her head, accepting the momentary defeat. The left ankle boot was the first to be tossed across the room, followed soon by the right. He stood and his boots came into her line of vision as he moved around to her front. Though they were dusty, the hint of a sheen that lurked beneath implied they were impeccably cared for.

Outlaws were scruffy creatures who could barely get their hands on two coins to rub together, because they drank away everything they stole. Who were these men?

Taking her chin in a chillingly gentle hold, he forced her to meet his gaze. He wasn't smiling as he held the knife he'd found in its leather sheath before her face.

"Ever use this before?" His warm breath fanned her cheek.

"A few times." She jerked her chin from his grasp. "I'm used to dealing with unsavory men."

But none so handsome as him, an inner voice chided. With him standing so close to her, it was difficult not to notice his beauty. The planes of his face, his cheekbones, the bow of his lips, the strong jaw and chin, he could have been sculpted in granite by a master craftsman. The coarse sprinkling of a few days' worth of beard only made his classic beauty more rugged and masculine. *Oh, dear Lord, Em, of all the men Ship has brought home to you, you pick this one to become a fool over?* A pretty face did not equal pretty intentions, and this one had some fairly dubious intentions toward her. The fact that he was beautiful was an atrocity against nature, not something to become weak in the knees over.

Without warning, he unsheathed the blade

and threw it across the small room so that it embedded itself in the wall, the wooden handle vibrating.

"Do you have anything else in that dress that I should know about?" His smooth, deep voice caressed her ears in a way that was entirely too unseemly for their current situation.

Her locket! Her eyes widened before she could stop them and her heart gave a jolt in her chest. She'd been so concerned with physically fighting him that she had forgotten all about her locket and the sleeping powder it contained. Of course! It should have been her plan all along. When she turned twelve her mother had presented her with a pouch of white powder, left over from her days at the brothel. With shrewd eyes and in a conspiratorial whisper, she had shared with Emmaline its secret. A little bit put into a man's drink would leave no taste and would leave him well rested and certain that he'd had the best tumble of his life, albeit too embarrassed to admit that he didn't remember the actual act itself. Too much and he'd be left groggy, disoriented, and suspicious the next morning.

Emmaline had used it before and knew that it worked well. While her mother had lived, the men Ship rode with had kept their distance and usually slept in the barn if he brought them home. After her death, they found their way inside more often than not. Generally they kept their distance from her, regarding her as the child of their boss and off-limits, but occasionally—especially if Ship was drunk or preoccupied—one would make an advance. Sometimes she was able to verbally put them in their place, sometimes a flash of her knife had done the trick, but when that hadn't worked she'd smiled and sweetly offered them a drink. Thinking they had won her over, they had eagerly accepted and grinned lecherously as they anticipated the night to come. Emmaline had always slept well on those nights.

She'd been stupid to forget the powders and now she was terrified of losing her only advantage. "No, nothing." She shook her head as vigorously as she was able given her awkward position. When his gaze narrowed, she held a breath and forced a calm she didn't feel, lest she give herself away. "The knife was all I had."

He didn't seem convinced and she tried not to gasp when his big hands tore at the lacing on the front of her corset, before pushing up underneath. "What the hell are you doing?"

He didn't answer but reached behind her to the ties in the back. Panic gripped her as the strings gave way. "Please, don't!" His arms were around her almost like an embrace, and her struggles only seemed to emphasize that as with every movement she somehow twisted closer to him. Suddenly he became every nightmare she'd ever had about the men in Ship's gang. She was trussed, more helpless than she had ever been, and this man was so much stronger than her. Making sure to get both sets of toes on the ground, she pushed upward with her last bit of strength and bent her knees, hoping to catch him in his groin or middle, anywhere soft where a kneecap could hurt.

His hands dropped immediately to catch her, gripping her at the top of her thighs and pressing downward, holding them steady so that her one jolt of momentum had been lost and she flailed helplessly until she could get traction on the floor with her toes again. Except that when she did, her front was almost entirely pressed to his, so there was no space to attack him. "Whoa… easy… I won't hurt you like that, Em." His voice was low and deep.

She was so shocked when he spoke her name that she gasped aloud. His lips tipped upward in an attractive smile. It was knowing and teasing, hinting at an awareness between them that she had no intention of acknowledging aloud. Damn him, it made her aware of the hard, strong length and breadth of his body pressed against hers and the way his big hands held her thighs tight against his own, and the fact that those things weren't entirely unpleasant. Nothing about the moment should have reassured her about his intentions, but it did. He didn't mean to force himself on her.

"You know my name."

"The man at the saloon called you Em." He explained. "What's it short for? Emily? Emma?"

The fact that her eyes had slipped down to watch his mouth form those words only made her angry. "That's none of your business."

His brow rose and with that same lazy amusement, his hands slipped from her thighs and he moved to stand behind her to deftly finish unlacing the corset until it fell to the floor at her feet. She closed her eyes and bit down on her lip when his hands roamed her torso, making sure that there were no pockets hidden in the dress where she had stashed a weapon. He was back to being a ruthless outlaw when he stood before her again. She tried not to notice how the dress gaped open now that the corset wasn't there to hold it in place. She wasn't as buxom as her mother had been, but the corset had held the extra fabric in place nicely. Without it, well, there wasn't much to keep the bodice from exposing her. He had no qualms about noticing and allowed his gaze to roam at will. When he reached toward her bodice, she sucked in a quick breath, but he only fished the locket out from between her breasts and turned it over in his fingers.

She held that breath, willing him to put it back. Finally, he looked up from his study of the tin trinket with its faux onyx locket. The stone would open on a hinge to reveal the real treasure of the powders inside and his thumb absently stroked that very hinge, taunting her as she imagined just how easily it would pop open to reveal her secret. "Please, don't take it. It was a gift from my father."

"Stolen no doubt," he remarked as he examined the locket in his palm.

"Not Ship," she corrected. "My real father. That's all I have of him. Please don't take it."

"Not Ship, huh?" His knowing glance filled her with dread. "You mean not Ship Campbell, the man you claim to know nothing about?"

Dammit! She wasn't any good at this. She'd walked right into that. This was the worst night of her life and she was being a complete idiot. First the powders and now this. She was always the one in the family with a level head. The one making sure they had canned enough food to last through winter, making sure the eggs they sold in town went for the best price, but now she was being an idiot. The fear she had been holding back so well was finally starting to wear on her.

He grinned and gently tucked the trinket back between her breasts, the backs of his fingers stroking against her skin as he did. Biting down on the inside of her lip to stop the shiver that threatened to move through her, she watched his face for any indication of what he planned to do next. Taking a step back, he crossed his arms over his chest. "All right, you can keep it, but only if you tell me what you know about Campbell."

It was on the tip of her tongue to tell him to go to hell again, but that would simply be letting her anger talk and do her no favors. He might even take her locket, leaving her situation even more dire. Anger wasn't the way to handle him or her predicament. It was time to start using her head and stop simply reacting to what was happening. She was smarter than this, smarter than *him.* She just needed to get herself out of her bonds and the only way to do that was to appear to cooperate and earn his trust.

Swallowing back the words she longed to hurl at him, she managed a grave expression and gave him a contrite nod. "Ship Campbell is my stepfather."

"How long have you known him?"

"About thirteen years."

"When did you last see him?"

"Five weeks ago. He was supposed to be home last week, but he hasn't come back yet."

"What do you know about his plans when he left?" he asked, continuing his rapid-fire assault.

Torn between playing along and risking revealing something that he shouldn't know and possibly compromising Ship's safety, she bit down on her bottom lip to contemplate her answer. His gaze immediately darted to the movement and she froze as an intangible and warm current moved between them. Lord, this man was dangerous in more ways than one. In completely inappropriate ways that didn't bear thinking about now trussed up like she was.

With an infinitely gentle touch, his thumb pressed against the flesh just below her lip and pulled it free. "No lying. Tell the truth and I promise you'll be safe."

Just the touch of his thumb felt a thousand times better than it should. She took in a shuddering breath as a ripple of pleasure moved through her from that touch before answering him. It wasn't as if she knew that much anyway. "He was going to rob a bank in Crystal

City, I think. It was supposed to be a quick job and then back."

"It takes about a week and a half to ride to Crystal City from here. A week and a half back. What did he plan to do with that extra week?"

He'd mentioned a detour to meet an old friend, to hide out so no one followed him from the bank, but the presence of the Reyes Brothers made her wonder if that hadn't worked out. "I don't know," she answered. "He doesn't share the details with me and I don't ask."

"Why doesn't he share the details? Aren't you involved with his gang?" That same thumb traced a lazy path across her chin before he grimaced and drew his hand back, as if just catching himself in the act of touching her.

"No," she snapped at him, unreasonably angry at herself for missing his touch.

He was quiet for a while, his gaze piercing, making her want to fidget beneath his scrutiny. He didn't believe her. The skepticism was plainly written on his face. She couldn't blame him, though, because she knew herself to be a horrible liar. She wasn't involved with his plans, but she knew where his friend lived. Ship had always told her to look for him there if he ever went missing. If Ship was actually visiting that friend, she had no idea, but it was something she needed to keep to herself, which was why she needed a distraction. She'd feed him faulty information about the farm, make them go somewhere else so they would leave her alone.

"Go to the farm if you don't believe me. He's not there. But he keeps a chest at the foot of his bed and it's full of notes. You might find something there that will tell you where he's gone."

His expression didn't change as he brought his thumb up and slowly ran the side along the crease below his well-formed bottom lip. Perversely, the movement held her mesmerized until she forced herself to look away. "You still don't believe me?"

"Your sudden cooperation seems a little too convenient."

It was too convenient. She was planning to lie. "My hands are numb and my arms hurt. That changes things."

"Where's the farm?" he asked, without addressing her complaints.

"Oh, no, you don't get that information so easily."

Raising a brow and crossing his arms over his chest again, he was apparently willing to stare her down as he awaited her capitulation. When she didn't speak, his gaze went to the dangerously gapped-open bodice and the locket gleaming in the firelight. Unwelcome butterflies fluttered along with the nerves in her belly. "You wanted to keep your trinket," he reminded her.

"Please." She tugged on the bonds at her wrists, wincing at the pain. "This is horribly uncomfortable. Cut me down and I'll tell you where the farm is."

Chapter Five

Hunter allowed his gaze to linger on the swell of her breasts before bringing it upward to settle on her eyes. They held his attention just long enough to make her squirm as he pretended to weigh her request. He'd cut her down because what had begun as a game to expediently get information from her had turned into something more dangerous. There was something provocative about having her bound before him, but he'd never taken a woman by force and he wouldn't start now. The same instinct that made him want to protect her made him want to make her his.

Despite her attractive face, he'd expected her to be different than she was. These past years, they'd traveled through many backwater hells avoiding the law, avoiding outlaw hunters, avoiding all the sons of bitches looking to make a name for themselves by taking one of them out, but all the women he'd ever come across in those dark places were just like their men. Un-educated, coarse and almost willfully ignorant in their spurning of the outside world.

She was different.

The way she spoke made him think that she'd had some education, but he didn't know how that could be, considering what he'd seen of Whiskey Hollow and what he knew of her stepfather. Her deep blue eyes sparkled with an intelligence that was intriguing with the challenging way she looked at him, as if taunting him to figure out her secrets. Those eyes coupled with the unexpectedly soft curves that he'd felt as he'd searched her for weapons had been damned pleasing. The mere memory made blood rush to his groin. The firelight flickered, gave her skin a golden hue as she hung there, tied like an offering to him. Her unbound breasts begged for his palms, as they were all but revealed to him, the black lace at the edge of her bodice only just managing to keep the pink of her nipples hidden. The locket taunted him from its prized position nestled between them. It didn't help that the looks she gave him said she was as attracted to him as he was to her. She tried to hide it, but she wasn't as afraid of him as she should be, at least not afraid for her safety like a normal captive would be. Her fear stemmed from what crackled between them.

Pushing a hand through his hair, he forced a breath out and decided he'd been too long without a woman, a situation he'd have to wait until he got back home to Helena to rectify. Damn Campbell to hell! He'd happily kill the man with his bare hands once they recovered Miguel. She startled when he made a quick grab to pull his knife from its sheath strapped to his boot. He approached her more slowly so she knew his intention, the knife raised to the rope securing her to the wood beam above her head.

When her arms fell free she stumbled forward into him. "Whoa, I've got you." He wrapped an arm around her small waist, his fingers noting each fragile bone as his hand rested along her rib cage, and a shard of anger tore through him. Campbell had done a piss-poor job of taking care of her. It was clear that she hadn't had a decent meal in months. He could break her in two if he wasn't careful. He gentled his hold as he half bent to sheathe his knife. She was trembling, but probably more from muscle fatigue than fear, or at least that's what he wanted to believe.

Before he could suppress it, a wave of tenderness for her moved through him. She must lead a very lonely life with Campbell gone for months at a time. The thought brought back unwelcome memories of his own childhood. With his mother living so far away in Boston and his father working all hours of the day and night, he'd known what it meant to be lonely. His hands tightened on her waist as he straightened.

Nostrils flaring, he took in her scent, a faint undercurrent of wildflowers. The silken waves of her dark hair brushed against his knuckles, giving him the urge to tangle his fingers in it and pull her head back to taste her. He closed his eyes as he stifled the notion. She was his captive, not his woman. That line could not get blurred. What in hell was wrong with him?

Slipping a fingertip underneath the rope that still held her wrists tied together in front of her, he made sure that it was loose enough that it wouldn't hinder circulation while still keeping her somewhat restrained. His palms settled on her hips, helping her to find her footing before moving on to her arms, stroking up and down her forearms in a massage to help get her blood flowing again.

"Thank you," she murmured a few moments later, her voice slightly hoarse.

He stifled a twinge of guilt that she would thank him for cutting her loose, as the soft catch in her voice brought his eyes to hers. He saw reflected there the same awareness that thrummed through his body, that attraction that refused to be cowed whether it was appropriate or not. Like lightning drawn to iron, his gaze moved down to her small mouth and lush, red lips that made his breath quicken. As if readying themselves for him, they parted and it was all he could do not to take them.

But he wasn't that man. He didn't need to take advantage of a woman who was at his mercy.

Annoyed at his own response to her, he demanded in a low voice, "The farm. Where is it?"

Caught in their dangerous spell, it took her a few seconds to realize what he had said. He was so close that his scent enveloped her. Leather, the subtle salt of perspiration, the spice of some long-ago applied aftershave—none of which were overpowering, but combined in a heady blend that was pure male and unexpectedly appealing. It was more than his scent and his handsome-as-sin looks that intrigued her. Though he was an outlaw and danger poured off him, she recognized gentleness beneath the harsh exterior. He'd not been rough with her at all, when any one of Ship's men would have gloried in their power had they been in his position. And, though at first she hadn't been sure of his intention, she knew he wouldn't force himself on her.

A grudging respect for him had grown within her. True, she was his captive, though she didn't really think that was a situation he had wanted. But she also knew that he was an outlaw, probably wanted from here to Texas, and she couldn't forget that. And despite the fact that he had checked the bindings on her wrists to make sure they weren't too tight, *he* had put them there.

Buying some time to get her thoughts in order, she pulled away from him and rubbed her hands together. "I'm cold." It was true, but she said it more to stall because she had no idea what she planned to tell him about the farm.

His nostrils flared slightly as he took a deep breath and moved away, walking backward the few steps it took him to reach his saddlebags. When he stood back up, holding the winter dress that she was sure had been lost back when they'd taken her, she found herself smiling for the first time since she'd left the saloon. The brown wool was a welcome sight. It wasn't the prettiest dress in her paltry wardrobe, but it was warmer than the dance-hall costume and much less revealing. "Here." She automatically held up her wrists so that he could cut the rope free.

Except he didn't move but to raise a brow at her.

"Well, how else am I to get that on?" she challenged and reached for the dress, but missed because he raised the wad of fabric higher.

"I'll help." The lazy, teasing smile had returned to his mouth now that the fire had been banked...slightly.

"Thank you, but, no." Holding her hands out for him again, she nodded to the knife sheathed to his boot. "Just untie me. You can tie me back up after I'm done, if you think I'm such a threat to you. Please," she added at the end when he just stared back at her.

Faster than she had imagined possible, even having seen him grab it before, he smoothly reached for the knife and stood with it in his fist. Slowly, not quite so certain now that he held the weapon, she offered him her wrists and he held them tight with his left hand, stuffing the dress beneath his arm, as he sawed at the rope with his right. The rope loosened and partly fell away, aided by her when she was finally able to get a hand loose. She threw the rope into the fire before he could stop her, but she needn't have worried because he only smirked at her as he handed over the dress. "Change."

"Turn around."

The smirk didn't leave his face as he half turned, facing the door and giving her his shoulder.

"All the way around."

He only gave her a shake of his head and kept his eyes on the door. "You haven't earned my trust yet, sweetheart. This will have to do." Then he gave her a glance and a wink. "Unless you've reconsidered my help."

When she only glared at him and began unbuttoning her costume, he gave a low laugh and looked back toward the door. Turning her back to him, she did her best to shield herself from him in case he dared to look back over at her. It wasn't difficult, she left her drawers and camisole on while quickly stepping out of the costume and shimmying into her dress. She made quick work of the buttons up the front and turned back to him just as he turned to her, making her wonder if he'd been peeking. He wasn't smirking anymore though. In fact, his brows were narrowed over his eyes, bringing to mind the fierce outlaw she'd seen walking into her saloon.

"The farm."

Just like that, she missed him smirking and a little playful. She hadn't realized he'd backed her across the tiny space until her spine touched the wall and she let out a little sound of surprise.

Eyes wide, she took in the breadth of him as he loomed above her. Her heart pumped hard in her chest as he crowded her even more until her entire body was flush with the wall. His greenish eyes had darkened, with the fire at his back, making him appear almost otherworldly for one brief moment.

"You don't scare me." It was a brazen lie and they both knew it. Though she didn't think he would physically hurt her, this man wielded too much power over her present and future, and inexplicably too much power over her body.

"Really? That's interesting." His hand came up out of the darkness, and she watched as his long, tapered fingers came toward her to reach for her locket. She grabbed his wrist before he reached it, but she couldn't get his hand away no matter how hard she pushed. Before she realized it, he'd grabbed both of her wrists in one hand and pressed them flat to the wall above her head. All she could do then was watch as his palm closed around the only weapon she had, the backs of his fingers resting against her breasts. She was certain he could feel her heart threatening to pound out of her chest. Her eyes were glued to his fist, well aware that one tug was all it would take to break the slender chain so that it would fall away from her neck and he'd hold her only hope of escape. "Tell me again how I don't scare you."

She couldn't help but to raise her chin, refusing to be cowed by him, even though it was a different experience entirely to be totally restrained by *him* rather than the rope. It gave the situation an intimacy that the binding hadn't. While fear pounded through her, it was tempered with something else that she wouldn't dare to allow herself to think about. "As I said, I'm used to dealing with men like you."

"Sweetheart, I seriously doubt you've met anyone like me."

"All men of your ilk seem to think that they're an original."

A quick breath tickled the hair at her temple, a laugh. "Men of my ilk," he repeated. "You talk like a schoolmarm, not a saloon girl. Who are you, Emmy?" His voice lowered a bit on this last question, so that it was soft, but still so deep that the vibrations rumbled through her.

Emmy? A name that he'd made up. Something about the way he whispered it made it more of an endearment. The notion was ridiculous, but it wasn't the outlaw looking back at her anymore. She saw *him*. Time stood still as he stared right back at her, his greenish eyes locked to hers, seemingly caught up in the same realization eating away at her rationality. That, maybe, this was someone she'd like to know better. That maybe there was more to him than his good looks and dangerous exterior. Slowly, his gaze moved down to her lips, touching her with the sudden heat that flared in their depths before moving back up to her eyes again. Attraction arced between them. When he licked his lips, her own lips tingled as if he had touched them. His heavy gaze fell to her mouth again. That look was so hooded and dark, she was sure that he was going to kiss her. He moved forward so slowly that she was certain he was giving her time to object. There was no chance of that, because she was caught and couldn't even breathe.

His breath brushed across her lips, tinged with the whiskey he'd drunk back at the saloon. He didn't kiss her though, leaving her bereft for that touch when he simply stopped and let his breath touch the sensitive flesh just below her bottom lip. It wasn't a kiss. It was too soft to be a kiss. It was more like a restrained exploration, an acknowledgment of want. When he moved along her jawline, still not kissing, still just that gentle almost-there touch, she turned her head to allow him access, eyes falling half-shut as the flicker of warmth that had begun deep in her belly began to flare higher. The stubble on his jaw rasped pleasantly against the softer skin of her cheek. He stopped when he reached the sensitive shell of her ear, his breath hot and somehow loud in the quiet space of the room. Chills of excitement ran through her body. Not even realizing she had moved until it had happened, her back arched, pushing her breasts into him. Immediately, his fist unclasped, settling his palm against her chest over her pounding heart. He still covered the locket, but his fingertips were so close to the tip of her breast that her nipples beaded, begging for his touch.

"Still not afraid of me?" His words were a hot whisper, followed by a gentle scrape of the stubble near his mouth against the tender lobe of her ear.

Her heart plummeted and she wanted to whimper, but was too proud to utter a sound that would give her secret pleasure away, although she was fairly certain it wasn't so secret. He was so confident it must be plain for him to see. Or maybe she was simply that easy to read. Maybe he didn't feel anything that she did and had been playing her the entire time. This was her greatest fear come to life. That she would fall for someone like him, only to be used and discarded, exactly as her mother had been by Ship. Emmaline had spent her entire life being guarded. Why had this one man been able to sneak right past her defenses and make her want something more? Her mother had been a whore who had lost herself to exactly this type of man. Maybe Emmaline's fate had been sealed the moment she was born in the brothel.

"Please…don't take my locket." She kept her eyes closed and said the only thing she could think of that wouldn't give herself away.

He took a deep, ragged breath, not immune to her after all. His breath shifted, hot against her throat now. The back of his fingers gently stroked a circle around the smooth metal and faux gemstone of her locket, teasing her skin through the material of her dress and drawing a shiver from her though she tried to hide it.

"You lied to me. This is your last chance to tell me the truth."

Whatever he might have done to make good on his promise, the knock that shook the thin door in its frame cinched her decision. A firm, single knock that made her imagine the giant or the angry Spaniard standing out there waiting to interrogate her. "It's two miles northeast of where you found me," she blurted out.

Just that quickly, he released her from his hold and turned just as the door was opening. She didn't miss that the smirk was back on his face, but sagged with relief that his attention was away from her, however briefly. What was happening to her?

Chapter Six

The knock on the door didn't come as a surprise. Castillo and Zane weren't patient men and with Miguel's life in the balance, Cas wasn't inclined to wait any longer than necessary to have the information they needed. Hunter didn't blame him. Miguel was like a brother to him as well, but he knew that the girl didn't have any idea where Campbell was keeping the foolish boy. His gut said that she was innocent in Miguel's kidnapping. It was obvious that she was hiding something from them, but it wasn't about Miguel.

Facing his half brother, he made sure to keep her shielded behind him. He acknowledged the move as soon as he'd done it, but he refused to examine why she stirred up his protective instincts. Her tiny hand automatically went to his back, not to push him away, but he thought to reassure herself in some way that he was there between her and danger. He knew he was right when she moved a few inches toward him, her smaller body almost completely hidden behind him. Without thinking, he moved his left hand back a little until his fingers found the thin, rough wool of the skirt of her dress. The strange thought went through his mind that she should be clothed in something finer, something softer.

"Has she told you anything?" Cas spoke in Spanish, his eyes hard as they sought those of the girl. From the corner of his eye, Hunter caught her glaring back at his brother over his shoulder.

The entire gang spoke Spanish, so Hunter was fluent after riding with them for years, and replied back in that language. It was best the girl not know what they were saying. "She admitted to being Campbell's stepdaughter, but she doesn't know anything about Miguel. This was a waste of time."

Cas's booted feet sounded heavy on the bare wood floor as he took a step to cross the few feet separating them from the door until he stood before them. "She's all we have."

"Campbell took your brother to get to us. Miguel didn't have anything to do with the shoot-out. Campbell will make contact soon enough once he's figured out what he wants."

Cas scowled, the anger vibrating off of him

almost tangible. "And that coward will pay with his life." Nodding to the girl, he said, "We'll keep her until he comes out of hiding."

Hunter swallowed a curse, even though the proclamation came as no surprise. The last thing he wanted was to sit with the girl while they waited for Campbell to crawl out from whatever hole he'd disappeared into, though he knew his brother was right. They needed leverage when dealing with Campbell. He still thought they had a chance to track him down, a chance that dwindled the longer they wasted time chasing the wrong lead. There were still plenty of scum out there who knew Campbell and someone knew where he was hiding. "Send Zane back to town and put out the word that we have her. Afterwards, we can take her to a safe place and keep looking. Campbell will come out of hiding soon enough. He wants you more than he wants Miguel dead."

Cas shook his head and his brow furrowed. "I'd like to believe that. Hate is a bitter thing. He could kill him just to spite me."

"He won't. We'll find him, Cas. Campbell's been around too long to hold a death grudge over Hardy's death. There were witnesses there that day. They saw him draw on you first. Campbell just wants to shake us up. It's extortion."

Cas nodded and his gaze jumped back to the girl. "Has she told you where she lives?"

"Northeast of town. We hadn't got to the specifics yet."

"You believe her?"

Hunter smiled. "Not a damn word. She's smart."

"You seem impressed, Brother."

"Intrigued."

"Don't get too intrigued. She's not just another one of your women. She could be the key to Miguel."

"She could be." Hunter shrugged, aware of the heat of her small body at his back. "Doesn't mean I can't enjoy her company."

"Save it for Susanne Harris when you get home."

Grimacing at the reminder of Susanne and all the other scheming socialites waiting to throw themselves at him upon his return to Helena, he shook his head. Their attention came from the fact that he was heir to a mining fortune and almost no one there knew he was an outlaw. It didn't hurt that he wasn't hard to look at as well, but his looks weren't what had them all scheming for marriage. Aside from a couple of indiscretions when he'd been too young to know better, he gave socialites a wide berth. "You're an ass. You deserve Susanne."

Cas flashed a smile, but the moment of levity was gone as quickly as it appeared. "Just don't forget our purpose."

"I've never let you down, brother. This one is smart, but she's also afraid. If she knew where Miguel was taken she would've given him up. I have the feeling her loyalty to Campbell doesn't extend as far as you think. I'll find out where she lives and you can ride out there."

Cas nodded in agreement. "I'll take Zane with me. If Campbell isn't there I'll send him into town and come back here to question her myself."

Hunter leveled a long stare at his brother. Though they'd only discovered each other's existence in adulthood, Hunter knew him as well as if they had been raised together. It was Cas's loyalty to his younger brother mixed with a heavy dose of guilt that made him talk so hard.

Switching to English, Hunter turned back to the girl and asked her exactly where her farm was located. Still glaring at his brother, she told them, keeping her voice firm and full of the contempt she felt for Cas. A little spark of pride surprised him as he watched her face them down. Fear and uncertainty shone in the depths of her eyes, but she kept her voice steady and her body didn't tremble. Her chin even rose a notch in that cute little way she had. He found himself smiling at her before he even realized it and crossed his arms over his chest, glancing down briefly as he forced himself to look as fierce as he was supposed to be.

Despite what had happened before they had been interrupted, Cas was right. She was Campbell's daughter. As much as Hunter would enjoy that seduction and especially how it would rankle the old son of a bitch, he wasn't in the habit of seducing his enemies. Besides that, there was a purity about her. She must have seen horrible things living with her stepfather, but they seemed to have left her unmarked. She wasn't like the others in her world and for some reason he admired her a little.

"If you're lying, *querida*, you'll have to face me come morning," Cas warned in his slightly accented English, a wink and the hint of a smile softening the words, but not the threat. Hunter placed a hand on his brother's chest and lightly pushed him back, not stopping until they reached the door.

"We'll find him."

Cas nodded, holding her gaze just a little longer before turning to leave, but the moment he opened the door, a shot rang out and a bullet splintered the flimsy wood at the top of the frame.

"Get down," Hunter called back to Emmy, and drew his Colt as he moved back to crouch in front of her. Cas drew his own gun and immediately shot back, the inside of the cabin filling with the explosion of the bullet being fired, before he laid himself flat against the wall. Another shot quickly rang out, this one so close that it had to be Zane returning fire.

"He's taking off!" Zane's voice carried inside as he ran toward his horse. "I'll get him."

Cas looked out, keeping an eye out for any other shooters. "Campbell's man. Looked like O'Brien."

Hunter looked to the girl for any reaction, but she didn't seem particularly upset if she recognized the name. "We can't stay here. There could be others out there." Staying could put her in danger and they couldn't risk that.

Nodding in agreement, Cas said, "Go to the cavern. We'll find her farm, get the word out that we have her and meet you there."

Cas took one more look into the darkened clearing around the shack and then made for his horse. Hunter holstered his gun, intending to collect the saddlebags.

There was another shot, this time much further away in the direction Zane had ridden chasing O'Brien. He looked up to make sure there were no riders coming toward them and saw that her face was pale. "You okay?"

She nodded, a jerking motion that she tried to disguise by turning her face to the fire, making him think she wasn't.

Pausing in the act of repacking, he gripped his hands into fists to keep from reaching out to her. "Do you know him?"

"O'Brien? No, I mean, the name is familiar."

At that, he rose to his feet and walked the few steps to stand beside her. Before he could stop himself, he was touching her shoulder. "This isn't me interrogating you. I just want to make sure you're okay." To his surprise, she didn't flinch away from him and her eyes were wide with fear when she looked up at him, making his gut tighten with something he couldn't risk identifying.

"Ship only just met him a few months ago. I don't really know him."

"I don't like that you had to be pulled into this." He wanted to tell her that he wouldn't allow Cas to hurt her, that everything would be fine, but he couldn't. He couldn't say a damn thing to reassure her until she told them everything she knew. Yet, even knowing that, he couldn't stop himself. Before he quite realized what he meant to do, he was lifting her chin up just a fraction higher so that she looked him in the eyes again. "Campbell took someone very important to us." The flair of surprise in her eyes confirmed what he had already suspected—that she knew nothing about what her stepfather had done. "I believe that you had nothing to do with it, but you will be with us until we can get him back."

Her heavy eyelids sank closed as she realized exactly what he was saying. In the flickering light of the fire, he could faintly see the blue veins beneath the pale and delicate skin, only emphasized by the fan of her incredibly long lashes. Dark smudges of color marred the skin beneath her eyes, fatigue making her appear only that much more delicate, but strong at the same time, he conceded when she opened her eyes again to stare up into his. The spark, the fight, was there just as strongly as it had been before. He wanted to tell her that she didn't have to fight him. There were so many other more enjoyable ways they could spend their time.

Hell, all he really wanted to do at that moment was kiss her. He wanted to pierce the heat of her mouth with his tongue and taste her. He wanted to pull her tiny body against his and feel her melt into him as her resistance faded and hunger took over. Only the realization that he was on the brink of closing the short distance between them and taking her mouth made him rein in his thoughts, but he still couldn't stop touching her. His thumb traced along the line where her alabaster skin met her red bottom lip, smudging the rouge a bit, touching her without crossing that ever-changing line in his head. He imagined the blunt tip slipping into the wet heat of her mouth to press against the rough silk of her tongue.

"And what if something bad happens...what if you don't get that person back?" Her voice was barely above a whisper.

"Do you think that will happen? Would Campbell risk you like that?" She flinched, jerking her chin from his grasp and making him feel like an ass for asking the question. She was worth so much more than Campbell's petty vengeance. Hardy had been a consummate drunk and an incompetent bank robber who had almost been strung up twice before. He'd wanted to make a name for himself by taking out one of them and Cas had responded in the only way he could. By drawing faster. It wasn't fair that she would pay for that.

"Let's get out of here while we can. Put your

boots on." He grabbed the bedroll and saddlebags and went out to tie them to his horse. Once
they were secure, he went back inside and used
his boot to scatter the small fire until it went out
and then turned down the lantern. She had put
on her boots and looked ready to bolt, so he took
her arm and led her to the horse. Grabbing her
waist, he lifted her up and then mounted behind
her before taking one last look around. There
were no signs of any other men, but he wouldn't
rest easy until they were miles away.

He took a moment to put on his gloves before
pulling her into the cradle of his thighs and picking up the reins. "Tell me your name." He didn't
think he imagined the slight jump she gave at
his question, but when she answered her voice
was as firm as before.

"Tell me *your* name," she challenged, turning her head just a bit to catch a glimpse of him.

This was the girl he liked. He liked her bris-
tly and challenging so that he could break down
her defenses as he had earlier. He liked how she
had become almost supple in his hands. He liked
teasing her.

Dammit, he liked her.

Fighting a smile, he inclined his head in grace-
ful defeat. "All right… Emmy…we can do it your
way." He pressed his knees to the black, nudg-

ing the horse forward to take a path along the creek. It'd be the best way to hide their tracks.

"No, tell me your name. What am I to call you? It seems like we'll be spending a lot of time together."

"Will we? Is that because you just gave us the wrong directions to your farm?"

But she was quick and didn't rise to that particular challenge. "It's because Ship isn't at my farm. I told you I don't know where he is and until you believe me—which I don't see happening—we'll be spending a lot of time together."

A vivid image of all the many ways he wanted to spend time with her came to mind, but he pushed it aside and cleared his throat. "My brothers will be back tomorrow and we'll see. If you've been truthful then you have nothing to worry about."

But she wasn't being truthful and he could sense the guilt on her as she quickly turned her head away. She was a terrible liar. He didn't know if he should be pleased or worried for her. It seemed to him that anyone associated with Campbell and his men would need to be proficient at lying if nothing else. Their survival would depend on it. It occurred to him then to wonder what her life with her stepfather was like. Was he cruel to her? Did his men treat her harshly?

His gaze wandered down her pretty profile, the light from the half-moon making her skin alabaster, before moving further down and noting the softness of her breasts, the trim line of her waist and the flare of her hips pressed against his thighs. She was pretty in a silent way that drew him in the more he noticed her. Had she had that same effect on one of those men? Did she belong to one of them? The thought was distasteful, but he had to acknowledge that it was probably true. One of them would have laid claim to her. And, damn his baser impulses, the fact that she had known a man's touch made her seem a little less out of reach, a little bit less of an innocent whom he'd be debauching.

Needing a distraction, he reached behind him to dig out some of the dried beef in his saddlebags. "Here." She eyed him warily and he couldn't stop the slight upturn of his mouth. "Take it." Shoving it into her hand, he grabbed another piece for himself. "Eat it, sweetheart. We won't get more than a couple hours' sleep if we're lucky and you'll need your strength for tomorrow."

"Stop calling me that. I'm not your sweetheart." She gave a haughty toss of her head as she brought the beef to her mouth with her loosely bound hands.

"Until you tell me your name I can call you whatever the hell I want." He couldn't resist chiding her, wrapping his arm tightly around her waist again until she settled against him, slowly relaxing.

"You called them brothers. Are you really? The big one doesn't favor you at all in appearance."

He was surprised at her question, but even more surprised with how he answered her. "No, he's not my brother. But he might as well be."

"But the Spaniard is your brother?" When he didn't answer she continued, "He has your eyes. There's something about the jawline, too, that's similar."

She was smart. He'd been surprised as anyone the day a man looking very similar to himself had shown up at his home demanding to see their father.

"He's my half brother." There was no real good way to explain the fact that their father had abandoned Castillo and his mother when his greed got in the way of family life. Tanner Jameson had been born the son of a poor dirt farmer in Texas, whose future had looked even grimmer once he'd been wounded in the war and discharged from the military. When he'd heard of the fortune to be made in Montana Territory, that's where he'd headed, leaving a young wife and child behind and damning the consequences.

A lucky hand of cards had won him a claim that began the Jameson fortune almost overnight. Soon after, he'd befriended a politician from Boston who'd been on a hunting excursion and wooed his daughter—though it was really the family money he was wooing; Hunter had the impression that his parents had never particularly liked one another. With a better marriage arranged, his father forgot all about his first family.

It shook him to the core that he wanted to tell her all of that. Instead, he said, "We only discovered the other's existence a little more than five years ago. I trust them both with my life. To survive what we do, you have to."

"And what is it you do?"

"We protect people from the likes of Ship Campbell and his band of thieves."

She looked back at him over her shoulder, her brow furrowed. "I think Ship would disagree with you. I think a lot of people might disagree with you. You're not lawmen."

"No, we're not lawmen and I'm sure that Ship would disagree. Doesn't mean it isn't true."

"Why do you do it?"

"Someone has to. Can't let the outlaws take over the world."

"But if you're not a lawman then you're an outlaw, too."

"If you want to put a fine point on it, then yeah, we're outlaws, too. But the work we do is necessary."

"Necessary or self-serving?"

He shrugged. It was really one and the same. "Both."

He met her challenging gaze and though it was too dark to see the emotion they held, he felt that look in his gut. It scorched a path all the way down. He wanted her beneath him. His erection swelled against the confines of his pants with the need to claim her. Not tonight, not while she was his prisoner, but already the fact that she was his enemy was beginning to hold little sway over his desire, a situation he'd never faced before.

He'd never met anyone like her. It was jarring just how much he liked her. He'd never turn his back on his brothers, and his loyalty to Cas was more important to him than anything else, but something about her made him want to think of a different future. A future where he could have her.

The intensity of his stare should have sent her screaming into the night. It should have at least warned her that she was in over her head. It did neither. It left her body throbbing with a need she was too smart to give in to, but not too ignorant to completely understand. How she could want to give herself so completely to this man, to this enemy who had abducted her solely for the purpose of reaching her stepfather, should have filled her with a self-disgust that would shame her for years to come. But it didn't, or it hadn't yet.

She swung her gaze forward to break his hold and did her best to move forward, to keep space between them. She'd been completely unprepared for how he would overwhelm her. His torso pressed against the length of her back as he leaned forward, a move she thought was deliberate until she realized he did it to navigate them up a slope. Regardless of the reason, he was all around her at once. His smell, the heat of him, the solid reassurance of his large body behind her.

Reassurance. It was a tricky word and one she wouldn't have thought to attribute to him, but once it crossed her mind it felt right. No one would harm her as long as he was there at her back. The truth of that was as unsettling as it was comforting, so she tried not to dwell on it and took another bite of her jerky.

"Look…" he sighed and his voice sounded

weary "…just because Campbell and I are enemies, doesn't mean that you and me can't be friends."

"I'm not usually friends with people who tie me up and hold me captive, but I can make an exception given there really is no other choice."

"Fine." The word came out a bit clipped.

His sudden anger made her unreasonably angry. "My apologies. Should I not have reminded you that until half an hour ago you had me bound from the rafters and even now my wrists—"

"Enough."

She opened her mouth to reply but shut it just as quickly. *What are you doing, Em? You're supposed to make friends, make him trust you.* All hope of escaping that night had long since drained away from her, fading with the echo of the first terrifying gunshot back at the shack. He was so large there was almost no chance that she could forcibly push him from the horse, and without a weapon she didn't dare try it and get herself tied up again. Instead, she would bide her time until she could use her powders and in the meantime get information from him. If she put an end to their *friendship* he'd be less likely to tell her anything.

Swallowing the bitter dredges of her pride, she

said instead, "You're right. I'd like it if we could be friends. I'm sorry, I'm just tired and irritable."

He grunted behind her, but didn't say anything, and she knew their tentative peace was over for now. They rode throughout the rest of the night, keeping close to the trees when they could and only breaking into a gallop when the trees gave way to open grassland.

By the time the sun had made its way above the flatlands to the east, she was aware that someone must be following them. She never saw or heard anyone, but he kept looking backward and twisting back and forth across the creek so often that she was certain he was trying to cover their progress. When she asked, he gave another noncommittal grunt that she decided meant he didn't want to talk about it.

Finally, about midmorning, when she had already nodded off more times than she could count, he turned them toward the mountains and they began to make an ascent into the foothills. Never comfortable around horses, and even less so on the steep climb, she wrapped her hands around the steely arm that held her tight. Sometime just after sunrise when they had stopped briefly, he'd shoved a handful of dried apples at her and ordered her to eat them. They churned in her belly now, threatening to make an unfortunate reappearance.

"I've got you," came his reassuring voice behind her.

It probably wasn't that steep. The horse never skidded or lost its footing at all, but every change in elevation seemed more dramatic from the back of a horse. They didn't go very far, but the path was treacherous, forcing them to move slowly and making him tense behind her.

"Where are we going?" she only managed to ask once she'd closed her eyes.

"There's a place just up here where we can take cover for a bit."

Her hopes of escape plummeted, because she had absolutely no idea how far they were from town at this point. She knew they had headed north, but had no idea when they had actually passed Whiskey Hollow and her home. The girls would be worried sick by now, but she knew that Jake would have gotten to them. He was a man of his word and he'd always looked out for her and the children. At least they were safe. "Is someone following us?"

"Doubt it. I obscured our trail, but if someone is looking for us, they'll find it eventually. We'll stay hidden just to make sure."

When they came to a stop, she opened her eyes to see the tops of the chokecherries and spruces just below them. They went blurry for just a moment before she blinked the exhaustion away and made herself look forward, away from the drop off. The mountain rose up ever higher, one giant mound of rocks and dirt covered in grasses in every shade of green and brown. There was no path here and a near-vertical slope, but he sensed her question and raised his arm to point ahead. Just in the shadows along the side of the sheer slope was a gouge in the earth, really just a natural separation of the rocks that would give them a small roof over their heads and an opening at each end to crawl out of. With the mountain at their back, the side facing the world was partially obscured with rocks.

"Don't worry. We'll have an excellent view if we were followed." With those words of optimism, he dismounted and helped her down.

Her knees immediately threatened to buckle and every muscle in her body protested the long ride. He grinned at her as he grabbed her hips to steady her, that flash of white that managed to transform his granite face from stone to something close to human. Her stomach flipped despite her discomfort as she bent over to rub her thighs.

"Come on." The smile was still in his voice as he put an arm around her waist and helped her to the makeshift cave. Waiting until she crawled her way under the overhang of rock, he walked back to grab the gear from the horse, making an extra trip for the saddle. "I'm taking the horse back down to the trees. I'll only be a couple of minutes."

It occurred to her then that now would be an excellent time to escape, but she couldn't so much as lift herself from the unladylike sprawl her muscles had frozen into. She watched his head bobbing as he walked away, waiting for it to disappear from her line of sight, telling herself the entire time that as soon as it did, she'd get up and run. But when it did, she closed her eyes for only a moment and allowed the overpowering bliss of sleep to overtake her.

Chapter Seven

The sun was starting to sink behind them when she awoke. She sat up with a start, never having meant to go to sleep at all. The shadows weren't that deep yet in the valley below them; it had to be early afternoon. He stirred behind her, voice husky with sleep as he said her name. *Emmy.* Not her name, but the name he'd invented for her, the one that she secretly liked more and more every time he said it. Only when she looked over at him did she realize that at some point he'd laid out the bedroll and put her on it before covering her with his coat. It sat crumpled in her lap now with him lying right beside her.

She tried not to imagine him moving her practically unconscious body from the ground to the bedroll. Had he watched her as she slept? Had he lingered over the task or performed it in a perfunctory manner with no care at all? For some reason she kept imagining him moving her gently, with the slow touch of a lover, spreading the bedroll and cradling her to his chest as he placed her tired body upon it. The thought was so clear she had to wonder briefly if it was a memory flitting through her mind, even going so far as to try to remember what position they had been in when she'd awakened and sat up, before giving it up to a notion of her ridiculous imagination.

This bizarre attraction to him, to this man who had *kidnapped her*—a sane person shouldn't have to keep reminding herself of that small detail—was intolerable. It didn't matter that he was handsome. It didn't matter that he had handled himself in a way that had earned her grudging trust. It didn't matter that she kept imagining him as a knight in battle, like in the few adventure novels she read to the girls. None of that mattered. He was the enemy. He was her captor and she very much needed to get herself away from him as soon as possible.

The enemy in question wasn't smiling as he looked up at her with those strange eyes, deep pools of transient color that changed from green to gold on a whim. That intense gaze was taking its time tracing every contour of her face. Long, dark blond lashes rimmed the heavy lids making him appear deceptively at ease, while the shadows of fatigue beneath his eyes, along with the extra day's growth of beard, gave him a fierce look.

"Thank you for the bedroll and the coat." She spoke, to break his spell as much as to thank him for seeing to her comfort. When he didn't move or answer, she grabbed his coat and pushed it toward him.

"You should sleep," he finally said. "There will be more riding tonight. Rest while you can."

She nodded, but it wasn't at all what she intended to do. Her muscles still ached and her body craved rest, but to willingly give in to it would be accepting her place as his hostage. If there was a chance to escape, she needed to be awake and alert to seize it. Her gaze flitted around the small space, taking in every hard nook where rock met more rock. The low ceiling kept it dark and cool inside their little cavern. Light penetrated from each end, just beyond his head and feet, and along the drop-off edge where boulders kept them from rolling out and down the mountain in their sleep.

"Have we been followed?"

"No. I've been checking, but so far no action." He rose to his knees then, the space too low to allow him to get to his feet, and pushed the coat back at her. She accepted it because she was cold and held it to her front, draping the wool over her shoulders. Walking the few feet needed to reach the edge on his knees, he picked up a small, leather-wrapped case and pulled out what could only be a pair of binoculars. Two sets of lenses, one small and one larger, were set into twin cylinders rimmed with a thick edge of gold at either end, fastened to a middle wrapped with rich, brown leather. He gripped the leather in his fingers as he raised the smaller lenses to his eyes and looked back into the distance in the direction they had come. A few minutes later he lowered them, giving her a nod. "Still no sign of anyone."

"Are those binoculars?"

He seemed surprised by the question, his brow furrowing a bit as he looked down at the object in question. "Of course. Have you never seen a pair?"

She shook her head. "We've never had need for them." Not that they would have been able to afford them had there been a need. After food and clothing all other *necessities* became frivolities. The only exception being the occasional book Ship, or even Pete during one of his sober spells, would sometimes bring back for her, but if those small treasures were bought or stolen she didn't know. She'd made a point of never asking. She'd heard Pete mention needing binoculars before, though, and had wondered about them ever since.

"Have a look." He raised them toward her.

She tensed to refuse, but her curiosity won out and she tossed his coat aside and accepted the binoculars. Going to her knees beside him, the expensive smell of leather and polished metal greeted her as she brought them to her eyes and peered between the boulders, barely managing to keep her mouth from dropping open at the sight that greeted her. The entire countryside was before her—*right there* before her eyes—just an arm's length away, or so it seemed. She could even make out each distinctive white petal on the thimbleweed across the valley below them as they swayed in the gentle afternoon breeze.

"It's amazing, isn't it?" She couldn't help but smile as she pulled the lenses from her eyes, only to bring them back again as she compared the different views.

"I suppose it is," he answered in a voice that made it clear he didn't think so at all.

"It…everything is just…just right there and it's almost as if you can touch it." She held her fingers out before her, wiggling them in front of the lenses and smiling at how large and blurry they were.

After a moment, she noticed that he had become strangely still beside her and she pulled the lenses back from her eyes to look at him. He sat back on his heels, his face stoic in an expression she couldn't quite place as he watched her. "You think I'm silly." Not for the first time, it occurred to her how worldly he seemed for an outlaw and she felt quite silly in her ignorance. The smile fell from her face as she handed the binoculars back to him.

He shook his head "no" in answer to her accusation and placed them back into their case.

"It's fine."

"No. I don't think you're silly."

"It doesn't hurt my feelings." What a simple, pathetic girl he must think her.

"I don't think you're silly. I think you're…"

After an appropriate amount of silence followed, she prodded, "What? What am I?" She realized she was holding her breath for his answer, but couldn't seem to make herself not care. She was being a dolt over this criminal.

"You're unusual."

She let out a disappointed breath, but acknowledged that "unusual" was better than silly. Why did it even matter? This wasn't a Sunday picnic. He hadn't bought her basket at the church auction, not that Whiskey Hollow had those anymore after the pastor had left them one spring night a couple of years ago.

"That's a compliment. I've met Campbell. I've met your brother, Pete, and men like them, you're nothing like I was expecting."

It spoke volumes for Ship's character that she knew exactly what he meant. Ship was a big talker, but he wasn't known for being particularly eloquent or honorable. "My mother wasn't always a prostitute. She was a schoolteacher first."

His eyes widened for a moment in surprise before he hid the reaction and she realized that he hadn't known that. She was used to people in Whiskey Hollow knowing all about her mother and how Ship had brought her and her bastard daughter to town from that fancy Helena brothel one day years ago. She still remembered how difficult it had been for her to leave the women at the brothel behind, the only family Emmaline had ever known. Her mother had thought she was doing the right thing for her daughter, giving her a real home with a real family. She hadn't realized until it was too late that a legitimate husband and shelter wasn't what made a family. Ship had never been intentionally cruel to them, but his crassness, his inattention and boorish nature had never made them feel at home.

Shaking herself out of the memory and to cover the gaffe, she continued on. "She brought her books along when Ship married her and we moved to his farm. She taught me what she could. Ship never really cared to learn anything…from her or anyone else. Pete let her teach him to read, but only just barely, and that's only after she threatened to shoot his horse if he didn't learn."

He laughed, a gentle breath of air that made her smile. Their gazes met and held over that smile. "She sounds like a…special woman, your mother."

"She was." Her smile faltered as she experienced a pang at the loss all over again. A cough had ravaged her mother's body one summer and hadn't let up until she was gone. It had been over seven years now and it still hurt.

His green eyes darkened, becoming solemn. "I'm sorry you lost her."

She nodded, trying to determine why that look from him touched her so deeply.

"If your mother's gone, why do you stay with him?"

She shrugged, not daring to mention her sisters. She and the girls had been alone when her mother had died, Ship hadn't come back until weeks later. She'd asked to leave then, to take the girls with her and go back to the brothel knowing that Glory, the brothel's madam, would help her find respectable work with her connections. Through the madam's regular letters to Emmaline's mother, she knew that while she ran a functioning brothel, women in trouble went to her all the time in search of aid. Sometimes they decided to become prostitutes, sometimes they simply stayed for a brief sanctuary and a train ticket out of town.

Ship had refused to even consider it, telling her that she could be a whore if she wanted, but she wouldn't take his girls. After that, he hadn't delivered any more letters from Glory. She couldn't blame him for not wanting to part with his children, even though she knew their best chance at a good life was to be away from him. She'd resigned herself then to life with Ship for a little longer. Just until she could figure out a way to get the three of them away safely.

But that opportunity had never presented itself and here they were in danger. She couldn't wait anymore. She had to get them to safety, even if it meant doing something unspeakable.

"Where would I go? I don't have binoculars edged in gold." That wasn't completely true.

Though she didn't have money, once a man had asked her to leave with him, a widower who had worked at the stable in town for a few months before moving further west. He'd become a regular at the saloon and one night, slightly drunk and missing his wife, he'd kissed her. It had been pleasant and repeated on other nights as well, but when he'd suggested that she leave with him, she'd gently refused because she couldn't leave her sisters. Besides, leaving with him would've been unfair, because she'd only be using his affection to take her away from Whiskey Hollow.

"No, I suppose you don't." Suitably chastened, he looked back out over the valley.

"How is it that you do? You're an outlaw like Ship. How is it you're so successful? I always thought outlaws barely got by on the money they steal."

"Some do. We earn a decent living."

"No, there's more," she prodded. "I could believe that from the Spaniard or even the giant—"

"The giant?" He laughed and whipped his head back around to look at her.

"The big one," she explained and raised her hand to the low ceiling of their little hideaway. "He dresses fine, but there's something else, something underneath, a lack of refinement."

"You're good, Emmy. I was educated back East." He wasn't laughing anymore, but he still smiled at her. It was the brief half-smile that she was coming to crave from him.

"Then why did you leave that world and become an outlaw?"

He shrugged. "There's more to life than binoculars edged in gold. My brother needed me. I had to help him."

She studied him closely, trying her best to see what lurked behind those words. It was on the tip of her tongue to ask more, to find out all there was to know about him, but she knew that he wouldn't answer. The situation they found themselves in wouldn't allow him to answer. Why was she so willing to forget that with him? She looked away from his mesmerizing face and drew in a breath. "I suppose that includes stealing people who don't belong to you."

Instead of letting it drop, he touched her chin, his fingertips making her pulse race as he tilted her face back to him. His eyes were heavy and intense as they pierced hers. "I want you to understand that I never wanted to take you. I promise that when this is over I'll take you back home if that's where you want to go. In the meantime, I'll keep you safe."

* * *

As if fate was giving him a chance to prove true to his words, a bullet ricocheted off the boulder beside them, spraying them with bits of rock. The explosion of the gunshot seemed to fill the entire valley below them. Before she could react, he grabbed her and rolled with her in his arms, his larger body taking the brunt of the fall before coming to rest on top of her, his arms cradled around her head as another shot tried to find its way into their sanctuary.

Waiting just long enough to make sure that a third shot wouldn't attempt to find them, he rose up to his knees, just to sprawl back down on her as another bullet attempted and failed to find them. "Goddammit!"

Her eyes stared up into his when he rose to his elbows above her to double-check that she was fine. "Are you hit?" she asked.

"No." He should have been watching for the bastard tracking them, not letting his captivating charge distract him. If he didn't get his head on straight he wouldn't get them out of this alive, much less return her home. "You're not hurt?"

"No."

Now that the shooting had stopped, he moved to his knees, his body continuing to shield hers as he leaned forward to take a peek through the narrow gap between the boulders. The view was obscured, but he could just make out the shadow of a man just below the tree line, his body partially hidden by a ridge of rock nearer the bottom of the slope. Hunter wouldn't be able to get a clear shot, but neither would he. The rocks would protect them as long as they stayed low.

Moving back into his original position over her, he opened his mouth to reassure her, but the words hung in his throat. Beautiful wasn't the word that would've come to mind when he'd first seen her. That word was reserved for the debutantes with their practiced smiles and perfect coiffures. Arresting had been more appropriate for her. She was pretty, but there was something about her that made you look twice just to make sure the glint you saw in her eye hadn't been imagined. She was real in a way that no other woman had been for him.

Looking at her disheveled hair and her wide, blue eyes as she lay beneath him, he couldn't help but imagine how it might be if she was lying beneath him for an entirely different reason. They were in the middle of a shoot-out and he still wanted her. Apparently his depravity knew no bounds.

Wrenching his gaze away from her, he nodded to the bedroll and moved off of her. "Stay down and move back to the bedroll. That'll keep you far enough away from the possible range of gunfire."

"Is it Ship? Please don't hurt him if it is."

"I can't get a good look, but he'll poke his head out soon enough." He didn't wait for her to obey him before reaching for the binoculars and pulling them from their case. Moving as close to the entrance of the cavern as he could without exposing himself, he held them up and waited. He didn't need to wait long. The man was obviously impatient to complete a task that had already taken more time than he wanted, so he popped up above the ridge to take another shot. Hunter didn't even flinch, knowing the bullet wouldn't find him. The shooter had pushed his hat back on his forehead to aim his shot, revealing a face that Hunter was sure he'd never seen before. Greasy brown hair streaked with gray and a grizzled face that could have belonged to any one of the men who might want him dead.

"I don't recognize him." Shifting on his knees, he looked back at her over his shoulder and reached out a hand. "Come take a look. Do you know all of Campbell's men?"

She nodded. "There are a few who shift in and out of his gang, like O'Brien, but most of them have been riding with him for years."

He made sure to keep himself between her and the outside of the cavern when she joined him and passed the binoculars to her. "He's there, just at that ridge." His hand automatically went to rest at the small of her back and he had to force himself to not breathe her in, no matter that she still inexplicably smelled like flowers. They stayed like that for a few minutes waiting for their adversary to make another move. When he finally rose up, this time to get a better look without taking a shot, she lowered the lenses and passed them back.

"I'm not sure."

This was getting out of hand. They'd had her for less than twenty-four hours and already she'd been shot at by two different men. When Cas and Zane arrived later they'd have to have a serious discussion about what to do with her. "Move back to the bedroll."

He brought the binoculars back up just in time to see the muzzle of the gun glinting in the afternoon sun and ducked instinctively just as the next shot fired, the blast echoing against the rock of the mountain. Dropping the binoculars, he pulled one of the guns from the holster he'd shed earlier and propped against the boulder. Then he moved forward as far as he could without exposing his shoulder to the shooter and took aim at the spot the man would appear when he tried to shoot again. Over the next several minutes Hunter got off a few shots, but none of the bullets found the narrow swath of the faded blue shirt his target would occasionally reveal and gouged craters in the rock the coward hid behind, instead. He forced a deep, slow breath, counting the beats of his heart as he waited for the man to show himself again. He was rewarded a short while later when the barrel of the revolver came over the edge of the rock followed quickly by a flash of blue. Hunter fired and the barrel disappeared behind the rock only to come back up a moment later. He'd missed.

A bead of sweat rolled down his neck as he took advantage of the break and opened the chamber on his Colt to reload. He'd been in shoot-outs before and knew that patience was the only way to win, but he'd never had to worry about an innocent's safety before. It gnawed at him that he was the reason she was in danger.

Another shot fired, the dust from where the bullet grazed the rock spraying over his shoulder as he finished loading the gun. "You okay?" He spared a glance in her direction to see her nodding, her wide-eyed gaze fastened to the shooter's hiding place. Smothering a curse, he took aim and waited for the son of a bitch to reappear.

Six shots later he sat back on his heels, cursing again as he reloaded. He had bullets left, but at this rate they'd run out before Cas and Zane got to them. Movement from behind him caught his eyes, but he didn't bother to look at her and just yelled back, "Stay down!"

He pushed in two more bullets before a shot rang out, so close that it left his ears ringing, too close to have been from the man trying to kill them. As he pulled his Colt up to fire at whoever had shot, his gaze landed on the girl holding his spare gun.

Chapter Eight

Emmy was on her knees near the boulders with the gun pointed toward the shooter, its muzzle still smoking from the shot. Automatically, Hunter's gaze followed the line of fire and saw bushes rustling and flashes of movement as the man made his way on foot down the mountain and to his horse. The heavy brush at the bottom gave the man natural cover so Hunter couldn't get a clear shot, so he grabbed the binoculars and watched him make his way to his horse. By the time he reached it, he was out of revolver range, making Hunter wish he'd had his rifle. As the man awkwardly pulled himself up with one arm, Hunter could tell that he was seriously injured. A bright stain of red marred the blue on his right shoulder as he rode off, hunched over the reins.

Dropping the binoculars, he looked back at her. "Shit! You got him."

"I hope I didn't kill him." Her face was pale and her hands had started to shake as she watched the rider retreat.

"No. No, you didn't, it was only his shoulder," he hurried to reassure her. "He won't be aiming a gun anytime soon, but he'll be okay."

She looked at him then, finally taking her eyes from the retreating horse once she was assured that he spoke the truth.

"That was an expert shot," he said.

"Of course it was. I'm an excellent shot."

The arrogant yet somehow innocent grin she supplied with that remark was enough to make him stare. She *was* beautiful when she smiled like that, her eyes shining with confidence. He found himself smiling in return just because she was so damned enticing with that smile, but caught himself as he remembered their roles.

"But how? Last night you didn't even come close when you shot at us."

She shrugged, the apples of her cheeks turning a light shade of pink. "I'm better when the targets aren't moving and there aren't animals involved. Last night I didn't want to hit the horses."

He couldn't help it; he laughed then, practically doubling over as the hilarity of her statement hit him. She'd rather not shoot their horses—animals he'd gathered she didn't particularly care for—than save herself from being kidnapped. Her brow furrowed, but then she laughed, too. The tension of the moment needed an outlet. The light sound of her laugh was just husky enough to rake pleasantly across his senses while something warm tugged deep in his gut. It was beyond appealing.

The moment their eyes met, they both realized the exact same thing: she was his hostage and she was holding a loaded gun. Before she could move, he lunged and knocked her backward, one hand moving to cup the back of her head and cushion her fall while the other grabbed her wrist, holding it pinned to the ground above her head.

The laughter was gone and just inches separated his face from hers, his lips from hers. She didn't struggle and she let go of the gun so that it dropped to lay on the ground. Of its own volition, his hand inched up from her wrist until they were palm to palm, surprising himself when his fingers laced with hers. She squeezed him back and he was dropping down to her as if she held some magic that was pulling him in and he didn't even think about resisting. All he wanted was to finally claim her as his.

Her gasp filled the air between them just before his mouth touched hers. Despite his need, it was a gentle touch, slow and soft, giving her the chance to pull away the moment she didn't want it. Except that she did want it. Soft lips parted beneath his and desire immediately tightened deep in his groin as his heart beat a fast rhythm against his rib cage.

Excitement pulsed through her veins like a power that couldn't be contained. The fear that had only compounded with each bullet fired, followed by the exhilaration of firing the shot that had saved them, had combined to form this heady mix of energy she didn't know how to control. She didn't want to control it.

With his warm palm pressed to hers, his hand at the back of her head and his large body covering hers, imprisoning her between his powerful thighs, she briefly realized that she should have felt very much at his mercy, his prisoner, but what she felt was quite the opposite. She felt protected and wanted. A small gasp escaped her when his tongue brushed against her bottom lip and she craved more. Her free hand went to his chest, palm reveling in the hard muscle as she moved on to his shoulder and then the dark blond hair at the back of his head, where her fingers clenched in the short, thick waves to pull him closer.

His soft growl of pleasure made a spark of pleasure shoot through her belly and she touched him back, stroking the tip of her tongue against his full bottom lip. Immediately he deepened the kiss, tightening his own fingers in her hair as he chased her tongue with his, moving in and out in a sensuous rhythm. A new and strange need began to pulse within her, warmth unfurling in her belly and moving downward to pulse between her thighs. She wanted to be closer to him, to feel the hardness of his body against the softness of hers.

He must have sensed what she wanted, because he lowered himself so that his elbow was no longer supporting him and his weight fell softly on her. She almost groaned with how good he felt on top of her. He was hard everywhere: his chest and stomach, his unforgiving thighs entrapping hers, the unmistakable shaft of steel pressed against her belly. For the first time in her life she wanted to explore that part of a man. The strange urge gave her a moment of pause, until she let the excitement overtake her again, forcing herself to lock her reticence away and to just let him make her *feel*.

Letting go of his hair, she curled her hand around his impossibly wide shoulder and held him close. It was his turn to groan when he pulled his lips from hers and buried his face in her neck. His breath on the sensitive area sent goose bumps prickling across her skin, but then it was followed by the wet heat of his mouth and she gasped aloud at the unexpected bolt of pleasure that shot through her middle, pushing her hips up into his. He groaned again and pressed his pelvis into her. This time her lips parted on a soft moan she tried to contain by biting down on her bottom lip. His mouth moved down her neck, his tongue coming out to stroke her just before his lips closed over the spot, sucking lightly. Finally, he reached the coarse wool of her dress and she actually sighed with disappointment when he stopped, his forehead coming to rest briefly on her shoulder as he took a deep, shuddering breath and raised up to look down at her.

She knew that she must look a mess if the heavy breaths she was trying hard to get under control were any indication. His brow was furrowed, drawing his eyebrows together in a way that made him seem bewildered, and she couldn't help but smile at how the look transformed him from hardened outlaw to ardent lover. It didn't seem to matter that they shouldn't have been kissing at all or that their hands were still locked together and she wasn't behaving like a proper hostage at all. It had happened and neither of them seemed to quite know how it had come about.

When he smiled back, a tentative grin that revealed far more of his uncertainty than he probably intended, she had to resist the urge to trace the curve of his shapely bottom lip as desire shot through her core. Everything about that desire was wrong.

"That shouldn't have happened." The words were automatic and not at all what she meant even though she knew they were true.

"No. It shouldn't." Releasing her hand, he brought his to rest gently on her jawline and the curve of her neck. His fingertips rested there for a second, stroking back and forth before he roused himself and slipped off of her. "I shouldn't have kissed you."

She opened her mouth instinctively to tell him that it was fine, that she had wanted it. Her body still throbbed with how "fine" it had been, but bit lightly on her tongue to stop the words. He was still the outlaw who had kidnapped her. Instead of saying anything, she pushed herself up and pulled her knees to her chest. She had to get away. The locket rested heavily between her breasts, reminding her of the plan she had made.

He pushed his hand through his hair and let

out a deep breath. A tiny flutter of pleasure winged its way through her at the tangible evidence of how she affected him, but that wasn't the only evidence, she reminded herself, and discreetly glanced to the bulge still obvious in his breeches. It shouldn't matter and, really, it didn't matter, but it was something she could take with her and relive later.

When she didn't absolve him of his guilt, he nodded and retrieved the gun she had used to return it to his holster lying near the saddlebags. "I'm glad you know how to shoot. It was good that Campbell taught you." After he was finished he gave her a quick glance and flashed a grin. "Care for a drink? I sure as hell need one."

The flask! She faintly remembered seeing it at some point when she was on his horse and realized that it would be the best way to get the powders into him. "Yes, please."

Lips still tingling from his kiss, she watched his impressively wide shoulders as he dug through the saddlebags with more than a little regret. It really was unfortunate that she hadn't met him under different circumstances. That kiss had been…unbelievable. But it was stupid to pursue that line of thought. She had to get away— and not just to get back to her sisters. If the past hours had taught her anything, it was that she wasn't safe with Ship anymore. Money or not, she had to get herself and the girls away from his chaos. She shuddered to think what might have happened if someone like Ship's men had kidnapped her, or worse, her sisters.

Taking a deep pull on the flask, he handed it to her and watched as she nodded her thanks and took a small taste of the whiskey. It burned going down, warming her from the inside out as if she'd needed it after that kiss had heated her blood. She had only just begun to worry about how to get the powders into his drink, when he turned to pick up the binoculars, bringing them to his eyes to look in the direction the shooter had ridden. She couldn't resist admiring the view he presented, wide chest, narrow waist and the tantalizing way his breeches pulled tight over the curve of his backside.

Shaking her head, she fumbled with the locket, pulling it out of her bodice and carefully pressing the catch to open it. How much should she add? One quick glance to make sure he hadn't moved and she emptied the entire powdery contents into the whiskey, just managing to stow the locket back in her dress before he turned around. Swirling it, she made a show of bringing the flask to her lips again, making sure to keep her lips closed as she pretended to drink before handing it back to him, stifling her pang of regret. "No sign of anyone?"

"No." He held the binoculars loosely at his side with one hand while bringing the flask to his lips with the other and taking a drink. The muscles working in his throat held her mesmerized as he swallowed and she knew then that it would be her life's regret not to see more of those glorious muscles of his.

When he lowered the flask, she realized that he had caught her staring at him. His darkened gaze settled on her lips briefly before meeting her eyes, both of them reliving that kiss. His eyes were hot, blazing across the few feet separating them. "If my brothers are the giant and the Spaniard, who am I?"

"What do you mean?" Her heart pounded in her throat once before it skidded to a complete halt.

Taking another pull off the flask, he grinned. "I understand why you'd name him the giant. He's one of the biggest men I've ever met. And the Spaniard, well, that's obvious, too. But what have you named me?"

"I—I—what? Nothing. Nothing! I haven't named you anything." Her entire face flamed as her heartbeat seemed to have returned to beat an absurdly loud tempo in her ears. If she had to admit to naming him "The Pretty One" she'd die right here in this cave.

He was smiling as he looked down to screw the cap back on the flask and set it beside him. He was laughing at her and she was torn between dying of embarrassment and panicking because he wasn't drinking the sleeping powders and she knew as diluted as they were, the little he'd had wouldn't be enough.

"Let's see." He was still amused when he looked back up at her, seeming to consider his options. "You've named us based on our obvious physical attributes, so what's the most prominent thing about me?"

She squeezed her eyes closed, certain that her nickname for him would be obvious. He knew he was pretty. Hell, *Jake* had known he was pretty.

"It doesn't really matter, does it?"

"That bad, huh?"

"No, not that bad." She opened her eyes to see him still watching her, one arm draped lazily over his knee, the whiskey still at his side. How was she ever going to get him to drink more? "Take another drink and I'll tell you." She blurted those words out before she could figure out anything.

His brow furrowed and he looked down at the whiskey and then back at her. *What a way to make him suspicious, Em!* Dear Lord, she was horrible at this, whatever *this* was. Subterfuge. Finesse. Being clever.

"It's embarrassing." It was the only explanation she could offer. Still unable to get her brain wrapped around a coherent thought tight enough to formulate a plan, she walked on her knees to sit beside him while still facing him and grabbed the flask. Her fingers worked to unscrew the cap as she met his gaze. Lord, she couldn't force him to drink.

Or could she? Her gaze shot to his mouth and her lips tingled as she imagined it on hers, a hasty plan formulating. "Will you promise not to say anything if I tell you?"

He nodded once. The mood had sobered and she wasn't entirely sure what it meant. "I promise." His deep voice filled the small gap between them, vibrating across her senses.

Staring at the stubbled hair on his chin, she whispered, "You're 'The Pretty One'."

He kept his promise and didn't answer. His lips parted as if he might say something, but he paused and closed them as he took the flask from her, tipping his head back just enough to take a long drink.

She felt like a ridiculous little girl admitting she'd taken a fancy to the older gentleman in one of the Gothic novels her mother had favored.

Chancing a look at his eyes, she saw they weren't laughing at her. Not anywhere close to laughing. He was staring at her with that same intoxicating look that made the green appear so vivid. The one that made her think he was imagining kissing her. That look didn't make her feel like a little girl at all.

Taking the flask back from him, she took a swig of the laced whiskey, the rich, oak taste of the amber liquid sitting on her tongue as she held it in her mouth. Her gaze locked on his lips, she leaned forward slowly, anticipation making her skin prickle until her lips pressed to his. They parted beneath her and she fed him the warm liquid. He made a rough sound in the back of his throat as he drank from her. When he'd taken it all, his tongue teased across her lips, dipping inside to brush against her tongue. She wasn't prepared for the answering flare of heat deep in her belly and a small moan escaped her.

His hands immediately seized her waist and dragged her astride his lap, strong fingers unyielding on her hips as he pulled her into him. She gasped aloud at the shock of his hard arousal pressed against her so intimately, but he chased her mouth with his, covering it with his as he pushed up against her. The flesh between her thighs grew wet with her desire, making her ache from the rough contact and the need to be closer. Her fingers clenched tightly in his hair as she stroked his tongue, needing more from him.

Only the need for air drew them apart, then he just pressed kisses to the corner of her mouth and then her chin as he pulled back far enough to look at her. His scent was all around her and she realized just how much she craved it. Need burned hot in his eyes as they held hers briefly before he took her lips again, devouring her with his kiss. His hands moved in a slow circular caress up and down her hips, finally moving to fill themselves with her bottom which he squeezed gently as he rocked her into his hard arousal. A whimper escaped her as the ache increased in intensity.

"Emmy." Her name whispered against her lips made her stomach flip pleasantly. "When this is over with Campbell... I want you." He took her mouth again in a rough kiss, his tongue slipping between her lips to brush hers.

"I want you, too." The words were out before she could stop them. It would never happen. When this was over with Ship she'd be long gone. But it was a pleasant idea, even if it was wrong in so many ways. She wanted him so badly that it was taking away her reasoning. Would it be so bad to lie with him just once?

Yes! The accusation was so loud in her head that it made her draw back from him. She wouldn't become her mother. She wouldn't become a whore. Her virtue was the only thing she had any control over and she couldn't let this happen.

"I'm sorry." She pulled back so abruptly that she felt the need to apologize. But the wounded look on his face made her offer a jumbled explanation. "I...my mother... I shouldn't."

"What's wrong?" His hands were so tender as they touched her face that more words poured out.

"I'm so afraid of becoming like her...a whore." She had no idea why she was giving voice to her deepest fear. To *him*. Probably because she knew that he wouldn't remember any of this. His voice had thickened as the powders were already starting to take hold.

"Dear God, Emmy, do you really think that you ever could be?" The intensity on his face was as if she had blasphemed.

Furrowing her brow, she nodded. "Yes, sometimes it's not a choice."

"That's not who you are."

"You don't know who I am."

"No, I don't." He eyes held hers and refused to let go. "But you're not a whore. No matter what happens, that's not who you are. My own mother used her body for profit. Believe me, I'm familiar with that type of woman."

"Your mother worked in a brothel?"

He smiled and it was distinctly self-depre-cating. "No, nothing so honest as that. She did her work in a marriage bed with a husband she didn't want. It's rather the same thing, don't you think?" He paused then and stroked his thumbs over her cheekbones, trailing fire across her skin. "That's not who you are. You could sell your body every night and that's not who you would be."

She couldn't stop the sudden ache in her throat or the blush that stained her face. No one had ever paid attention to who she was before. No one had cared to notice. Words wouldn't move past the thickness of her throat, so she kissed him instead. A slow, lingering kiss that she hoped let him know her gratitude.

He groaned softly and put his arms around her again, squeezing her bottom to pull her against him and deepen the kiss. Pulling back slightly, he blazed a path of hot kisses down her neck. "I want to know all about you," he whispered against her skin.

She knew the feeling. She wanted to lie with him and talk to him for hours, for days. She wanted him to open up to her even more. Pressing her face to his hair, she breathed in the intoxicating scent of leather and man, knowing it was for the last time. If only they had met some other way. If only Ship wasn't his enemy. If only she had a different life.

"And I want to know you." She pulled him up to kiss him again, stopping whatever other silly promises he might want to make. She knew they weren't real. His eyes were clouded and muddled. He'd forget everything that happened.

His hands moved back to cup her face and he was surprisingly strong when he pulled back to look at her. "When this is over—"

"When this is over," she agreed, cutting him off before he could finish.

Then he gave her a tongue-tangling kiss that sent tendrils of longing through her whole body, making her long for a few more minutes with him, but sooner than she would have liked his hands dropped to his sides and his body relaxed beneath her. Pulling back to make sure his eyes were closed in sleep, she gave into the urge to brush her lips against his one last time before getting to her feet. She covered him with his coat and picked up the canteen, debating on taking it or leaving it. He'd seemed confident that his brothers would find them that night, but she wasn't sure and knew the powders would leave him dehydrated and thirsty when he awoke, so she placed it beside him, giving him one last lingering look. She did take one of his guns, extra bullets, most of the jerky and the bedroll before heading down the mountain to where he'd tied his horse.

The large black snorted at her when she tried to put the saddle on his back and pranced to the side. It took her four tries, her arms burning from the exertion, before she finally made it. She tried to calm him just as she'd seen his master do it by running her hand down his neck, but he was having none of it and tossed his head away. Grumbling under her breath, ever aware of the sun sinking behind the mountains, she tied her supplies down and took a firm grip on the reins to lead him downward. There was no way she was chancing a mount until they were on level ground.

The narrow path seemed to take hours to navigate, but finally she was wading through the grass, grasshoppers jumping out of her way. "Okay, beast, just hold still and I promise this won't hurt either of us," she whispered to the animal as she put her foot in the stirrup. With a quick prayer, she swung her other leg over his back, holding on for her life when he pranced beneath her. It seemed he didn't like what was happening any more than she did.

Once she was settled she glanced to the south, toward her home and her sisters. Her heart clenched with the pain of the decision she had to make. She couldn't go back there just yet. The outlaws would find her easily and even if they didn't, her problems wouldn't be solved. She had to find a way to get the girls to safety. That meant getting them away from Ship and his outlaw life. This could quite possibly be her only chance to do that. Her sisters would be fine with Jake for a few days, just long enough for her to do what she had to do and come back for them. With a quick glance of regret up the mountain and the man she'd left sleeping, she turned the horse north.

An idea had been forming in her mind over the past two years, but she'd never been brave enough to act on it. Never desperate enough. Now she had no other choice. She had to keep her sisters out of danger, she had to take back control of her life, even if it meant following in her mother's footsteps for one night. At least she'd have the rest of her life to be free of men like Ship.

Chapter Nine

Hunter opened his eyes to a searing headache and a heavy feeling deep in his gut that said something was wrong. Horribly wrong. His eyelids felt as if they weighed ten pounds each, but he managed to open them with some effort. When he did his eyes were gritty and his mouth was as dry as if he'd eaten a bucket of sand. The world swung precariously as he sat up, hanging his head between his knees until his stomach settled and everything righted itself.

What the hell happened? It took a moment longer for the fog hanging over his brain to lift and for him to get his bearings. He lifted his head and realized that he was still in the cavern, then it all came rushing back. The saloon, the kidnapping, the woman who'd been such a complete surprise, that kiss. Holy hell, that kiss.

Emmy! He rose so fast he banged his head on

the rock ceiling of the cavern. "Dammit!" Pressing a hand to the wound, he crouched, looking around to see if he could find her, but the cavern was empty. Maybe she'd gone out to stretch her legs.

He prayed—*prayed* for the first time in years—that the bastard who'd been shooting at them hadn't come back and found her. He wasn't entirely certain the man had been one of Campbell's. If he wasn't, there was no telling what he'd do to her. Heart beating a harsh rhythm in his chest, he moved on his knees to the opening and peered out. It was mostly dark though, only a small sliver of sunset lighting the mountain. But it was enough to see the shadow coming up the path.

For one blessed moment relief filled his chest, but then Cas called his name and Hunter realized his earlier calls were what must have woken him.

"Hunter, you are here!" Cas called with relief. "We didn't see the black and I thought something had happened."

"He's not there?" Tension coiled tight in his shoulders as he realized exactly what that meant.

"No, he's not under the trees." By this time Cas had come close enough that he could make out his brother's furrowed brow. "Did you leave him somewhere else? Where's the girl?"

"She's gone." The girl had poisoned him with something and then stolen his horse. That kiss had only been to catch him off guard, to make him take whatever drug she had put into his whiskey. It had all been an act. The little lying wench.

As he turned to grab his gear, a tiny light in some dark recess deep within him wondered if he was judging her too harshly. He'd looked deep into her eyes, he'd seen the uncertainty and longing within them, and he *knew* it had been more than just a kiss for her. Molars grinding together, he silently vowed to find her no matter what it took. He needed to get to the bottom of whatever this was between them.

Hunter stood in the foyer of Victoria House and seethed, his rage threatening to burn out of control. The girl had left him days ago and only one person stood in his way of getting her back. Social etiquette required that he at least wait for the woman descending the steps to actually reach the bottom before he strangled her.

"Now, Mr. Jameson, you're not actually suggesting that I turn over the poor little dove who came to me for sanctuary? I'm sure it doesn't bear repeating, but you know my stance on such matters." Glory Winters, the madam of the most exclusive brothel in Helena, couldn't have been more than thirty, but held herself like a queen. Stepping off the bottom step of the elaborately curved staircase, she came to a stop a few feet before him. The heels of her silk-encased slippers left tiny divots on the Persian rug in her wake. She was elegantly dressed as always in the latest fashion from Paris, in a gown of royal blue silk. The shining red of her hair, her crowning "glory", was twisted up in a thick pile atop her head, impeccable as ever. He'd never wanted to shake it out of place as badly as he did right in this moment.

"Cut the bullshit, Glory. She's mine and I want her back." Days of dead ends and hard riding had left him short-tempered and ready for murder.

"Are the rest of you gentlemen as sociable as Mr. Jameson this evening?" Calm and collected, her rouged lips parted to flash a white smile as she looked over at Cas, who only scowled back, and then on to Zane, who raised a brow. Zane was the only one of the group to look as if he wasn't fresh off the trail. He'd returned the day before and had had a day of food and rest.

Hunter knew that he himself must look at least as bad as Cas, neither of them having had a decent bath or shave since his brothers had found him in the cavern. They had left Zane to continue on to Helena with his charges while he and Cas had followed the girl's tracks north. They'd lost them once she'd hit the train tracks. It had appeared she had followed the railroad east, her tracks leading them that way until they had disappeared. Once they had reached Billings, Hunter had checked the depot and found a telegram from Glory waiting.

The madam was the only one in Helena who knew they were the notorious Reyes Brothers. She had come to him once for help when men with money and greedy appetites had moved into town hoping to take over her business. Since then they had coexisted in Helena as associates, helping each other out when the need arose, which was rare since they generally kept their outlaw activities further south. But because of her unique position, she'd occasionally have access to information they needed.

During their cooperation, they had set up a system of alerts, just in case they ever needed to communicate. Glory had recognized his horse when the girl had arrived and sent a coded telegram to him that would be received at each stop along the railroad, both east and west. She hadn't mentioned the girl in the telegram, just that his horse was in Helena and he'd hopped on the first train headed in this direction, hoping like hell that she was there, too.

There had been no time to send for his personal train car, so they'd endured the trip with minimal food and no baths. Once the train had reached Helena they'd found Zane waiting at the station and had come directly to the brothel. The comforts of home would have to wait until he found her.

"Glory." It was a warning growl. The only one she'd get. He wouldn't physically harm the madam, but he'd smash through every polished wood door in the sprawling, three-story mansion until he found Emmy.

She didn't so much as bat an eyelash and the large specter of a man, who had shadowed her for as long as Hunter had known her, took a warning step away from the wall, the soft light from the electric chandeliers shining off of his dark skin. Hunter spared him a look. "Evening, Able." As impeccably clothed as his mistress, in his evening dress with a roll-collar coat and waistcoat, Able gave him a nod, but the warning in his eyes was clear. No one was allowed to disrespect Miss Winters.

Giving her hired man a dismissive wave, Glory let her smile slip away and her eyes hardened. "That young woman came to me for sanctuary, I won't allow you to come in here and do her harm. I sent you the telegram as a professional courtesy because she rode into town on your horse. The horse is waiting for you down at your town house. Emmaline, however, is not coming with you."

Emmaline.

Her name was Emmaline. The green fist of jealousy slipped its fingers around his heart, only stoking the flames of his anger. He had no reason to be jealous that this woman had been given her name from her own lips while he hadn't, but he couldn't stop the emotion and ground his molars together to get a handle on it. "That woman stole my horse and ran from me. I will have her."

"No, you won't. She's not yours—"

A brisk rap on the front door silenced her and when the doorman opened the massive door to allow the newcomer inside, her smile moved seamlessly back into place, settling into the unlined mask of the welcoming madam that she wore for her clientele. "Mr. Westlake, how good of you to join us tonight." She stepped smoothly around Hunter and his brothers to greet the older man and accept his hat.

While she helped him with his outer coat, she made pleasant small talk, impressing Hunter with her knowledge of the banker's family, and he responded as if they were old friends meeting on the street. He'd never seen Westlake here before, but he shouldn't be surprised that he visited the establishment. Almost every man in town had been inside at one point or another and not necessarily for the company of the females who resided here. There wasn't a place in Helena to get a better beefsteak or game of cards.

"There's a fire blazing in the front parlor and a few men are already playing cards," Glory said, her Southern drawl a little softer and more evident now that she wasn't angry and biting her words out. "Go on in now and I'll send Jeannette with your usual Scotch."

Westlake greeted them each by name before addressing Glory again. "Oh, no, my dear, I didn't come for cards tonight. I came for the…" Sparing them a glance, he dipped his head closer to Glory's and continued in a whisper that everyone could hear, "The *other* entertainment in the Black Chamber."

Hunter's eyebrows rose in surprise before settling back into the impatient scowl he'd been wearing. In the years he'd visited Glory's establishment he'd never heard of the "Black Chamber". No doubt another scheme the clever proprietress had come up with to separate eager men from their money.

"Oh!" She seemed surprised. "Oh, that… I wasn't—"

"Of course, dear, I know it's only for a chosen few and I'll be the first to confess that the stakes are higher than I'm willing to part with, but I thought I could attend anyway." He paused and waggled his eyebrows good-naturedly.

"Yes, of course you may attend," she acquiesced and smiled so brightly Westlake fairly preened from the attention. "But I must ask you to be discreet. It wouldn't do to have the whole town talking." When the older man nodded, his jowls fairly quivering as he agreed and reassured her of his utmost devotion to secrecy, she darted a glance at Hunter, one that he was sure she hadn't meant to do because it was a dead giveaway. In that glance she revealed her uncertainty and a very real fear, and it set him on alert. A quick look to Cas, who raised a brow in warning, assured him that his brother had seen it, too.

The older man grinned. "Our good citizens here, particularly the fairer sex, don't understand the need for a bit of lively amusement now and then. I assure you I wouldn't dare ruin our bit of fun, but the prospect of an auction intrigues me so." At his inadvertent use of the word "auction" the banker brought the fingers of one hand to his lips, as if he'd said too much. He probably had because Hunter was imagining Emmy standing there as men bid on her and he clenched his fists at his sides as he assured himself that wasn't the case.

Glory waved to a fashionably dressed woman who seemed to appear out nowhere to escort Westlake past them to the hall leading off the left side of the foyer.

"What the hell is going on?" Hunter demanded of the madam as soon as he was out of sight.

"What happens here is none of your concern, Hunter." She dropped her friendly demeanor as she faced him again. "Now if you'll be on your way, I have business to attend."

"You kicking us out, pretty lady?" Zane's deep voice entered the fray.

To her credit, she swallowed once and plastered that serene look back on her face. She was too shrewd of a businesswoman to completely risk alienating the men who had come to her aid more than once over the course of her tenure as madam. "No, of course not. You are all welcome to have a drink…or a bath and a room." She gave Hunter's and Cas's dirty attire a once-over. "But you cannot persist in looking for Emmaline."

Hunter didn't bother with a retort and took off in the direction Westlake had been taken. That look on Glory's face when the banker had mentioned the Black Chamber told him more than enough. The word "auction" pounded in his skull and his gut churned in an unfamiliar mixture of fear and disgust, but when he turned the corner the hall was empty with no sign of which room Westlake and the woman had disappeared into.

"Mr. Jameson," she called a warning. "Hunter!" The click of her heeled slippers was loud as she moved from the rug to the gleaming hardwood floors behind him.

"Mr. Jameson!" Able's baritone voice joined in as he started forward.

Someone, Cas or Zane, drew a gun, the sound of metal being pulled smoothly from a leather holster filling the tense air while the heavy steps of their boots followed him into the long, dimly lit hallway. Pale blue textured wallpaper lined the walls between numerous doors leading to various dining and meeting rooms, a sconce lighting each one. He mentally ticked off the ones he knew to be dining or card rooms, targeting the last two as potential locations for the mysterious auction.

"Gentlemen, please!" Her voice rose enough for effect, but low enough to not disturb any customers on the lower level. "This doesn't have to—"

The closed doors rattled in their hinges as

Zane shoved Able's large body into the wall. Not to be stopped, Able grabbed the bigger man's shoulders and pushed back, ramming him into the opposite wall.

"Able! Mr. Pierce! I won't have a clash of giants destroying my house." She put a hand on each of them before remembering that she needed to appeal to the man leading the group. "Hunter, please, wait. I'll show you where she is, but I can't allow you to harm my business." The silk of her skirts swooshed as she hurried past Cas and grabbed his arm. "Please!"

Hunter stopped, but only to level a heavy look at her. "Show me."

She nodded and looked pointedly at Zane until he unhanded her sentry. "Fine, but the same rules apply as always. Hats and guns off, gentlemen."

The respect he had for her and the fact that time was of the essence made Hunter give his brothers a quick nod to unbuckle their holsters. He didn't like it, but as they stood waiting some man could have his hands on her. Besides, they'd be able to overpower anyone who stood in their way.

"Thank you. Please go lock those up, Able." Able gave them each a hard look before he turned back toward the foyer. She waited until he turned the corner before leading them to the end of the hall, putting herself between him and the last door on the right to look up at him. In a pique, she snatched his hat off and put her other hand on the brass doorknob. "You look horrible. You're going to scare the living daylights out of her."

She looked at him as if he were feral. He almost obliged her with a growl. "Says the woman who gave her 'sanctuary' only to throw her to the wolves."

"That's not fair. That's not what happened."

"You're telling me it's not her being auctioned?"

She had the decency to look chastened as she opened the door and let them in. The glare she gave his brothers as they followed him inside had them taking off their hats. Zane grinned as he placed his on her head. Whatever she did after that was lost on him because the sight greeting him stopped him cold.

Emmaline was thankful for the darkness in the room. There were no harsh electric lights to cast a judgmental light on the horrible thing she was doing, just candles and soft lanterns placed on the raised platform meant to be a stage.

Glory had adamantly refused when she had initially discussed the idea of the auction and had offered to lend her the money to flee, but she could only spare enough to get them to another town. It wouldn't come close to providing for them long enough for Emmaline to get on her feet. If it had only been just her, then she could have accepted it and left. Without enough money for security, then Emmaline risked taking the children away with her only to place them in greater danger. She refused to do that. They didn't need to simply get away, they needed to disappear, to abandon the outlaw life altogether before someone else came to collect a debt and maybe next time kidnap one of her sisters. The brothel had been the only place Emmaline had known to run. It was where she had been born.

As strange as it might seem, the brothel had seemed like more of a home than the farm ever had. She'd been taken care of here, had been given lessons and a family. She still remembered the nights after closing they spent around the piano singing hymns while one of the women played. Ship had promised her mother that family, but all they'd gotten was a dirt farm and a lot of time alone while he gallivanted across the countryside. Each trip home he'd brought with him even more dangerous men and done nothing to alleviate the poverty to which they were slowly succumbing.

Part-gentleman's club, part-brothel, Victoria House prided itself on being the only first-class establishment of its kind in the territory. Every wealthy man in town had spent nights within its walls, whether to have a meal, play a hand in the card room, or spend time upstairs. Little had changed in the twelve years Emmaline had been gone, except that Glory had made the place even more luxurious somehow. This was the place she could earn the most money.

Now staring out into the blackness of the room, she was having second thoughts. It wasn't a big room, a simple parlor transformed into something dark for the evening and would go back to being used for whatever its purpose was the next day. Its walls and furniture had been draped with a dark, velvety material of inde-terminate color, because the decor wasn't to be the focus on this night. No, the focus was to be solely on the woman on stage, perched atop a velvet divan and draped in a simple robe of white satin with a matching half mask cover-ing her eyes.

The robe reminded her of those worn by the ancients in drawings she'd seen and she'd been surprised when Glory had brought it to her in her bedroom. She'd imagined all sorts of attire, all of them much more revealing. Falling to her bare feet and leaving just her arms and a bit of her chest bare, the clothing had been a relief. For a little while. But then she'd sat down on the stage's divan and the slits on either side revealed the entire length of her legs and the deep V where the fabric crossed over her breasts fell open to reveal the tops of the slight mounds. She left it open. Better to overcome her modesty now, before it was really put to the test. At least she'd have the tiny slip of a mask that covered the upper portion of her face so no one would recognize her come morning. It was a requirement of the covenant that she be allowed to wear it all night.

The parlor had already been filled when she'd taken her seat. She had heard the men on the other side of the curtain, shuffling and murmuring. The smell of their mingled colognes had made her stomach churn, but she suspected nerves had just as much to do with that. And then the curtain had dropped and she'd stopped thinking of anything except for Rose and Ginny and how she'd go to get them when this was over.

The light from the stage only allowed her to see shadowed forms as they shifted in their seats to get a better look. She took only shallow breaths, the weight on her chest constricting her lungs. A man's voice filled the room, and though she couldn't focus on his words, she knew that he was relaying the terms of her service: one night to begin at the auction's end. Horrible thoughts tried to interject themselves, but she forcibly pushed them away. Whatever happened, it would only be for one night and then she'd have enough money to take Rose and Ginny away to somewhere safe where she could find work and they'd never have to worry about Ship's antics destroying them. It would be worth one night of her life. She repeated that mantra to herself over and over as men began to call out amounts. One thousand dollars. One thousand five hundred. It continued until the bidding went over ten thousand dollars and the voices slowly whittled down to three men, their voices pitching back and forth across the room as they bid, hurling taunts at each other as they called out their bids.

Ten thousand dollars was the amount Glory had told her to expect. The difference between a life of uncertainty and one of stability to her, but a pittance to the bidders so wealthy from mining that they routinely earned that in a week. That amount could mean a whole new life for her and the children. They wouldn't want for anything, not for a very long time.

Then the door to the room swung open, light

from the hallway illuminating the outlaws as they filed in. There was no mistaking the three tall men. Glory came in on their heels, and Emmaline realized that trouble had found her again. Her stomach dropped and her breath stopped altogether as her gaze locked on the one in front, her mind unable to comprehend the fact that he'd found her until her heart gave a jolt in her chest. For one terrible moment, she was actually torn between relief and horror. Horror that he had found her and meant to return her to Ship. Relief that he was there to save her from these men and the choice she had been forced to make.

Then the door closed, blocking out the light so that he was in darkness again, freeing her from the spell of his eyes. Horror was the proper emotion, she assured herself, and braced to run, prepared to flee the mansion in her robe if she had to in order to escape him. There was a collective murmur in the room as the men, particularly the active bidders, turned to see who the latecomers were. They were quickly called to order by the auctioneer with the booming voice who was cloaked in shadows just in front of the stage.

He was still watching her. The weight of his gaze fell heavy on her and she knew that he hadn't moved from his place just inside the door.

"We're up to fifteen thousand dollars if you

gentlemen would like to enter the bidding." Then his voice rose to address the parlor. "Do I hear sixteen thousand? MacDowell? Connors? You're not allowing McNally's fifteen thousand to best you. What's your best bid, gentlemen?"

MacDowell and Connors both threw out numbers, but *his* voice was louder. "Fifty thousand dollars."

"No!" Her heart screamed the word and her lips formed it of their own will, but no one heard or maybe she hadn't actually given voice to it.

There was collective silence in the room for a moment before the three original bidders' voices rose to protest this latecomer daring to enter their domain. Calls of "He can't bid!" and "Fifty thousand dollars? The blazes you bid fifty thousand dollars!" were all drowned when her ears picked up the words, "You weren't invited to this, Jameson!" So his name was Jameson. She locked that information away. One of the men rose to his feet, the legs of his chair scraping harshly on the hardwood floor as his shadowed form swayed.

"Gentlemen, please!" Glory's voice cut through them all, soft and yet somehow authoritative as she walked to the front of the room. "Remember that you are all gentlemen. Mr. Jameson was invited to this particular event, I assure you, as were his associates. He was simply running late, but I'm confident you gentlemen won't mind a little friendly competition." She had made her way to stand in front of the stage to address the room. Two gunmen appeared, one on each side of her, the only guns allowed in the establishment strapped to their hips, ready to keep order if anyone attempted to go against the madam. A few more lamps were lit by an impeccably clad manservant, providing enough light so that Emmaline could now make out faces in the audience. And, she imagined, light for the gunmen to aim properly if such action was needed.

"Fifty thousand dollars is not friendly competition and you know it, madam." This was from the man who had taken a stand, the words drawled with a deep Southern accent and she knew he was McNally, the lead bidder until her pretty savior had offered that ridiculous amount. His dark moustache curled at the ends over lips thinned with anger. "It's insulting. Who would pay that for a night with a whore? Have you even proof that she's pure?"

Someone else agreed with him, his voice joining in and questioning her virtue. She didn't so much as flinch. After all, she couldn't blame them. Virgins weren't known for auctioning off their bodies for a night of pleasure. Her face warmed, though, and her mind churned as she wondered what to do, avoiding looking out, afraid that she would meet *his* gaze.

"I'm not accustomed to having my integrity questioned, Mr. McNally. If you are so concerned with that, perhaps you should consider taking your business to another establishment."

That silenced him briefly. Everyone knew that there were no other establishments in Helena of the same caliber as Victoria House. To be forbidden from its walls was the same as being relegated a social outcast, at least among the society of the quality men in the city.

The madam raised a well-shaped eyebrow and continued. "I assure you all that you will be quite satisfied if you choose to consider bidding, but if no one else—"

"How do we know he can put up that sort of cash?" another man demanded, his face red with anger.

To this Jameson laughed, a bitter sound that raked down her spine. "You know that I can, Connors. Perhaps our good banker, Westlake here, can reassure you, unless you'd rather I come do that myself."

An older man rose to his feet then, his face alight and his cheeks rosy with the drama playing out before him, seeming eager to be included. "I can vouch for Mr. Jameson, as I can for each of your bids."

A shiver ran through her at how easily he was willing to part with fifty thousand dollars. How wealthy was this man and what was an outlaw doing with that sort of money? Did everyone here know that he was an outlaw? Did Glory know? If she screamed it out, would they help her?

"Well, then," Glory interjected, "let us continue." She motioned to the auctioneer and he stepped forward. Emmaline stared at her, trying to decide if the woman was betraying her by seeming to take his side, but then the auctioneer began to talk.

With his dark hair slicked back with pomade and his evening suit, the auctioneer could have been a wealthy financier. He was a slight man to have such a strong voice. It boomed out in a deep baritone as he smiled to the crowd, thanked Glory, then proceeded to ask if anyone intended to outbid Mr. Jameson. No one spoke or moved and she finally brought herself to look back at the man who had haunted her for the past week.

His gaze was livid, the green so intense as their eyes clashed that her heart jumped to her throat. He was furious. Blood rushed loudly in her ears so that she barely heard the auctioneer announce the closing of the bidding. "No." The word came out a bit stronger this time, but she repeated it louder until every eye in the room turned to her. "I don't accept his bid."

Clearly at a loss, the madam's mouth fell open in an O before she regained her composure enough to say, "But, my dear, it's…" Her voice trailed off when Emmaline interrupted her.

"You assured me that I wouldn't have to accept a bidder I didn't want."

"Of course you don't. But why wouldn't you…?" Seeming unable to complete a thought, Glory looked back to Jameson. Even Emmaline had to admit he was the most handsome of the three who'd been vying for her. But they hadn't planned to send her back to her stepfather. He did.

The auctioneer smiled up at her, a salesman's smile trying to convince her to just go along with things. "We've already closed the auction, dear. Not to mention, it's *fifty thousand dollars*. You won't get a better offer than that." Laughing boldly, he swept her body with a glance and she wasn't sure if he found her lacking or simply ridiculous for thinking to refuse.

Impulsively, she looked at Jameson again and he smiled, though it was more of a sneer, just revealing a slash of white. Every instinct she possessed urged her to run until she finally did. Her bare feet hit the soft, pale gold rug spread beneath the divan and she jumped down and ran out the door near the stage, back the way she had come into the tiny hallway that led to the servants' staircase and her bedroom. Away from the man hunting her, the same man who owned her for the night.

Chapter Ten

The instinct to follow her had driven Hunter forward through the men in the room, but the gunmen at Glory's side drew their guns to halt his progress. "Dammit, if she gets away—"

"She won't go anywhere. I'll go talk to her." Holding both her hands up, Glory turned her attention to the manservant and said, "Please show these men to a suite of rooms and have supper and baths sent up to them."

"Glory…" Hunter's warning filled the parlor.

She was already rushing to follow Emmaline out the back door of the room. "I said I'll talk to her, Hunter! Just go clean yourselves up and I'll come find you. If you come after her, you'll only make her even more upset."

He'd talk to her himself and he opened his mouth to tell her that, when Zane stepped forward, placing a hand on his shoulder. "I'll go

with her, brother." And he walked around him
to follow the madam through the back doorway,
the familiar gunmen standing down when Zane
nodded to them in greeting and gave them a grin,
showing that he had no guns on his hips.

Cas said, his voice low, "We've already given
them enough to talk about." He nodded toward
the spectators staring at them in rapt attention.
"We have her. She can't escape. Now, let's go
upstairs. I could use a decent meal and a bath."

No one in Helena except Glory suspected he
was anything more than a wealthy man's son. He
wanted to keep it that way, so he reluctantly followed the manservant and Cas back to the foyer
where they were led to their rooms.

An hour later with his belly full of a meal of
ham and potatoes, the beard scraped from his
face by the hand of a pretty woman, and the
water cooling in his tub, his patience was running dangerously low. He knew Zane wouldn't
let her escape, but he was anxious to see her.
He kept imagining Emmy sitting on that stage,
her deep blue eyes as wide as saucers with fear,
chin proudly raised as she stared out into the
darkness. It infuriated him anew every time he
thought of Glory throwing such an innocent to
those animals. He couldn't believe that the proud

woman he knew Emmy to be would allow it. They both must be mad.

Staring down the redheaded woman who had busted into his room minutes ago, he told her as much. She hadn't so much as flinched to find him in the bath as she informed him that he wasn't taking Emmaline out of the brothel. He hadn't told her yet that the woman was their hostage, preferring to keep that information to himself if he could. It seemed Emmy hadn't told her either.

Choosing not to respond to his taunt, she raised her chin instead. "She doesn't want to spend the night with you and I won't have her forced to do anything she doesn't want to do. That's not how I run my business. You know that." Glory folded her hands before her, clearly nervous. It was one of her tells.

He gritted his teeth, biting his words out. "This isn't about your business. It's about mine. I played by your rules and that isn't working for me, so now we play by mine." Gripping the edges of the tub, he sat up straighter and the soapy water sloshed dangerously close to the edge, nearly spilling out over the porcelain rim.

"I won't let you take her out of here against her will. That wasn't what the auction was about."

"What the hell *was* the auction about? She

came to you for safety and you helped plan her slaughter." The memory of her small body revealed in that robe, those men practically panting to get their hands on her, was enough to make him see red.

"No," she clarified, fixing him with a harsh stare. "I was helping her secure her future."

"You'd better start explaining real fast what that means."

Pursing her lips as if she was debating on refusing, she finally sighed and began to pace the length of the small bathing room attached to his room. Her heels clicked on the slate tile. "She was born here, Hunter, in this brothel. Her mother worked here. I'm sure you understand what that means."

"Her father was a client of her mother's?"

"Yes. I think Charlotte, her mother, knew who he was, but he'd been gone years before I got here. She always referred to him as her miner who'd got away. Anyway, I came here only a few months before Charlotte married and they left." She paused then and gave him a knowing look. "I trust you know who Ship Campbell is?"

"Of course." Hunter gave a half nod in acknowledgment. Campbell was fairly well-known as a criminal in the region. He wouldn't be known in the finer parlors and ballrooms, but a place like this would know all about men like him.

"Emmaline was a young girl then, like a younger sister to me. When Charlotte married Campbell they left and I never thought to see Emmaline again. But then she showed up here asking for help, saying that she needed to get her sisters away from Campbell. She had this plan of selling herself for a night and taking the money and running. I offered to give her money, Hunter, but I could only spare enough to get her to San Francisco. She wasn't willing to risk placing them in danger and I don't blame her. She wants to offer them security so they won't have to deal with the life she has."

Her sisters. Emmy was going to be so angry with him when she found out about them. Shaking his head, he leveled a glare on the madam. "That doesn't excuse anything. Do you know what those men were thinking? What any one of those bastards would have done to her?"

Raising a brow, she gave him an empty laugh. "I do know, yes."

"Her fear was that she'd become a whore. She comes to you for help and you turn her into one?"

"Do you know what it's like to want nothing more than to take control of your own life, but have no means with which to do it?" she shot back. "Do you know what it's like to have your future decided by someone who doesn't care what happens to you? No, you don't, because you have—" She paused to take a deep breath and control her voice, which had been rising steadily.

"Because I have money?" he finished for her.

"Among other things, yes." She gestured to his nether regions, hidden beneath the soapy water, implying the fact that he was male was an advantage in itself. "You've always had privilege, stability. It's not that way for the rest of us, especially if you're a woman, and sometimes we have to make difficult choices."

"This was the wrong choice, Glory. You knew she rode in on my horse. You sent me a damned telegram. You could have had the decency to wait for me to get here." His fingers clenched into the porcelain and he paused to keep his temper in check.

"I could have, but she seemed afraid. She wouldn't talk about you or what had happened, and there was the very real evidence that she was running from you. Look." Holding up her hand to stop whatever he planned to say, she took another calming breath. "I'm not asking what happened or why she had your horse. I'm only asking that you leave her alone. Whatever happened between you two, she doesn't seem interested in renewing the acquaintance. I will not allow you to leave here with her."

"You can't stop me. She's mine." Dammit, he kept saying that. He didn't mean it like those words implied, but he kept saying them and they kept sounding right. Some long-buried part of him wanted to keep her safe. It was the same part of him that wanted her to run to him for comfort, the part that despised that he had abducted her and would one day be forced to hand her over to someone else.

"That's exactly what I'm talking about. She's not *yours*. She doesn't belong to anyone!"

"I paid for her." The words ripped out of his chest before he could call them back and he rose to his feet in the tub.

"The hell you did!" Emmy burst into the bathing chamber still wearing the robe she'd been wearing on that stage, though the mask was gone. Her cheeks were flushed with anger and he followed that pink all the way down to the low V of the robe's neck where it ended deep between the soft mounds of her breasts. His mouth went dry as he imagined filling his hands with them and he even had to clench his hands into tight fists to keep himself from reaching out to her. She *wasn't* his to touch, he reminded himself. But that didn't stop all the blood in his body from rushing down to his groin.

The fact that he was naked brought her up short and her eyes widened in shock. She must not have realized she was storming into his bathing chamber. As she took him in he couldn't help but push his chest out a little more as he stood still for her scrutiny. Her gaze jumped back up sharply when she got down to what he was sure was a very noticeable erection, but she didn't appear frightened. The pupils of her eyes were dilated, making the blue seem darker, but most telling was the way she parted her lips to take in a long, ragged breath. The sound moved through him, making a fresh pulse of desire lengthen him even more.

Glory was the first of them to come to her senses. "Jesus, Hunter!" But instead of continuing, she shook her head and pushed her charge toward the door. "Come on, Emmaline, you don't have to talk to him."

Emmaline didn't resist as Glory pushed her back into the bedroom and closed the door of the bathing chamber behind them. She couldn't have resisted had the woman pushed her all the way across the room to the low fire smoldering in the fireplace and shoved her inside. The image of his gloriously nude body was too busy burning itself into her memory.

It wasn't that she hadn't seen shirtless men before. Ship didn't exactly run a very strict household and when his men helped work the farm they often did it without a shirt. But, dear Lord, none of those men had ever looked like the outlaw. None of them could compare to his wide shoulders and sculptured chest. Though she'd never seen any of their more manly parts, she suspected that none of them could compare to the shaft of perfect masculinity she had just seen. As she'd watched, it had grown, doubling...no, tripling in size as it stood proudly reaching for his navel.

"Did you hear me?" Emmaline shook her head, trying to get him out of it as she focused on the madam who was staring at her with tender concern. "You don't have to talk to him. You don't even have to see him again."

No, she didn't have to do either of those things. Glory had just spent the past hour with her in her room, reassuring her that she did not have to follow through with the night ahead. When she'd left, Emmaline had felt much calmer, much more rational, than when she'd run from the stage. The outlaw might have found her, but that didn't mean she would be his hostage again. They were in civilization now and the men in that room had seemed to know him. They called him Jameson and she was betting everything on the fact that they didn't know he was an outlaw. The entire territory had been lobbying for statehood, with Helena the capital of that new state, and it wouldn't look good to outwardly harbor an outlaw in their midst. So, while her screams in the brothel might go unheard, on the streets of Helena the good men of the town couldn't allow them to go unchecked. He couldn't take her out of the house without exposing to everyone in town what he was doing.

She was safe and the reminder fanned the dampened sparks of her anger until they flamed back to life. He had some nerve barging into her auction and bidding. He had some nerve thinking he had any rights to her. She had come here to his room to tell him just what she thought of him and, come hell or high water, she was telling him and then their brief acquaintance would be at an end for good.

"I know. I want to talk to him."

"I'm not sure it's a good idea." Glancing at the bedroom door and then the bathing chamber door, Glory lowered her voice and closed the gap between them. "Unless you do want to honor the auction. Fifty thousand dollars is enough money that you wouldn't have to work again. You could even get the girls an education. I won't take commission. It's all yours. And I can make sure he allows you to leave in the morning." She paused, her green eyes holding Emmaline's and her voice lowering to a whisper. "This wouldn't be a bad option, if it's what you want. He's an ass in many ways, but he wouldn't treat you harshly."

Sucking in yet another shuddering breath, she nodded. That argument had been turning itself over in her mind throughout the past hour. It would be a simple solution to her problem. Spend a night with him and leave the next morning with her fifty thousand dollars. It was so much money she'd have plenty of time to get the three of them settled somewhere. Ginny could go to some fancy finishing school for girls where she might have a chance at a respectable marriage one day and Rose could have toys, real dolls with real hair. It all could be so simple.

The only problem was that it made her worse than a whore. It seemed an absurd problem given that she had been the one auctioning herself off to the highest bidder. Yes, she had intended to spend the night with one of those men, but she had never intended to enjoy it. She'd anticipated sacrificing herself for a good that was so much greater than herself, not reveling in the act which was just what she would do if the man was *him*.

Revel. That's exactly what she had done with his decadent kisses back at the cavern. Reveled in each and every taste of his tongue as it stroked hers. That's exactly what she had done the moment her gaze had settled on his body, bare as the day God had made him. Reveled in not just the sight of him, but in the way her body had come alive at the sight of him. The way her nipples had beaded and a spot deep between her thighs had begun to thrum in anticipation.

"No, I can't do that." *I would enjoy it too much.* She couldn't admit to that out loud so, instead, she said, "There is too much between us for that to ever work out smoothly. I'd rather just return the bank draft." It was there in her room, waiting on top of the old and scarred bureau. The auctioneer had tapped on her door soon after Glory had arrived and handed it to the madam without a word. Glory hadn't mentioned it either, just set it on the bureau. And it had stayed there throughout their conversation, staring at them with his bold signature across the bottom.

"No," she said again, taking a fortifying breath and squaring her shoulders. "I just want to talk to him and—"

"Leave us, Glory. I promise not to eat her

alive." His deep voice cut in before she could finish.

They both turned toward the now-open door of the bathing chamber. He stood there between the dark wood door and the frame draped in nothing but a towel riding low across his hips, leaving the broad, well-developed planes of his chest bared to them. There wasn't a muscle she couldn't see in his torso, as it narrowed from wide shoulders to the tantalizing ridges of muscle crossing his stomach, a path of dark blond hair disappearing beneath the sanctuary of the plush, white towel. She dared not allow her gaze to linger there, remembering all too well what it hid.

Dragging her gaze back up the path it had traveled over skin that was smooth and sun-bronzed, she wondered how that was possible given that there was still snow in the foothills. Oh, yes, he was an outlaw, part of the Reyes Brothers. A gang that operated somewhere south along the Mexican border where it must stay warm all year long. It was strange and more than a little infuriating that she had to keep reminding herself he was an outlaw. He might not look like Ship and his men, but he was that type of man. Transient, irresponsible, reckless...everything that she didn't want.

"Do you want me to go, Emmaline?" Thankfully, Glory's voice broke into her inappropriate thoughts about the man before her.

"Yes, please, just for a little while." She wanted the woman to stay, but was a bit afraid and ashamed of what might come up in their conversation. While she was mad at him and intended to let him know just how much, she also needed to clear her conscience. She *had* left him unconscious in the wilderness and she wanted to apologize. The irony didn't escape her that *he* had kidnapped her and *she* was the one feeling guilty. But the reality was that she really did wish they had met under other circumstances, that he wasn't an outlaw and that they could be free to explore their strange and wonderful connection.

And, yes, if she was being honest, she wanted to kiss him one last time as she told him goodbye. Was that so terrible?

Glory squeezed her shoulder, and turned to go, her footsteps muffled as she crossed the thick carpet, then closed the door behind her. The metallic click of the lock was unmistakable in the silence of the room. Glory shrieked in anger, her voice muffled a bit through the door as she cursed the giant outside to every ring of hell. His answering deep laugh chilled her to the bone, but she couldn't focus on that because her captor stood before her.

"You have some nerve having your henchman lock me in here." Emmaline glared at the almost naked man in front of her.

The giant had been waiting outside her bedroom door when she'd walked out to find the room where Glory had told her Jameson was staying. She had ignored him, intent on the idea that she was free, but he had shadowed her the entire way, never hindering her progress or saying a word. Apparently he'd just been biding his time.

"Zane does what he wants. I don't think I have to remind you that you came here of your own will." Jameson moved forward into the room and she backed up, keeping a steady distance between them.

"That's right, I came here to talk to you. There was no reason to lock me in." She crossed her arms over her chest, wishing that she had changed clothes. She felt so exposed in the virginal robe with its deep neck and high slits up each leg, but she hadn't even been thinking of that.

He stopped walking when he reached the foot of the bed and leaned back against the curved, mahogany footboard. "Talk." One word. An order. His face gave nothing away, save his restrained anger, as he watched her.

Nodding to indicate his towel, she asked, "Don't you want to get dressed first?"

"No. I want you to talk."

The skin on the back of her neck prickled as if it was stretched too tight and her cheeks suddenly felt too hot. She gritted her teeth to bite back an angry retort and forced herself to remain calm, remembering why she had come to see him and that, despite Zane, she could leave when she wanted. Glory had gunmen ready to help her if needed. In fact, the woman would probably be back with them any moment.

To keep herself calm, she turned away from him and took her first good look at the bedroom. Decorated in shades of cream and muted blue, it was tasteful if a little on the dramatic side with its heavy, dark wood furniture. It held a writing table with an overstuffed chair upholstered in rich blue fabric pin-striped with gold, a bureau, an armoire and the oversized four-poster bed with spindly-legged bedside tables each holding a crystal lantern. There were windows on either side of the bed hung with heavy dark blue drapes that were pulled shut.

It was a perfectly civilized room. He was the only uncivilized thing in it.

There was such an air of wildness about him that she shivered and debated the merits of talking to him at all. The contrast of his clean-shaven jaw paired with his still damp hair, hastily towel dried and pushed back with his fingers, and the fury blazing in his eyes, made him appear as dangerous as she knew him to be. Somehow the effect only made her heart flutter. He was even more handsome than he had been at the cavern, as the shave had emphasized his strong jaw and the barely there indention at the bottom of his chin.

He looked restrained, just waiting for the moment she might step too close.

"I'm not 'yours', *Jameson*," she finally said once she'd gotten a handle on her temper, emphasizing his name because it was one less layer between them. "The contract I signed gave me the choice to accept the bid or not."

"You forget, Emmaline…it's not the contract that makes you mine." His green-gold eyes darkened and captured hers in that way he had that made her belly flutter.

She blinked to escape his spell and shook her head. "I escaped you."

"You did, until I found you."

"We're not in the middle of the wilderness anymore. You can't take me back, not here, not with all of these people."

One corner of his mouth tipped upward, but he didn't challenge her. He was so damned confident he didn't have to. Panic flared within her for one brief moment before she managed to get a hold of it and remind herself of all the reasons he wouldn't get away with her. Deciding not to give rise to her anger and tempt an already unstable situation, she changed tactics.

"I came to see you because I wanted to tell you I'm sorry that I had to put sleeping powders in your flask. I didn't want things to go that way between us, but I had to get away. I'm sure you understand my desperation." She waited what she thought was an appropriate amount of time, but he said nothing. She hadn't exactly expected a noble acceptance of her apology, but when a flicker of acknowledgment didn't so much as cross his face, her anger boiled over. "Well…" she prompted.

He raised his eyebrows in question.

"This is the point in the conversation where you accept my apology and—"

"Accept your apology?" he scoffed. "For drugging me and leaving me in the wilderness at the mercy of any animal or criminal who wanted to pick me off? No, I do not accept." He pushed off the footboard and took a threatening step toward her.

"How can you not accept?" Tightening her hands into fists at her sides, she attempted to keep the reins on her fury. "You were perfectly safe. You said yourself that your brothers were returning that night and it appears that they found you."

"A man had just tried to kill us. For all you knew he was going to come back with his friends before nightfall to finish the task."

"Oh, that's ridiculous! I shot him for you."

He laughed and it made her so angry she wanted to strangle him. "You don't know there weren't others close by."

"One: If he had come back to finish the task he would have found your horse gone and followed the tracks to look for you, which put *me* in greater danger than you. He wouldn't have known you were on the mountain to climb up there and look for you. Two: You *kidnapped* me! Is there some etiquette I'm unaware of that says I'm supposed to get permission from my kidnapper before escaping?"

"Before trying to escape, you mean?" He grinned, making her suspect that he wasn't taking this seriously at all.

"I did escape. You had no idea where I was, until... How *did* you know I was here?"

He just kept stalking closer. "You can't get away from me."

She wasn't sure if he meant escape in general or in this room right now. Either way, she took a step back and stifled the panic threatening to claw its way up her throat and escape in a scream. "But I did get away from you."

"Briefly. I admit you got the best of me. I wasn't expecting to be drugged, especially not after you sat astride my lap and kissed me so sweetly, but it won't happen again now that I know what you're capable of doing." His gaze flicked down to her chest and he nodded toward the place where her locket used to be. "Looks as if you've lost your locket."

"You left me no choice. I won't be a pawn in whatever game you and Ship are playing. I'm sorry he took someone from you, but I won't be a part of this."

"You already are. The message has been sent and he thinks that we have you." He came closer as he talked, slowly as if drawing it out.

Her heart pounded faster with each step because she had no idea what he planned to do once he reached her. It wasn't fear that made it pound. It was excitement. With every step it strummed through her veins, settling low in her belly, especially as she had become more aware of the bulge beneath his towel and the heady way his eyes pulled her in. Her resistance was hanging by a thread and he hadn't even alluded to anything physical happening between them.

Bumping up against the low back of the chair that sat at the writing table, she held her hand out to ward him off. "Stop, you don't have to come any closer for us to talk."

He did stop, but not until he'd walked right up so that his warm skin pressed against her palm. Her fingers settled into the indentation chiseled between the twin muscles defining his chest. Immediately her throat dried and her breathing increased. The contact sent a blaze of seductive warmth from her fingertips all the way through her body to where it settled in her core, pulsing as it waited for his touch.

This was bad. This was very, very bad.

"We're finished talking, Emmy."

Chapter Eleven

"No, we're not finished talking."

"Yes, we are. You ran from me. You led me on a wild chase and, what's worse, you left yourself vulnerable to ruthless men who would hurt you." He ran a hand through his drying hair in agitation and his fingers shook slightly. It was the first time she realized exactly how furious she had made him by running, but, instead of scaring her, the knowledge sent an inexplicable thrill of desire through her belly. "So you see, I can't decide if I should throw you over the bed and spank you, or throw you over the bed and take you because you've been looking at me like that's exactly what you want and I can't get it out of my head that I bought you."

She slapped him. It was a reflex that happened before she could stop it or even question it. The crack of skin on skin filled the room, drowning out everything else until it faded away leaving only the tense weight of silence.

Touching the imprint of her hand on his cheek, he shook his head, a low laugh escaping him. "Damn, but you're not making it an easy choice."

She let out a shaky breath, half-sigh, half-groan, as she realized in his answer exactly what she had done. She hadn't slapped him because he'd offended her, though he had, she'd slapped him to prove to herself once and for all that he was just like those horrible men Ship brought home with him. None of them had ever struck her, but only because she had never pushed them that far. If she had slapped them, they wouldn't have stood for it. By slapping Jameson she was trying to prove to herself that he was exactly like those men, even if he didn't appear to be on the surface. If she could prove that to herself, then she could stop her perplexing desire for him.

But he wasn't like them and his next words proved it.

"Get the hell out of here, Emmy." His voice had lowered to almost a growl, but he was allowing her to leave with no retribution.

What the hell was wrong with her that she didn't want to leave? It was as if striking him had released the valve on her anger, so that it seeped out, leaving room for everything else she was feeling to grow and take its place. He hadn't yet touched her, but her body was alive as if he had. The very idea of him throwing her across the bed had lit her up inside and made her realize that this might be her last encounter with him. No one else had ever been able to make her feel these things.

What if she walked out of here tomorrow and spent the rest of her life never knowing what his touch could do to her if she let it? What if no one else ever could make her feel like him?

So instead of leaving, like a sane person would, or even giving voice to her desire, she stayed. Backing away until she pressed so hard into the chair's back that it moved forward a little on the carpet, she shook her head. "We're not finished."

He clenched his jaw, his eyes humorless and full of warning, desire and all manner of dark things. "You really want that spanking, don't you?"

Her intimate muscles clenched at his words. Then when she dared to imagine his hand on her bare bottom, caressing and touching, a flood of damp heat accompanied the action. "No." She shook her head and paused before continuing, "Not the spanking."

His nostrils flared as if scenting her capitulation and his gaze shot to hers, pinning her in place. Pressing her thighs together, she shifted under the weight of his scrutiny and felt the telltale moisture from her arousal on the tender skin between her legs.

"Emmy." Her name was almost a groan on his lips. "This isn't the time. You've made me too angry." Yet even as he warned her away, he stepped closer, the movement slow and measured. The tension moved like a tangible wave from his body, touching her skin and thrilling her. This was his last effort to make her leave; she could sense his near capitulation. But he didn't know how much she wanted him.

Her gaze stopped on his mouth, fixated on his full bottom lip. Standing just inches from her now, warming her front with the heat from his body, he was so close that she had to crane her neck to look at him.

"You've no reason to be angry. I'm the one who's been wronged."

His large hands had already grasped her hips, strong fingers digging in gently as he pulled her across the tiny gap toward him. She grabbed his biceps and a secret thrill shot through her at how hard they were. She just wanted to run her hands all over his body and feel how hard he was everywhere.

"I still think what we said in the cavern holds true. We can be friends after this is over." She meant to say more, to explain how badly she felt about having to put the powders in his flask, how she had really meant everything she had said to him. But he took her words away by kissing her and she didn't even mind.

Letting her hips go, he cradled her head and tilted it upward so that he could deepen the kiss. His tongue pressed inside, brushing hers and she couldn't help but kiss him back. It had been days since she had kissed him. Days of remembering the simple pleasure of his mouth and missing it and coming to terms with never having it again. But now here was that pleasure returned to her, washing over her again, turning her into a puddle of need and want and desire and she didn't even care. She just wanted. She wanted everything he could give her without having to think of all the reasons she shouldn't have it.

Just as her fingers were curling into the damp hair at the nape of his neck, just as her tongue had begun to tease with his, just as she was noticing that he always seemed to taste of whiskey, he pulled back a hairbreadth. His breath came in heavy pants that filled the space between them. "It's impossible. We'll never be friends."

"What?" Wits scattered by the kiss coupled with his unexpected words, she shook her head to focus on him.

"We can't be friends," he repeated. "Not after you drugged me, not after you ran."

That cleared her thoughts. Pulling back the few inches she had so that her back was pressed to the chair again, she glared up at him. "You kidnapped me! And you have the nerve to be upset about the fact that I escaped?"

"Come on, Emmy. You seduced me so that you could drug me. You expect me to be fine with that?"

The pain of his rejection surprised her.

He must have seen the pain on her face, because his voice gentled as he spoke. "Don't lie to me. I won't let you. Not now."

"I never planned to seduce you. I only intended to earn your trust, to get close enough to give you the sleeping powders. Everything else… just happened." The kissing, the things she had revealed to him. She hadn't had to pretend anything because he'd made her feel safe enough to be who she was. The kissing had happened because she genuinely liked him, or thought she did at the time.

"And yet you left me anyway. *You knew* I wouldn't hurt you by then, but you left me unconscious."

That was the moment she realized that she'd hurt more than his pride when she left. Was it possible that he'd felt something more for her? That he still did? Laying one last olive branch at his feet, she reminded him, "You kidnapped me. I had to get away."

"*I* didn't know you when I took you."

"Just kiss me," she ordered. None of this mattered anymore.

"Emmy." It was that low warning again, but she didn't care to heed it.

"Fine, we can't be friends. I don't want to be your friend anymore."

His hands dropped back to her waist and he stepped forward until her hips were pressed back against the plush fabric of the chair's back. The harsh pant of his breath filled her ear and she became aware of that very aroused male part of him, impossibly large and unyielding against her belly. Her body immediately responded to him, flooding the ache between her thighs with more wet heat as she throbbed to the beat of her heart.

"Dammit, what do you want?" His voice was ragged as the weight of his right hand moved up from her waist to pause at her rib cage, just under the curve of her breast. The strength in his body restrained as he awaited her answer.

He was staring at her mouth, making her feel the touch of his lips from the weight of that stare. She wanted them on her and for the first time in her life, she allowed the rational part of her to lie quiet.

He wanted her. She wanted him. It was simple. Easy.

This is what she wanted and she was taking it before she never had it again. Moving her hands up his arms, she tightened her fingers around the back of his neck and pulled him down those few inches until their mouths touched, their breaths mingled for a second before the hot slide of his tongue touched her and she let him know exactly what she wanted.

It wasn't gentle and, Lord help, her she didn't want it to be. She wanted the power and intensity of this man. She parted her lips and his tongue ravished her, conquering and taking, staking a claim that was his to take. Before she realized his intent, his hand slid into the V of the robe and his fingers were touching the bare skin of her chest, then her breast, closing around it. She gasped into his mouth as his warm palm settled over the tightly pebbled nipple and he gently squeezed.

He murmured something against her lips and pulled away, only to grab her by the hips and lift her to sit on the back of the chair. A thrill shot through her belly at how easily he could lift her. It was a strange thing to be excited about, she thought just before he fisted the sleeves of the robe and pulled them down each shoulder to her elbows, baring both of her breasts to him. An embarrassed flush quickly stole over her. She'd never thought to bare herself to a man with all the lights in the room blazing and she realized she really hadn't thought this through at all.

What if he kept the lights on the entire time? The door was locked from the outside. What if Zane came in? About a million other questions rushed through her mind at once, but every single one of them fell away when he buried his hand in her hair and brought her mouth to his again. Her hesitation was forgotten completely when his fingers went back to her breast, this time plucking the tightened peak and then rolling it between his thumb and forefinger. Seductive pleasure moved through her body like warm honey, turning her limbs heavy and making her entire body pulse and come alive.

She didn't even realize she'd parted her thighs, seeking to get closer to him, until he stepped into the cradle of her hips and pressed his impossibly thick erection against her center which was already throbbing. When he pressed forward, she cried out softly and he tightened his fingers in her hair, pulling her head back, baring her neck to his hot, open mouth. She shifted restlessly. Even through the barrier of her robe and the towel she could feel herself become more aroused from the weight of him pressing against her, then from the friction as he moved, hitching his hips a bit forward to rock against her.

His mouth and tongue roved over the sensitive skin of her neck as he made his way downward, his tongue flicking into the hollow above her collarbone. When he kept moving downward, her breath stopped as she realized his destination. Every muscle in her body tensed, her hands clenching tight to his shoulders, almost afraid that he would stop. Then his mouth was there, his breath warming her skin, making her flesh prickle in anticipation. His fingers relinquished their hold on her nipple to move down to cup the flesh of her breast as an offering, just before his mouth closed hungrily over the sensitive tip, pulling it into the incredibly soft heat. Her cry filled the room as he sucked deep, sending pleasure shooting directly to her core, somehow making her ache even more for him. Of their own volition, her hips pressed forward, seeking that wonderfully hard part of him and he groaned with her nipple still in his mouth, the vibration of his voice tantalizing her already sensitive flesh. He flexed into her, pressing against her throbbing core, as he let go of her nipple only to move to the other one and start again.

Her legs had gone around his waist, struggling to somehow bring them into closer contact, but their clothing was in the way. Feeling her way down his shoulders, her palms skimmed over his broad chest and flat stomach to the towel knotted at his hips. She tugged blindly until it finally gave way and she pushed it down so that he sprang gloriously free. His manhood was both hot and silky smooth against her palm as she explored him. He was so much larger than she'd thought a man would be. When she wrapped her fingers around him, they didn't quite meet, giving her a quick burst of panic that he quickly extinguished by releasing her breast and taking her mouth again, forcing her attention back to him and his kiss.

Tightening her fingers around him, she stroked gently and he broke the kiss with a curse. She paused, thinking that she must have hurt him, but his hand covered hers and in a voice rough with pleasure, he whispered, "Again," against her lips. More than happy to oblige, she repeated the movement with him guiding her, elated to realize that she could give him pleasure.

After a few more times, he groaned, biting her lip as he broke away. Reaching for him to pull him back, he brushed his lips against hers almost tenderly as he placed his hands beneath her bottom to pick her up and walk her to the bed. His eyes were dark, the pupils almost obliterating the ring of green, and the effect made him look so intense that another shiver of desire mingled with a bit of fear that she wouldn't know how to handle this man once he was completely unleashed shook through her. Without breaking eye contact, he reached down and pulled the bedspread back, revealing the snowy-white sheets underneath. Then he sat her down on the edge of the bed, pulling purposefully at the robe. She tried to help, but her arms were caught in the sleeves.

"The back, the tie is in the back," she managed to explain, grabbing at the belt. She gasped in surprise when he turned her so that her front pressed down into the mattress, but she didn't care anymore when she felt him tugging at the knot. It gave way and he pulled the satin robe down, freeing her arms as he pulled it down her legs and then off completely. She started to turn around, but he pressed a hand to her lower back.

"Stay there." His warm palm roved downward and she had a quick thought that he did indeed intend to spank her now. But he only squeezed the flesh of her bottom while his other hand caught in the bend of her knee and pulled it up to rest on the edge of the bed. "You're beautiful." There was unmistakable awe in his voice.

She somehow blushed anew at his observation. But he continued to look, the weight of his stare like a physical touch. The pause made her quite aware of her position and that she was open to him, nothing hidden from his view. Pressing her forehead to the bed, she went to move anyway, but his grip held firm on her knee. Then he did touch her, his fingers skimming over her bottom and downward to dip just a fingertip into her tight channel before moving down to the swollen bud that had been throbbing for his attention since he'd kissed her. "Jameson," she moaned into the sheet.

Stepping forward and bending over her, his breath hot against her ear, he took the sensitive lobe between his teeth. "Hunter."

"Hmm?" She pressed herself back against him, craving more contact.

"My name is Hunter." Bringing his knee up to the edge of the bed behind hers, the tip of his shaft nudged at her entrance. "Say it."

"Hunter," she gasped and jerked at the unexpected contact. His hips flexed again, pressing himself against her as he moved in a gentle back-and-forth rhythm.

"You're already ready for me," he whispered, pleased, just before he buried his fingers in her hair and turned her head, taking her mouth in a deep kiss.

She wasn't quite sure why that pleased him, but she didn't care to reason it out just then and arched into him when his silken erection nudged against that particularly sensitive spot he had touched earlier. His hand came around her thigh, parting her folds to allow his thumb to circle the swollen flesh, drawing a moan from her. He did it again and again, making her jump beneath his touch, until he stopped kissing her and lifted her other leg so that her knee pressed into the edge of the bed. Still bent over her, one hand held her steady while the other guided the tip of his shaft to find her. He pressed against her, pushing forward until it was just inside her. She groaned at how good the fullness of him felt, stretching her to fit him, and pushed herself back onto him, needing more. Both hands gripped her hips tight, holding her steady for him as he pushed forward, only stopping when the pressure turned to pain and she cried out.

"You really are a virgin?" His voice was rough with disbelief against her ear.

She nodded and tried to say something, but all that came out was "Mmm…" muffled against the sheets. The pain receded a fraction as he pulled back and she took a deep breath, but his fingers tightened on her hips and he pushed forward again, repeating the movement twice more until the strength of his hips pressed against her bottom as he sheathed himself completely within her with a soft growl. He fell forward then and was all around her. His chest at her back, the coarse hair of his legs against the backs of her thighs, his breath harsh and fast at her ear, his hard shaft buried deep inside her.

This was what it meant to be possessed by him, she thought as she lay there beneath him completely at his mercy. Then she couldn't think anymore. His fingers found her again and he played with her, exerting soft pressure until her hips were thrashing, caught between his fingers and the mysterious throb of that incredibly large part of him inside her. The more she moved, the more frissons of pleasure rippled through her. Panting, she arched toward him, begging for more, and he shifted, pulling out a few inches just to push back into her in slow, gentle strokes, rocking into her.

"Hunter," she moaned, burying her face against the mattress, but he tightened his grip in her hair and pulled back a little.

"Say it again," he ordered, his voice rasping against her ear.

"Please, Hunter, more." Her hips were restless now, searching for something she didn't understand.

Only then did he became rougher, abandoning his play, to grab both her hips as he pulled out almost completely just to push back into her. She cried out from the exquisite aching pleasure that washed through her. The tenderness was still there, but the pain was long gone, to be replaced by a relentless need only he could fill. Her voice filled the room with each thrust, though she no longer cared if anyone was in the hall to hear her as waves of pleasure crashed through her, her body moving with his of its own accord, seeking something she didn't know how to find.

But he did. He knew exactly how she needed him and his fingers teased her until she could think of nothing but him, until the ache was gone to be replaced by such pleasure that she screamed with it, her eyes closed so tight that she saw pinpricks of light as the waves broke over her.

"Emmy." He repeated her name over and over

against the shell of her ear as she found her release, making her breath hitch from the endearment as he drove himself into her until his breath stopped and he shuddered above her.

Chapter Twelve

Hunter didn't know how long he lay there above her. With his face buried in her neck, his arms on either side of her barely keeping his full weight from her, he was having trouble regaining his composure. With every breath he breathed in her heady scent, salt mixed with the undercurrent of wildflowers, and he couldn't get enough. His heart rate slowed as his breathing normalized, but he still couldn't get his mind around what had happened. One minute they'd been talking, arguing, but then he'd kissed her and hadn't come up for air until…well, until now.

Even now all he wanted to do was rock against her and keep her beneath him, some primitive voice in his mind repeating "mine" as he took her so many times she'd feel him for days. Even then he wouldn't want to give her up, not until he'd gotten enough, but something told him it would be a very long time before he got enough of her. A soft hum of pleasure brought him back down and he realized he was tasting the tender spot behind her ear, the tiny indentation just where it met her neck, the tip of his tongue making small circles there as if he couldn't help himself.

She shifted beneath him and he remembered how small she was and that he was probably crushing her. It took all he could do to pull himself out of her and then move to her side. Grabbing a pillow, he pulled himself up a few feet on the bed and grabbed her, hauling her up to lie next to him across the mattress. He caught a glimpse of red on her thigh and felt the first real twinge of guilt since everything had started. Christ, he'd never really thought that she was a virgin. Inexperienced, yes, but never had he thought that someone—anyone—in that godforsaken town wouldn't have tried to claim her as his. How had she escaped the attentions of Campbell's men? Was Campbell such a tyrant that none of them bothered with her? She was sweetness and gentleness wrapped in a package of strength and intelligence. It didn't make sense that she would still be untouched.

Though guilt tried to stir within him, he couldn't summon up the regret that he knew he should feel now. Looking down at her, his fingers trailing a lazy path up and down the silken skin of her back, he liked that he was the first man to claim her. He, who preferred women who knew what they were doing in bed, who preferred women who sought out lovers as aggressively as he did, was glad that she had been a virgin. It made that voice in his head all the louder.

Mine. Mine. Mine.

His hand curved over her bottom and he squeezed gently, the need to touch her so strong that he couldn't seem to stop. She was lying on her stomach, still and quiet, and he needed to know how she felt, if she was still angry. His anger had fled the very moment he'd pushed himself inside her, but it hadn't tamed his passion at all. He'd taken her as aggressively as he'd ever taken a woman when he should have been tender. Her first time with a man shouldn't have been him mauling her. If he had known beforehand—but, no, he'd known as soon as he'd encountered her body's resistance and the knowledge hadn't made him gentle. Still, she had cried out her pleasure and he had all night to make it up to her and show her how it could be between them.

"Emmy?" Pulling the strands of dark hair

that had fallen loose from her braid back from her face, he leaned over her and rubbed his lips along the delicate, peaches-and-cream skin of her cheek. "Are you all right?"

She opened her eyes slowly, sleepily, and turned her head so that she faced him. Settling back on the pillow next to her, he watched as she blinked and saw the exact second her gaze focused on his face and she realized what had happened. A moment of panic came over her, widening her eyes and tightening her jaw, but then just as quickly it fled to be replaced by something infinitely more serene. But he didn't like it any better.

"Yes, I'm fine."

She was shutting out her feelings, to push him away and keep him at arm's length. He didn't like it at all, but he didn't blame her, not after the way he'd treated her. True, she had kissed him when he would have pulled away and it was she who had unknotted his towel and taken him in her hands. But it was Hunter who had nearly lost control and not regained it again until he'd been panting over her, his seed spilled deep within her. He never lost control like that. Hell, he didn't even know if she knew how to take precautions against pregnancy. It wasn't like him to be so irresponsible. Making a mental note to talk to

Glory in the morning, he pushed the thought from his mind and focused on the woman next to him. When he found himself about to caress her face, he clenched his hand into a fist and pressed it into the sheet between them, determined to control the compulsion to touch her.

"I didn't realize that was your first time. It doesn't excuse anything, but I meant to be gentle. I'm sorry if I hurt you."

The brittle look of calm she wore dissolved and for a moment he was afraid tears would replace it, but she surprised him by smiling and then smothering a laugh against the pillow. He didn't know what was funny, but found himself smiling anyway because he was so relieved that she wasn't upset. Before he realized it, his fist had unclenched and he was rubbing a lock of her hair between his fingers.

"I'm sorry," she said when her shoulders stopped shaking. "I just… I've never seen you look so uncertain."

His smile widened. "Yeah, well, I've never taken a virgin before." Then his smile fell away as his gaze traced her face. She looked so damned innocent and desirable at the same time. "You're not hurt?"

Shaking her head no, the smile on her face faded as well. A strange silence grew between them. They weren't friends, they'd already established that, but they weren't even lovers, not in the way he'd ever thought of the term. There was no word to describe them now. Captor and captive seemed absurd at this point. The hell if he knew what they were.

"I'm going to..." She pointed to the bathing chamber and gave him an embarrassed look as she slipped off the bed and all but ran from the room and shut the door behind her.

Taking a deep breath, he sat up and ran his hands through his hair. They had crossed a line tonight that he'd never anticipated. He'd bought her at the auction because he'd wanted her off display from those bastards staring at her. It had been impulsive, but the only way he could reasonably get her away from them without jumping onto the stage and hauling her off, which would have created more questions than he wanted to answer. He'd have done it if there had been no other choice, if someone else had already claimed her. Buying her the way he had would create enough questions, but he could deal with those. Everyone knew him as a man who enjoyed his fair share of women, he could explain the novelty of a virgin's auction away and no one would question it. They all knew the Jameson accounts wouldn't so much as shudder at the loss of fifty thousand dollars. He couldn't so easily explain carrying her off as she screamed for help, which might very well happen once morning came and he had to take her out of here.

The patter of the slow trickle of water from the faucet hitting the porcelain bowl of the sink came through the bathing chamber door and he rose from the bed. Searching for his discarded towel, he retrieved it from the carpet near the chair. It was still damp so he cleaned himself and threw it into a corner. Deciding things might progress more smoothly if he wasn't nude when she came out, he grabbed the sheet from the bed and wrapped it around his waist. The clean clothes he'd sent for hadn't yet arrived from his townhome. Or if they had, he didn't want to open the door to check the hallway.

Picking up her robe, he decided he'd rather she didn't put it back on, so he threw it into the corner with his towel. The water turned off and a moment later the door cracked open. He sat on the edge of the bed, one foot braced on the floor as he watched her walk out. She was so beautiful, wearing nothing but a white towel. He hardened the instant her shy blue eyes found him and lingered on his naked chest. The memory of her small hand on him made his flesh tingle with the need to have her touch him again. This time he'd let her take her time to explore and he'd explore her. This time he wouldn't lose control and bend her over the bed like a savage.

Surprising him yet again, she boldly walked over to him, stopping only a foot away from where he sat. Her shy gaze dropped to his lap, no doubt taking in the massive erection she caused with embarrassingly little effort. The thin sheet did little to hide the bulge. Then she gave him a slow smile as she looked up to meet his gaze. "I really am fine."

He let out a huff of air—a laugh, he thought—but he didn't know what to think anymore. Grabbing her shoulders, he pulled her against him, burying his nose in her hair and taking a deep breath, filling himself up with the intoxicating scent of her. "You should be angry, sweetheart. Yell at me and tell me what a savage I am."

She shook her head against him and pulled back just enough so that her gaze could meet his. "I wanted what happened and I can admit that."

"I've never met a woman like you," he stated honestly as he stared down at her. She was such a contradiction of qualities he didn't know what to make of her. The women he'd known would have played coy or wailed at him, looking for more attention, more money, more time. He had been so wrong about her when he'd awakened to find her gone. He'd been angry, in large part because he thought she had used her body to get something from him, proving herself to be exactly what he had hoped she wasn't. He'd thought she had intended to seduce him all along so that she could escape, but now he realized what a fool he had been. Everything she had said to him that day had been the truth. Of the pair of them, he was the liar. He had taken while she had given. "You really didn't plan to seduce me, did you?"

"It's a rather moot point now, don't you think?"

"Not to me." The pad of his thumb drew tiny circles on her arm. "Why did you run, Emmy? Do you have any idea of the hundreds of terrible things that could have happened to you between there and here?" He did. The images had haunted him the entire time they'd been tracking her.

"Do we have to talk about that now?" She glanced to his arousal again, then looked away, but not before her face flamed pink, causing his heart to shudder to a stop in his chest. Finally gathering her courage, she met his gaze again. "We have the rest of the night, to, um, forget about everything for a while. Hours until we have to remember who we are. I thought we could enjoy the night we've been given… Is it possible to…you know…?" Her gaze strayed downward before jumping back up to his. "Again?"

"Hell, yes." He had her on her back on the bed so fast that she giggled, though when he reached for her towel, eager to see her body again, she stopped him by grabbing his hands.

"No lights this time. Please."

Shaking his head he looked down at the slight swell of her breast beneath the plush towel and then back up at her face. The need to see her, really see all of her, controlled him. "You don't know what you're asking. I need to see you."

She chewed her lip as she reconsidered, her gaze straying to his chest. "I want to see you, too," she whispered.

Smiling, he rose and turned off the electric wall sconces, leaving only a single oil lamp burning on a side table. Its gentle flame illuminated the bed like candlelight, casting a golden glow over her skin and making their small space seem more private, more intimate. He held her eyes as he stood by the side of the bed and tugged the sheet free, letting it drop to his feet. When she lowered her gaze to take him in, his chest swelled with joy when she approved of what she saw and smiled. "Now you."

Her eyes widened in surprise, but her smile stayed in place as she rose to her knees and loosened the towel. He didn't realize he was holding his breath until she dropped it and his breath came out in one low exhalation. She was beautiful, small and petite, but curvy and perfectly proportioned. Stepping forward to place his knee on the edge of the mattress, she grabbed his shoulders and they moved as one, him following her down, her legs effortlessly opening to make room for him and sliding around his waist as he settled into the cradle of her hips. It was as if they'd made love a thousand times, each knowing how the other would move. His lips brushed hers, parting them so his tongue could slip inside to taste her again. But it wasn't enough and already the need to have more was thundering through his blood, roaring in his ears. He wanted to devour every inch of her to give her everything she deserved.

Tearing his mouth away, he moved down her body, the silk of her skin under his tongue like an exotic aphrodisiac. Making his way down her body, he held her thighs open for him as he slipped down between them.

"Hunter, what are you doing?" She pushed up on her elbows.

He didn't bother to answer as he lowered his mouth to taste her. Her moan of pleasure filled his ears and her fingers gripped his hair as she fell back and arched into him. He sucked until she cried out, bucking against him, then let his tongue lap at her again. She whispered "please" over and over as she moved against him and he couldn't wait any longer.

Moving up her body, he pressed kisses along the way before settling himself between her thighs. He held her darkened gaze as he slowly pressed inside her. She was so tight still that he was sure he was hurting her, but her hands only grasped at him to pull him closer. It took three small thrusts forward before her body allowed him to sink in completely. When he finally did, he groaned through his gritted teeth and fell over her, one hand wrapped tight in her hair.

"Are you hurt?" she whispered.

He almost laughed. "No, God, no. You feel amazing." He tried to kiss her, but only managed to drag his lips clumsily across her neck. How she managed to reduce him to this raging marauder, he didn't know. He only knew that it would take surprisingly little to send him over the edge. He wanted to go slowly, but already his hips were rocking against her, eager to take her as hard as he had before. "Tell me you're ready." His voice came from somewhere so deep in his chest that he didn't even recognize it.

"Yes, yes," she breathed the words out and her arms tightened around him.

He moved inside of her then, awed with how easily she moved with him. It was like she had been made for him, as if they had been made for this. Tiny gasps tore from her lips and he was mesmerized watching her face flush with her pleasure. The complete abandon with which she gave herself to him made her even more beautiful somehow and was his undoing. Just moments after she cried out for him, he followed her over the edge of bliss.

This time he managed to fall to her side, tucking her slight body into his as he struggled to catch his breath. It had been a very long time since sex with a woman had left him feeling this way: weak and barely coherent as he struggled to sort out his thoughts. What was it about this woman that brought him to his knees?

After a few minutes, she stirred next to him, snuggling closer. He rolled and brought her against his chest, not even bothering to try to make himself not touch her. There was no hope of him keeping his distance from her. Absently, his lips brushed across her brow and his palm moved up and down the satin skin of her back just wanting to touch her. She brought out a strange protectiveness in him that he didn't quite know what to do with. He imagined McNally's pudgy fingers touching her, hurting her, and the very idea of it made him angry. She wasn't his to protect, but that thought didn't sit well at all.

"Why did you run?" The question came out before he could call it back.

She inhaled deeply, still trying to catch her breath, and nuzzled her cheek against his chest. "I had your gun when I left. I was safe enough."

He wanted to laugh outright at that, but figured it would be a very bad tactical move, so he settled for reminding her of the night they'd met. "You had your gun when we found you that night. Why run? You must have known I wouldn't have hurt you. Do you still think I would hurt you?" His fingertips brushed back wisps of dark hair from her face.

She shook her head. Raising up to look at him, he was almost leveled by the direct innocence of those blue eyes. "The men in my life haven't been overly concerned with my best interest. I needed to get away because I couldn't be a part of what was happening between you and Ship anymore. You have to understand." She paused and took a deep breath, as if debating what she would say. The uncertainty in her face tugged at something deep within him. "It's not just me.

I have sisters and I need to get them away from Ship and his men."

A horrible thought crossed his mind, making his heart pound as if it was trying to break through his chest. "Is it that bad with him? Has he hurt you?"

"No, I don't mean in that way. Life with him is unstable. They drink all the money they steal and I can't see anything changing. Once the girls are older he means for them to marry men in his gang and I can't let that happen. I don't want that life for them. He wants me to marry one of his men. I've put him off that plan for a while now, because I can't bear the thought, but..."

But one day she might not be able to put him off any longer. She didn't say those words, but she didn't need to say them. Clenching his teeth, he forced himself not to react and especially not to wince from the lie of omission he was about to commit.

She didn't know that he hadn't really needed to track her down. Zane had gone back into Whiskey Hollow that night after leaving them at the shack and had encountered Jake on his way to her farm. He'd followed the saloon owner and found the girls and brought them to Helena just in case Cas and Hunter never found Emmy. If they had the other two girls to exchange for

Miguel, it wouldn't matter if she had gotten away. She wouldn't know that, not until tomorrow when he had to tell her. He hated the lie, but it was necessary. He wanted one night with her before tomorrow came and they were back to being outlaw and hostage. It would happen. There was no doubt in his mind that the momentary truce couldn't last. Even if by some miracle it did persist, he couldn't offer her anything. He was an outlaw and he couldn't turn his back on the vow he'd made to his brother.

"With fifty thousand dollars you'll be able to buy a new life for your sisters."

"Hunter…" She squeezed her eyes shut before lowering her head back down to rest on his chest. "I can't take that money."

"You can." He squeezed her to him, choosing not to think of the day she would leave him and put that money to use.

Sucking in a deep breath, she held it and then let it out slowly, almost as if she was in pain. "Do you think that's what this was about? The money? I didn't do this for the money."

"I know, Emmy. I know. I *want* you to have the money. Consider it an apology for having to take you."

She laughed then, a sound he hadn't heard enough, but was coming to crave. It was strange how things between them could be so easy, as if they really could be friends. "Fifty thousand dollars for kidnapping me? That seems excessive."

He rolled her onto her back so quickly that she let out a yelp. "What can I say, I'm a man with excessive tastes," he murmured as he nipped her chin and slid into the space between her thighs.

Chapter Thirteen

E mmy awoke the next morning smothered in man. As she lay on her stomach, Hunter's arm was tucked firmly around her waist while his face was buried in her hair, which had come loose from its braid at some point during their night together. His scent was all around her, accompanied by something more, a soft musk that had to be the scent of their lovemaking. She blushed just thinking it and knowing that everyone would know how they had spent the night, but she had no regrets. Since she planned to disappear, it didn't matter that they knew.

Soon she would be someone else living somewhere far away and she'd have the memory of this magnificent man keeping her warm all night. Shifting beneath his weight, she turned to look at him, wanting to savor the moment before the melancholy of leaving him set in. Even in his sleep he took her breath away. His dark blond hair had dried awkwardly as they slept and stuck out in tufts. Sleep barely softened his features, though, he still looked dangerous, like he'd awaken with the slightest provocation and give her that smile of his that meant she was in for a long morning in bed. For a brief moment she imagined what it might be like to wake up with him every day, to spend hours in bed with him before sharing breakfast, but she didn't allow herself to dwell on the thoughts for too long. She knew men like Hunter Jameson. Even if she stayed with him, their mornings together were numbered.

Despite what he had said she couldn't quite believe that he wouldn't tire of her like Ship had tired of her mother. In the early days when Ship had courted her mother at Victoria House, there wasn't a thing he hadn't promised them. A fine house with fine things to fill it, a pony for Emmaline and fine dresses. He was charming enough and dressed the part so that her mother had believed him. She'd believed every lie he'd ever told, even after they arrived to find the farm dilapidated and complete with a surly son he'd neglected to mention at all. Her mother had believed him until the day years later he'd arrived home after having disappeared for months. He'd never mentioned what had happened, but her mother had found a barely legible letter written from some sweetheart in another town, hidden in his saddlebag. It had crushed her to learn that Ship had moved on. Hunter would move on, too, once the novelty wore off. Maybe he'd wake up and the novelty would already be gone.

It was that sobering thought that gave her the nerve to wrench her gaze from his handsome face and take the first step in walking away from him. Pulling her bottom lip between her teeth, she slowly slid out from under him. He tightened his grip and she whispered that she needed to use the bathing chamber, when he relented, grumbling as he rolled away. Gaining her feet, she threw a quick glance at the curtained window, which showed a gray sliver of light peeking in. It was still very early, but soon the town would stir. It was best that she get herself out of the brothel before then.

She'd stop by Glory's room and borrow enough money to get them to San Francisco. Before Ship, her mother had talked about San Francisco quite a lot. It had always seemed like a magical far-off place where anything was possible. Now, it was the only place Emmy could think to go. Especially since she'd learned that some of the women from Victoria House had

relocated there at various times over the years.
Glory kept in contact with them because she genuinely cared about the women she employed and
Emmy knew that their unbending loyalty would
allow her to impose on them while she gained
her bearings. Or she hoped it would, at least for
a little while. Surely in a growing place like San
Francisco she'd be able to find work as a govern-
ess or even a shopgirl very quickly.

A panic started to rise in her belly, but she
beat it down. A million things could go wrong.
She could not find work and be worse off than
now, because the children would be in danger.
The plan was less than ideal and was exactly
what she had been trying to avoid, but it was
her only choice now. She couldn't come this far
only to go back.

First she'd take a train to whichever town had
a station nearest the farm, then find a horse she
could ride home to collect the girls. Perhaps she
could arrange a temporary lease instead of buying one outright. She didn't even know if such
an arrangement was possible and couldn't allow
herself to think of all the things that could go
wrong with such a poorly planned escape. The
important thing was to get home to Rose and
Ginny, to collect them and disappear.

Retrieving her robe from the corner, she

draped it over her and belted it loosely at the waist before casting one last look across the room. One arm was thrown over his head, his entire torso bared as the blanket draped seductively low, revealing the light brown path of curls to his manhood. As if her body was instinctively responding to his, a twinge of pleasure chased with aching pain shot through her middle, reminding her of just how well he had used her. She smiled and blushed again as she tiptoed to the door, relieved to find it had been unlocked at some point during the night. She poked her head out first, half expecting to find the giant there, but the hallway was vacant except for a leather satchel set next to the door.

On bare feet, she made it all the way back to her room without being seen. A strange sort of euphoria settled in her as she cast off the robe and grabbed a borrowed dress from the bureau, standing before the small dressing mirror to pull it on. She didn't look changed at all, but somehow lying with Hunter *had* changed her. She felt alive in a way she hadn't before. Always before it had seemed like she'd been waiting for her life to start, like she was just a shell waiting for her spirit to find her, but that had changed. To be fair, it had started changing before she'd even left him that day in the small cavern. He had looked at her and she felt as if she was see-ing herself for the first time. Her plan to escape Hunter and his brothers hadn't worked, not ex-actly. Her plan to escape Ship hadn't worked ei-ther. Not yet. But now she knew that she could do something. She would go home and get her sisters.

It was better than waiting around for some-thing to happen, which was exactly what she'd been doing.

The room she had been given was an older room, plainer than those reserved for customers and the women who made their living at Victo-ria House, so it didn't have running water. She dumped the water left over in the pitcher from the previous day into the bowl and grabbed a cloth to scrub herself clean. Then she dressed and ran a brush through her tangled mess of hair. With nothing at hand to style it with and no time to waste, she braided it again and tied the end with a bit of cloth. The only thing she'd brought with her was the brown dress she'd been wear-ing, so she retrieved it from the bureau and rolled it up under her arm. She took one quick glance at the woman staring back at her in the mirror, gave herself a smile and set off to take control of the rest of her life. Though she did reach back to grab the bank draft that bore Hunter's name, just in case. Folding it, she tucked it into the bodice of her dress.

Taking care to pull the door closed softly behind her so as not to wake any of the servants who shared this wing with her, she gingerly let go of the doorknob and turned to make her way to Glory's room, but a broad chest and set of shoulders stopped her in her tracks. She shrieked, but managed to bring her hand up to stifle most of the noise. Looking up, she wasn't at all surprised when her gaze settled on Hunter's angry, green stare. He was dressed in clean clothes she hadn't seen before, a simple button-up shirt in dark blue with tan breeches and a coat pulled onto his wide frame.

"Where the hell do you think you're going?"

She tried to be angry that he would attempt to sway her, but she couldn't summon the sentiment, not with the memory of his body against her own, inside her, bringing her so much pleasure she thought she'd die from it. And especially not with the endearing way his hair still stuck out in all directions and she could still feel the sensation of those thick, silky strands sliding between her fingers as she held him close.

Dropping her hand, she felt her lips turn up in a smile that she couldn't stop and she clenched her fingers into a fist to stop from reaching out to touch him. She regretted not being able to experience waking up with him, looking over and catching his smile as his gaze found hers in bed.

"Good morning, Hunter." Heaven help her, even now staring at his perfectly formed lips all she wanted to do was kiss him.

His frown didn't let up. "What are you doing?"

"I'm going home." She had the almost uncontrollable urge to run her thumb over the deep grooves between his eyebrows and smooth them out. He wouldn't appreciate the gesture, though she half considered it just to see if it would make him angrier.

He had the nerve to look stunned by her admission. "Emmy, you're not free to go."

"I know you think I'm still your captive, but I'm not. I escaped."

For a moment the frown disappeared and his eyes widened, perplexed as if he didn't know what to say, his hand running through his hair mussing it even more, but then he dropped it so it smacked against his pant leg and the scowl was back. "You didn't escape. We found you."

Waving her hand dismissively, she tried to step around him, but the hallway was so narrow in this wing that he only had to shift to the right to block her path. "Look around you. We're in Helena now, in civilization, you don't just take people captive in the middle of civilization." She didn't want to mention the gunmen Glory employed, but she would if it came to it.

"You're saying that you refuse to be my hostage?"

"Yes, it's a perfectly reasonable thing to say. And that's exactly what I'm saying. Now if you'll get out of my way—" Her voice let off sharply with a squeak when he picked her up, tossed her over his shoulder and turned on his heel, stalking away with her. "Are you mad? You can't do this. Everyone will know that I'm going against my will. You can't get away with this." When all reasoning got her nowhere because he continued walking steadily down the hall, she yelled, "Put me down!" That only earned her a sharp smack on the bottom and a command to be quiet, which only renewed her struggles. "Hunter Jameson, you cannot mean to take me out of here. I'll scream at the top of my lungs until everyone hears. I'll yell the entire town down around you. I don't care if you're as rich as a sultan, you can't take me out of here and get away with it!"

A door opened along the hallway, just far enough for her to see a boot-clad toe. "Help me! Tell Glory." Before she even finished saying the madam's name, the servant stepped back into his room and shut the door, turning the bolt with a definitive click. For the very first time that morning her confidence faltered and she wondered if the madam actually would be able to save her at all.

Of course she would, she had men with guns and Glory had assured her that all of the women who worked there were perfectly safe. That didn't stop her from struggling. She twisted and turned and when that didn't work she pounded his back with her fists. The solid muscle that she had so admired the night before had become a prison from which there seemed to be no escape. After a couple of turns, the hallway widened and she recognized the fine carpet of the guest wing. Then he was opening his door and they were back in his familiar room where he sat her down a bit roughly on the bed.

She came up quickly, expecting him to hold her down, but he just stood there, watching her as she regained her footing. The door stood wide-open behind him, which surprised her. She had expected him to lock her in again. "You won't get out of here with me. Glory assured me that she wouldn't let that happen."

He wasn't angry anymore. His expression was suspiciously resigned as he watched her, making a foreboding tremor snake down her spine. Something was wrong.

"Glory won't have much to say about it," he said in a strangely calm, strangely soft voice.

She laughed. "Oh, I assure you that she will."

"No, Emmy, she won't." He crossed his arms over his chest and stared her down with those intense eyes. The thing was—she believed him. Something about that look told her that he was very confident in his words, but he wasn't overly arrogant. He just stood there with quiet reassurance in what he said.

"What have you done?"

"We found your sisters." That was it, no further explanation.

She shook her head in disbelief, though deep down inside herself something told her that he was speaking the truth. "I don't believe you. It's too convenient after last night. I only just told you about them."

"Their names are Virginia and Rose. They're about ten and eleven, give or take. Blonde."

"I still don't believe you. You could have asked anyone…" But he couldn't have. No one at the brothel or in all of Helena, as far as she knew, knew her or her sisters. There was only Glory and she doubted that the madam had told him anything about them. It was impossible unless he'd gone back into Whiskey Hollow and talked to someone there.

He went on as if she hadn't spoken. "Zane, the one you call the giant, went back into town the night we took you and found the saloon owner. He was on his way out to your farm."

"Dear God, did he shoot Jake?"

"Jake's fine," he hurried to reassure her. "Zane figured he was going after you and followed him to your farm where he found the two girls. He tied Jake up, then met up with us at the cavern."

"Where are the children?"

"They're here. In Helena."

It was almost too much to take in at once. Her mind was swimming with the idea that her sweet little sisters had traveled all that way with outlaws. They must have been terrified. They must *still* be terrified. "Have you no decency at all that you would kidnap children?"

"They're fine, unharmed and well taken care of at my home, just outside of town. My house-keeper raised me and I swear to you that she's the best there is. I wouldn't put them in danger."

"You put *me* in danger. I'd never been shot at until you took me."

"That's not fair, Emmy. Campbell sent those men."

"Don't call me Emmy! I can't believe that I let you…" Her voice choked off as she remembered all the ways she had touched him and had let him touch her. All the time she had led herself to believe that he felt something for her, when the entire time she had known better. She'd walked right into his arms with her eyes wide-open. She'd known it was possible he was only using her, but she'd done it anyway, telling herself that she'd just wanted to use him, too. He had known all along that he had her sisters and was just waiting for the right time to spring that trap. Conveniently that time had come after she had given herself to him. Men like him would always get what they wanted first.

"Emmy." His voice lowered to a soothing tone and he stepped forward, cupping his hands around her shoulders to pull her forward, but she jerked away.

"Don't touch me. You could have told me before we slept together, but you didn't because you knew that I wouldn't sleep with you if you did."

"That's not how I remember it. I never intended to sleep with you. We were arguing and then things got out of hand. You wanted me, Emmy. You wanted what happened between us as much as I did. Don't let this ruin last night."

"How can it not ruin last night? You taking me captive, you holding my sisters captive...?" Her voice rose with each word.

"It doesn't have to be this way."

"How else could it be?"

"I swear to you that they haven't been harmed, nor will they be harmed. We just want to exchange them for Cas's brother. I didn't start this thing. Campbell did."

"I didn't start it either, Hunter, but here we stand."

He stared at her for a long moment, his face stoic but with no shred of anger left, and despite her best intentions she felt that look all the way down to her toes. "What happened between us last night is real, Emmy. If I had wanted another woman in my bed last night, I would have found one. It's you I wanted."

"Well, congratulations. You had me."

"Dammit, it's not that way with us and you know it." His fists clenched at his sides.

"Then tell me, how is it?" Her breath lodged in her throat as she waited for his answer. He felt something for her, she wanted to believe that, but she also believed that whatever his feelings were, they wouldn't change anything. When Ship finally decided to hand over their brother, they'd hand her over and she'd go back to her life in Whiskey Hollow. Or perhaps, after everything was done, Hunter would ask her to become his mistress—his whore—and that couldn't happen. She couldn't allow that to happen, because—

what would become of her after he was finished with her?

She thought of her mother hunched over the washing board on the farm where everything seemed dusty and old no matter how clean and new it was. Everything there had been hard and dirty and colorless. Even her mother. After years of dealing with Ship's broken promises she'd become a gray shell of herself, lifeless even before death. She didn't want that fate for herself or the children.

He was just parting his lips to answer when Zane poked his head in the open doorway. "The boys are ready." His dark gaze looked pointedly at her as he raised his eyebrows in question and glanced back at Hunter. Though he didn't say the words, he was asking if she was coming peacefully or if Hunter needed his help.

Without taking his gaze from her face, Hunter spoke, his voice hard again. "We'll be ready in five. Have the horses by the back door."

Zane left, his footsteps receding down the hallway, and it felt like he took all of the air in the room with him. All of the fight left her, leaving her deflated. There was no use in fighting. She had to go with them because she had to be there for her sisters. She'd play hostage. If Hunter had his way, when the time came they'd hand her back to Ship without qualm and she'd go back to serving drinks in the saloon. Only this time it would be so much harder because she'd had a taste of happiness, a glimpse of freedom, and it had been cruelly snatched away from her. As she watched him gather his things, she kept telling herself that she should have known better. She was just a bastard born in a whorehouse; she didn't deserve to have good things happen to her.

He walked over to her when he was ready to go, reaching for her hand, but stopping just short. She didn't move the few inches needed to make contact, there was no point. She'd get through the next days or weeks by keeping herself away from him and doing her best to forget how good it felt to have him hold her while they slept. One day soon she'd be able to forget about him completely.

"I'm coming with you, but I won't be bound again." Wrapping her arms about her waist, she followed him when he turned wordlessly and walked from the room. She didn't say a word until Glory approached them at the back door wearing a look of concern. Thanking the woman for her hospitality and apologizing for the trouble she had caused, she walked to the familiar black horse. When Hunter would have lifted her on, she shrugged him off and pulled herself up. After taking a moment to speak with the madam, their voices so low that she couldn't make out what they said, he followed. Grabbing the reins, he clicked his tongue and they set off for his home. Closing her eyes momentarily, she prayed for the strength to stay away from him even though the heat of his body at her back felt so good.

Opening her eyes, she resolved to stay alert the entire trip, looking for landmarks to guide her back to town. Now that the shock had worn off, she realized that perhaps it was a good thing he'd brought the children. It would save her from having to go back and get them. Because returning to the farm wasn't an option. She would escape and take her sisters away from the madness.

Chapter Fourteen

Hunter tightened his arm around her waist, taking their last minutes on the horse to hold her slim body close as his home came into view. About a two-hour ride eastward out of Helena, the Jameson Ranch was set near the back of a valley with nothing but clear blue sky and the mountains behind it. Rolling hills sat at the edge of the wide valley before it so that the house could only be seen in glimpses from the road until the rider passed a natural break in the hills and then it appeared through the awning of cottonwood trees at the base of the hills. Two-storied and sprawling, with a wood and stone exterior, it was a product of its environment, natural and almost uncultured except for its sheer size. A wide veranda, along with its twin on the second level, circled the whole house and every bedroom had its own bathing chamber and sitting room, an excess that his mother had insisted upon. Not that she had stayed around long after it was built to actually enjoy the luxuries.

Hunter grimaced as memories of his mother threatened to spoil the joy he always felt upon first seeing his home after a long absence. Glancing down at the woman in his arms, he couldn't help but think that she wasn't anything like her, she wasn't frivolous or shallow at all. She stared straight ahead, taking in the view of his home, and he longed to ask her what she thought. To speak to her of how much he loved it. How he had rebuilt the stables with his own hands. How he had hand-selected every horse within it and saw a select few bred to produce some of the most sought-after racing stock in the country. He wanted to tell her that the Missouri flowed just a little over two miles behind the house and that he'd spent many long summer days swimming and fishing its banks. He wanted to take her there. He wanted her to be there long enough for the water to warm so they could swim together naked under the sun.

Jesus, Emmy. He wanted to keep her. One night with her had only whetted his appetite for more. But it was so much more than sex. The hours he'd spent talking to her just made him want to peel back more of her layers. The thought of giving her back to Campbell made him so angry he couldn't see straight. He tightened his arm, his fingers pressing gently into her hip, trying to get closer to her, only to have her stiffen in his embrace. He clenched his jaw and looked down at her profile.

For the very first time in his life, he could imagine a future with a woman that didn't only involve sex—and it was the wrong damn woman. Apart from her being a Campbell, there were two other very good reasons a future with her wouldn't work out. The first was that she wasn't his social equal. He almost laughed aloud at the thought, because he didn't give a damn about that. Something told him she would. She wasn't shallow and he couldn't imagine her embracing some of the social functions and mingling with the Susanne Harrises of his world. She was every bit his equal, though. She served drinks to men like him for a living. Her stepfather was a man like him. Hell, her stepfather was a man like his own father. It wasn't such a stretch to imagine his father might have turned out like Campbell had fortune not shined on him. Campbell was just like him, only he wasn't polished enough, lucky enough, or smart enough to turn his money into an empire.

The second reason, the important one, was

that he was an outlaw. Despite how he felt for her, he couldn't see that changing in the near future. His allegiance belonged to his brothers. Hunter would ride with them until Cas had restored his family home and found the man responsible for his grandfather's murder. That wasn't something he was willing to walk away from and Emmy wouldn't want to leave one outlaw life for another. He was gone from home for weeks, sometimes months, at a time. There was always the chance he'd be seriously hurt or even killed. There was always the chance that some bastard would come looking for his woman, exactly the way he and his brothers had found Emmy. There were too many dangers to involve a woman in his life. That only left them a few stolen weeks. They'd have the next few weeks and he hoped he could convince her to share them with him before he had to let her go.

Despite how bone tired he was from chasing her down the past week and how long she'd kept him awake last night, he grew rigid just remembering how it had felt to be buried inside her, her body soft and responsive beneath him. He grimaced again as he remembered waking up and finding her gone. For some reason, he'd imagined waking her with kisses and, if she was able, taking her again in a long, slow rhythm that

would more than make up for how rough he'd
been with her the first time.

After he had made love to her that morning—*made love*? Christ, he was in deep, he'd
never made love in his life—he had planned to
ask her to come home with him so they had time
to explore what was between them. It wasn't as
if he could have kept his identity from her at
this stage. She knew his name and any person
in Helena could point her in his direction, so
there had been no reason not to take her home.
In fact, he couldn't allow her to go free because
she was one of the few who knew both of his
identities.

Once he'd obtained her agreement to come
home with him, he would've explained about
her sisters. He felt sure that if he could have broken that news to her gently, tactfully, the conversation would have gone differently, and she
wouldn't be making herself uncomfortable by so
needlessly holding herself away from him. Every
time he pulled her back so that she could rest her
weight against him, she moved away. Perhaps
he should have let her ride in the runabout they
kept in town and given her distance, but he'd
wanted to touch her while he still could. Once
they reached his home, he had no doubt that
she'd hide away from him, determined to keep

her distance. He couldn't say that he blamed her after the way he'd treated her.

Maybe he'd been selfish thinking they could have more time together than those few stolen hours. She had every reason to hate him. Even though he understood that, he had an overwhelming need to make her his, to make her scream with pleasure, to hold on to her and never let her go. He'd never felt that before and it scared the hell out of him.

No. No matter what he wanted, he couldn't think of anything long-standing with her.

On impulse, he transferred the reins to one hand and reached up to run a gloved thumb over the gentle curve of her cheekbone, swiping away a lock of hair that had fallen loose from her braid. She jerked away and he clenched his hand in a fist when it dropped back to the reins. Damn Campbell, and all the lowlifes who'd made the Reyes Brothers necessary.

Thoughts of the man had him looking into the distance to check for trouble. He wasn't expecting any. Campbell had no idea he was Hunter Jameson of Helena, but even if he did, Hunter had no fear of him. Criminals and fortune hunters alike had been making threats against the Jamesons for as long as Hunter could remember. The men at the ranch were all well trained to handle any threat. Though Cas and Zane had headed out this morning, two men from the ranch had been there to ride back with him and Emmy had they faced any trouble.

Walking the black up the circular driveway, he came to a stop before the wide brick steps that led up to the double front door. Dismounting, he reached up to grip her waist and help her down, noting how she kept her eyes carefully from him. He opened his mouth to welcome her to his home, but a black lacquered door opened and two squealing girls dressed in ruffles, came running out shouting her name. Pushing away from him, she ran up the steps and stooped down to throw her arms around them both, a smile like he'd never seen lighting her whole face and making him catch his breath.

Clenching the leather reins in his fist, a bitter hollow opening up in the pit of his stomach, he realized that he was jealous. He wanted to make her smile like that. He wanted her to look at him like that and be happy to see him. Shit, he was losing himself over her and there wasn't a damn thing he could do about it. Perhaps it *was* better if she stayed away from him over the next few weeks. Even as he thought it, he knew it didn't matter. He wouldn't allow it to happen. They had days, weeks maybe, before they heard from Campbell. Just the thought of it made panic clench tight in his belly.

Willy stepped out behind them and raised her hand in greeting. "Welcome home, Mr. Jameson."

Willy and her husband, Ed, had come from Boston to work for them as soon as the house had been built. She'd taken over the role of his mother in addition to running the house and over the years Ed had come to oversee everything outside the house. Smiling at the older woman, he took the steps two at a time until he stood under the overhang of the porch, pulling her into his arms and breathing in the familiar scent of the peppermint candy she loved to eat. The scent always seemed to cling to her.

Her hair, which had been graying ever since he could remember, was pulled back in its customary bun and she wore one off her usual gray dresses with the white apron. As far he knew his father had never insisted she keep the uniform his mother had put in place, but the woman wore it anyway, whether it was from respect or habit he simply didn't know. "It's good to see you, Willy. I hope the girls weren't any trouble. I know you weren't expecting guests." From the corner of his eye he noticed Emmy look up sharply at the word "guests". Apparently, she disagreed with the term.

"Not at all. They were perfect angels." She smiled at her charges and earned a soft look from Emmy as well for her kind words.

"This is their sister, Emmy Campbell."

"Emmaline Drake," she quickly corrected him.

He stood silent for a moment as the housekeeper greeted her, realizing just how little he knew about this woman who was quickly becoming an obsession and just how badly he wanted to know everything. Inclining his head, he continued, "She'll be staying for a while, too, as our *guest*." He emphasized the word just to watch Emmy's back stiffen. Fighting a smile, he allowed his gaze to rove from her back to her bosom, which wasn't flattered the least bit in the drab, conservative dress she had borrowed. "She's a special guest. Please make sure she has everything she needs."

"Of course, Mr. Jameson. I'll have a room near her sisters' room readied for her."

He clenched his jaw at the formal salutation. They had discussed that nonsense before, but she refused to refer to him as Hunter in front of company. The woman had tended him through every childhood fever and illness. He saw the formality as fake civility while she saw it as a necessity to some nonexistent social balance he'd never understand. She had accused him once of being unable to see how life really was due to his privileged upbringing. Glory had accused him of the same. But life was too short for that nonsense, and if it was his privileged upbringing that made him realize that then he was all the more thankful for it.

"I hope you don't mind I sent Ed into town to fetch more clothing for them. Mr. Pierce failed to bring any with him."

Finally sparing a glance to the two young girls, he noted the blonde hair that Zane had mentioned, but he couldn't see any similarities between them and their sister. They stared back at him with wide grey-blue eyes, not the clear blue of his Emmy.

His Emmy.

He couldn't stop thinking of her as his no matter how hard he tried. If it kept up, when this was over he'd have to buy himself a week at Victoria House and pray that if the women didn't make him forget her, the whiskey would dull the ache of her loss. Somehow he knew that it wouldn't be easy to see her go.

The girls wore almost matching dresses of pink and white ruffles that must have come ready-made from one of the dress shops in town. He opened his mouth to ask if Ed had gone to

Madame Dauphine's. He had sent enough business her way that the proprietess would hesitate
to mention the odd request, if asked. The last
thing he needed was word getting out that he
had the girls here; he was already risking a lot
by keeping them all at his house. But then he
glanced at Emmy and figured the question could
wait until he was alone with the housekeeper.
She didn't need to know how many women he'd
bought dresses for in the past. Even as he thought
it, he couldn't deny that he wanted to take her
there as well. To watch as she picked out fabric
and designs, as she was measured and fitted. To
know that she wasn't reduced to hand-me-downs
and coarse material that abraded her skin. To tell
her that money was no object and she could buy
to her heart's content.

Raking a hand over the back of his neck, he
said, "It's fine, Willy. I hope you had him get
enough. They'll be visiting for a few weeks at
least."

"We'll be prisoners, you mean?" Emmy stared
at him, not flinching when he stared back.

"Of course that's what I meant." He spoke the
words firmly but softly and they settled into the
suddenly stale air of the porch. He hated that she
had pushed it to this, but she had to understand

that he was in control. As kind as Willy was, she was on his side.

Willy proved his point when she completely ignored the statement and assured him that Ed had picked up enough clothing. His heart ached when Emmy's bottom lip trembled just for an instant when she realized the housekeeper would be no ally. It was so subtle that he probably wouldn't have noticed had he not been so attuned to the woman's every damned nuance. He wanted to tell her that *he* would be her ally, that he only wanted to take care of her, but he knew she wouldn't believe him and he couldn't hold it against her because he had kidnapped her. Instead of replying, she stiffened her shoulders and her face hardened with them. She didn't say anything else, just turned her attention back to the girls who had started chattering again.

Without a word, he leaped down the steps and grabbed the reins of his horse, following his men to the stable across the open yard.

Chapter Fifteen

~~~~~~~~~~

Emmy watched him walk the dirt path toward the stables with a hollow pang of longing in her chest that she tried her best to ignore. It irritated her that as her gaze roved over his broad shoulders she still felt a tug deep in her belly and that she craved his tender words from the night before. How could he be so willing to send her back to Ship after their night together? She tried to tell herself that it hadn't really meant anything, but she couldn't stop seeing the intensity of his face as he'd held himself above her, or the way he had looked deep into her eyes as he'd moved inside her. Her heart along with her body still ached from him, but he seemed to have already forgotten.

She was a fool.

Instead of letting herself dwell on that, she turned her attention back to her sisters, who were each talking over the other in a bid to tell her about their adventure of the past week. The name Mr. Pierce was being shouted, who she was sure couldn't be the giant she knew. They described him as kind, having kept them entertained on their trip with stories of the noble men who used to ride the plains. He hadn't been stoic or threatening, the awful attributes she would have attributed to him. He'd been smiling and kind. Though she was very grateful that the girls had viewed their situation without fear and, indeed, with excitement, she couldn't reconcile their experience with what she knew to be true.

The housekeeper ushered them inside where Emmy stopped to admire the two-story foyer that was all polished, honey-colored oak and wrought-iron. Tall doors, two sets on each side, flanked the wide entry hallway that ran the length of the house. The first set, leading off from either side of the huge burgundy and gold Persian carpet, were open to parlors with tasteful, comfortable-looking upholstered furniture. But she didn't get the chance to explore, because the girls pulled her along to the staircase as she stared in openmouthed awe at the expense that must have gone into such luxury.

Curving and elegant, with a wrought-iron handrail with spindly, decorative supports, the stairs were wide and led them to the upper floor where a plush, burgundy rug covering the gleaming wood floor greeted them on the landing. A right turn would have taken them across the foyer to the south wing, but the girls pulled her to the left and stopped at the first door on the right.

One glance at the room and she knew that it had been a nursery at some point. A crib was pushed back into the far corner surrounded by baskets of baby toys: rattles, wooden carriages and horses, and even a brightly painted rocking horse carved from wood. Though Rose was nine and liked to consider herself as big as Ginny, who was three years older, the child still lurking within her came out as she ran to the horse clearly made for a younger child, making Emmy smile. "Look at this, Em! Do you think I could keep it when we go home?" Grinning, Rose mounted its brightly painted saddle and demonstrated how to ride it.

Ginny ran across the large room to the armoire and opened it to show her all the new clothes that a Mr. Ed had brought for them to wear. They were all dresses in various pastels with more ruffles and lace than she had ever seen in one place before. Ginny smiled and ran a reverent hand over the fabric. "Aren't they lovely?"

"Yes, absolutely beautiful."

"I gave Rose the ones with ruffles, but I'm keeping both of the pink ones. I've never had anything besides gray and dull gray. Do you think these will turn gray after we wash them?"

Every dress the girls owned was secondhand and had been washed so much their color had long since faded. Blinking back very sudden and unexpected tears at this show of how much the girls had been deprived of, Emmy turned her gaze to the rest of the room. It held two small, matching beds neatly made up in dark green bedclothes. A desk set against one wall was complete with a bookshelf filled with books on arithmetic, astronomy, biology and all the other subjects a child might need to learn. Another bookcase was filled to the brim with more toys: wooden drums with skins stretched tight across them, a brightly painted wooden flute, blocks, and even male and female dolls dressed in fine evening wear.

She stood horrified. This must mean that Hunter was married and his wife and children had been stowed away somewhere. Her heart dropped into her stomach as she made her way deeper into the well-appointed room. Every item a child might need could be found here. Walking to the desk, she picked up one of the books with a shaking hand. *The Young Man's Guide to Becoming a Gentleman* was embossed in faded letters on the drab brown cover.

Sons. He definitely had sons.

But as she was placing the book back, Rose called her name and she misplaced it so that it fell to the side of the stack of books. The cover flipped open, revealing Hunter's name written in the painstakingly correct yet immature handwriting of a child. Placing the book back in its spot, she noted the initials "HWJ" carved into the side of the desk with the uneven efforts of a child. She tried to imagine the boy he had been playing here in the room. She'd see a gangly boy with dark blond hair swept down over his eyes and that same mischievous smile and her heart would ache, but then the image would be replaced by the handsome, imposing man she knew him to be. This had been Hunter's childhood room. Did his sons claim the room now?

A voice warned that she shouldn't make assumptions, he'd have told her if he was married. But another voice reminded her that he would have no reason to tell a whore. The problem was that she didn't know which voice was the rational one. That scared her very much. For as long as she could remember, she'd lived by the idea that as long as she made the reasonable, rational choice then everything would turn out fine. Now that everything was turned upside down, she just didn't know which that choice was.

The next hour passed in a blur as the girls, who had already explored every inch of the nursery, showed her every toy and its purpose. She had never seen them so happy back home at the farm. Their toys there had been so limited it shamed her to think of it. They'd never held any sort of musical instrument or even had a book full of children's stories. Emmy had read some of her books to them, always editing so the plots were appropriate and interesting to them. They'd never even had free rein to just play, with chores and meal preparation always taking up so much of their time, especially when Ship and his men were home.

She was smiling at her sisters as they argued over the rules of a board game played with colorful marbles, when the housekeeper walked into the room and gently cleared her throat. Emmy rose from her seat at the small table and greeted the woman who gestured toward the hallway. Assuring her sisters that she'd return very soon, she followed the housekeeper out the door.

"I wanted to thank you for taking such good care of my sisters, Mrs....um..." Hunter had called her Willy, but that seemed too informal.

"Please call me Willy, dear. Everyone does. My name was Wilhelmina, but that's a name from back East. It never seemed to fit out here." She smiled easily and, it seemed, genuinely. "And no thanks necessary. It was my pleasure to keep them happy, they're wonderful girls."

"Well, thank you." Emmy nodded, but to call her Willy didn't seem right, so she skipped the subject.

"I apologize for the delay, but we weren't expecting another guest, so I needed to prepare your room. Follow me and I'll show you to it."

There was that word again. Guest.

Willy led her to the next room down the hallway and, following her inside, Emmy gently pulled the door closed behind her. She hadn't yet determined how to explain their stay here to her sisters, nor had she had the time to ask them what they had been told, so she didn't want them to overhear their conversation. It was time to figure out if the housekeeper was ally or foe, though she suspected she already knew the answer.

"I'm sure you'll find everything you need here," Willy was saying as she walked to the center of the small sitting room. A settee with matching chairs flanking each side was upholstered in a rose velvet and was the focal point of the room. The window behind the settee was

framed in matching drapes that let in cheery
late-morning light, making the regularly polished wood of the fragile-looking tables gleam.
The air was fragrant with the pleasant smell of
polish and sunshine. "And in here…" The housekeeper paused to open the door to the attached
bedchamber, revealing a four-poster bed made
up in golden bedclothes with touches of pink in
the throw pillows to match the upholstery in the
sitting room.

Emmy was pulled into that room by her own
curiosity, her feet sinking into the thick cream
and rose carpet as she stepped inside. A large armoire and dressing table took up one wall while
two large windows on the opposite wall allowed
light to flood the space. With its rich fabric and
beautifully maintained furniture, the bedchamber could have belonged to a princess.

"I'm afraid I've only been able to find a handful of gowns, but if your stay is long enough
I'm sure we can arrange a modiste to come and
attend you." Willy smiled a large grin as she
opened the armoire to reveal more clothing than
Emmy had ever had access to in her life. And
she'd called them "gowns", not dresses—that
must make them special.

As if stuck in that same trance that had led her
into the bedroom, she crossed the carpet to let

her fingers touch the array of fabrics and textures inside, with the same reverence Ginny had displayed earlier. The dresses were in every jewel-toned color she could imagine: sapphire, ruby, amber, emerald. There wasn't a single dull blue, brown or black in the lot. An irrational flicker of excitement flared within her as she imagined wearing them, but she hastily beat it down as she reminded herself that she was a prisoner and not a guest at all. She had no rights to these clothes nor should she want to accept them. They were bribery, plain and simple. Hunter wanted her to accept the luxuries in exchange for her cooperation, or perhaps he simply wanted to assuage his own guilt. No matter the reason, accepting would be inappropriate. The thought made her snatch her hand back and close it into a tight fist to resist the urge to touch them again.

"You must know that I'm here against my will." She kept her voice soft, but firm.

Willy's smile faded, but her eyes stayed kind as she nodded. "I'm aware of Mr. Jameson's *other* life, Miss Drake. There's almost nothing you can tell me about him that I don't know."

"Then how can you condone what he's done? He's taken me and my sisters from our home."

"It's not for me to condone his actions. I know that he wouldn't harm you and that's enough for me. Though he hasn't yet shared his reasons for doing what he's done with you, I can assure you that they are noble ones. Please don't judge him too harshly. You'll find him kind and fair if you give him the chance."

Kind and fair. The words echoed in her head. Was he kind? Yes, he had been once he'd stopped trying to scare information from her. Even then, he hadn't been as boorish as he could have been. Was he fair? No, it wasn't fair that he had taken her and it wasn't fair that he had loved her body so thoroughly the night before only to take her captive again when morning came. He wasn't playing fair at all.

Looking at the woman squarely, she demanded, "Whose clothes are these? And whose room is this?" It was unimaginable to her that such a magnificent room and such grand clothing were left unused.

"Mr. Jameson has…guests from time to time. It seemed prudent to keep clothing about."

Mistresses. The housekeeper hadn't said it, but the slight hesitation in her voice was enough, unless Mr. Jameson was in the habit of abducting female hostages on a regular basis. She didn't think that was true. The thought of the many mistresses he must have had rankled, even though she had no idea why. He'd made no commitment to her. Indeed, she'd given herself to him freely without asking for one, but only because she'd thought it would be for a night and then she'd never see him again. She didn't know how to deal with the awkwardness of still being forced to be in his presence, particularly under these circumstances. Or the awkwardness of still wanting him, if she had to be completely honest with herself. Which she didn't. She didn't want to remember how good it had felt to press her shoulders back against his chest the few times she'd allowed herself the small luxury on the ride here.

"And this is where his *guests* stay?"

The woman had the good grace to lower her gaze briefly. Wonderful. She was in the mistress's chamber. This captivity just kept getting better, but at least it wasn't his wife's. Suddenly she just had to know the answer to the question that had been worrying her since the nursery.

"Is he married?"

"He's never been married. I'm not sure he'll ever be married." Willy shook her head and gave a soft laugh, walking to the windows to open them to the cool morning air. "His parents are married, but they hardly ever see each other. I believe they've given him an unfortunate disposition on the matter."

"Oh? His parents don't live here?"

"Not his mother, she's from Boston and re-
sides there with her family. His father lives
here, but with all the hubbub about statehood he
spends most of his time in Helena or back East.
He's in Washington now." The woman spoke as
she made a turn of the room, straightening lin-
ens and checking the quantity of the numerous
pots and bottles on the dressing table, then the
housekeeper smiled at her and walked to the
door. "I believe you'll find everything you need.
Night clothes are in the drawers there," she said,
pointing to the bureau. "The bathing chamber
is through there, just let me know when you'd
like a bath and I'll have water heated. I'm going
downstairs to finish preparing the meal. Come
down with the girls in about an hour to eat."

With that, Willy strode out of the room, leaving Emmy to wonder if Hunter's father would
care that his son had taken her hostage, but
then quickly decided he wouldn't. Hunter was a
man who did whatever he wanted and everyone
around him had probably become accustomed
to it years ago. With a sigh of defeat, she walked
to the open window and the strange chair before
it. It was a soft rose color like the furniture in
the sitting room, but the back was only on one
end, leaving the sides on the other end com-

pletely open. She'd never seen anything like it, not even at Glory's.

Sinking down onto the soft velvet, she let her gaze move to the window and with no outbuildings to hold her interest, it roved to the mountains in the distance. The sun was just beginning to reach its peak in the sky, burnishing the hills in gold, orange and soft shades of pink. For the first time since her bizarre meeting with the outlaws that night at Jake's, Emmy was able to take a deep breath and feel her muscles relax as she breathed the air back out. She wasn't free and she wasn't even sure what the next day would bring, but she did feel safe and the immediate safety of her sisters had ceased to be a concern.

Laying her head back, she closed her eyes and breathed in the air of early spring. After a few minutes the tension began to uncoil in her shoulders and it was like a weight lifted from her chest. The rational voice in her mind began to talk the loudest and she could finally hear it. She'd slept with Hunter last night because she wanted to know how it would feel. The muscles between her thighs clenched at the memory of his powerful body moving over hers and she smiled at the tender ache he'd left behind. She wouldn't regret their night and she wouldn't let that other voice in her head make her think it was more than it had been. They'd both enjoyed it and it was over, never to be repeated again. She could live with that. It hadn't changed anything.

With her thoughts clear for the first time since she'd met him, she turned her mind to what she needed to do next. Perhaps she should be thanking Hunter. He'd saved her the trip back out to the farm. All she had to do now was get the three of them back to town and on a westbound train. She couldn't allow herself to think about what would happen if she couldn't find a source of income quickly. She couldn't allow herself to think of how that fifty thousand dollars from Hunter could help them.

The knot of tension returned to her belly, so she took several deep breaths and closed her eyes until it began to dissipate again. Taking it would make what happened last night something cold and unpalatable. Money would tarnish the joy. No, she'd have to accept the loan Glory had offered her and pay it back later.

Now she just had to figure out how to get the three of them away without Hunter following.

Chapter Sixteen

When she next opened her eyes, the sun had disappeared to the other side of the house, lengthening the shadows in the bedroom. She sat up disoriented and looked around the immaculate room, forgetting for a moment where she was until everything came back to her.

Oh, yes, kidnapped again.

Except this time the thought wasn't accompanied by dread or the powerful need to escape. She felt calm, secure even, and more rested than she'd felt in a very long time. Naps weren't a luxury in which she was generally able to indulge, so that one had been heavenly after so many days of pushing herself to the limit of her physical and emotional endurance.

Yawning and stretching her back which had stiffened in the awkward position, she found that a knitted blanket had been carefully placed over her while she slept. Willy. Though she was essentially her jailer, Emmy couldn't help a tug of tenderness in her heart at this kindness. The housekeeper had been nothing but kind to her and she'd been so thoughtful with the girls that Emmy couldn't fault her for the actions of her employer.

As if thoughts of her sisters had summoned them, Rose's squeals of delight found her through the open window. She grimaced when she stood and took a moment to rub her bottom and the backs of her thighs, which were a bit sore from the horse ride. Though that didn't quite explain the tenderness between her thighs and she couldn't help smiling about that. Pushing the sash higher, she craned her neck to see that her youngest sister was just inside the fenced stable yard off the end of the house, sitting atop a horse. A man with a wide-brimmed hat was leading her around and Emmy could tell immediately from the set of his broad shoulders that it was Hunter. Ship had always forbidden the children from riding his horses, because they were too valuable to risk them getting injured. As a result, Rose didn't know how to ride and, to her knowledge, had never even sat on a horse before, though she must have ridden one on the way here.

Her heart flipping over in her chest, Emmy rushed downstairs and ran the few hundred yards across ankle-high grass to reach the stables. By the time she reached the fence, Hunter was lifting Rose off the horse's back as she beamed with joy. Setting her on her feet, he turned to Ginny who had been patiently waiting her turn and helped her up to sit on its back. Emmy had already parted her lips to call out a warning, or admonish him for risking her sisters, but whatever she had planned to say died away when she saw the care he was taking with them. They were having fun.

"Em!" Finally noticing her, Rose called out and ran the few yards to reach her. "I rode a horse! Did you see me?"

Emmy smiled back at her. "Yes, I did! You looked like a real horsewoman."

"Isn't she pretty? Her name is Cinnamon. Mr. Hunter says it's 'cause she's the same color as cinnamon, but I don't really know what that is."

Emmy followed the girl's gaze back to the horse and found herself agreeing with her even though her own gaze had been caught by the man staring at her. He was just as breathtakingly handsome as she remembered. Though his eyes were shaded from her, his strong jaw and a day's growth of stubble was as tantalizing as ever. A secret thrill shot through her belly, making her jerk her gaze away to tame it. It also made her aware that her hair was probably a mess after her nap having been put into a hasty braid that morning.

"Be careful, Ginny," she called out and ran a hand over her hair.

"I will! This is my second time," the older girl proudly called out as Hunter began to lead her around the fenced space.

Emmy managed to keep her gaze from lighting on him again while Ginny rode around and Rose kept up the conversation. Apparently, the girls had spent the afternoon with Hunter in the stables, getting to know all of the horses. Rose told her about the two who were about to foal and the ones who'd won races. When he had told her that Cinnamon was the gentlest horse he'd ever known, Rose had asked to ride that one. Despite herself, a wave of tenderness rose within her when she imagined him taking up so much time with her sisters. She'd expected the indifference he'd displayed that morning when they had arrived. But she was forced to admit that despite the night they had met, he'd shown himself to be very gentle and caring.

Even the night they'd met he'd been such a contradiction. When he'd released her from hanging from the rafters, he'd made sure that the rope at her wrists was loose enough that she wasn't chafed. He'd never harmed her, never really even frightened her. He wasn't evil.

When it was time to put the horse away, Emmy was curious and followed them inside the large structure to see where the horses were kept. Fifteen stalls lined each side and it appeared that many of them were occupied. Ginny was telling her the names of each of the horses they passed, their velvet noses sticking over the low doors curious to see who had come to visit them.

They reached Cinnamon's stall and the girls followed Hunter inside. She watched from the doorway as he showed them how to take the saddle off and brush her down. Then he let them take over the brush and picked up the saddle. Stepping out of the way to let him out, she couldn't help but admire his well-sculpted backside as he walked away from her to swing the saddle over the bench where it was stored, lined up with a few others. The muscles in his back and shoulders bulged under his shirt as he did it, making her vividly recall how they had felt beneath her hands. Her body's attraction to him was as unfair as it was undeniable.

"Thank you for spending so much time with

them this afternoon. They enjoyed learning about the horses," she said when he turned and caught her watching him.

"I enjoyed it, too. They're very kindhearted. They'll be good with horses." He smiled back at her and crossed the short distance between them, coming to a stop just in front of her.

Emmy didn't know when they'd have the opportunity to be "good with horses", so she let the comment pass. Their excited voices came from just inside the stall, not far away but so engrossed in their activity that it afforded them a modicum of privacy. The sounds of men hammering came from somewhere far outside the back entrance of the stable, but they were too far away to be obtrusive. "Sorry I fell asleep. It wasn't intentional."

"Don't apologize. You were tired." He surprised her by reaching up to run the pad of his thumb along her cheekbone. Now that he was so close, she could see his beautiful green-gold eyes. Desire blazed in them, low and intense, but he wasn't teasing her about how long he'd kept her awake last night. There was nothing there that made her feel as if he was mocking her. She didn't move away.

"I'd like to talk to you about...things." She wanted to persuade him to let them go, but didn't want to close down the conversation before it got started. "Could we talk, privately?"

His eyes flicked to the girls in the stall and then back to her. Nodding, he said, "Tonight. I've got some work to do, but come find me in my study after dinner." Then he dropped his hand and walked past her into the stall where he helped the girls finish up. By the time they were done, Willy was calling them from the front porch, telling them it was time to eat. Her stomach grumbled, reminding her that she hadn't eaten since the night before. Even then, she'd barely been able to get any food down knowing what was waiting for her with the auction.

Much to her surprise, Hunter didn't join them at dinner. The table, which was large enough to seat twelve people, had only been set for three. The meal of succulent beef, roasted vegetables and biscuits, finished with apple pie and a light whipped cream, was the most delicious she'd ever eaten. Even the girls had cleaned their plates and asked for more, licking the sweetened cream from their fingers with relish. After dinner she took them back to the nursery where they all three played the board game with the marbles again and read a few stories from the children's storybook Rose picked out, before Emmy put them to bed.

Only as she was kissing them good-night did Ginny look up at her with her serious blue-gray eyes. "Will we stay here for long, Em?"

"I'm not sure. Do you miss home?"

The girl shrugged. "I miss Ship, I suppose, but I like it here. Maybe we could stay and he could visit."

"Me, too," Rose piped up from her bed. "There's so much to do here. I love Cinnamon. And all the food."

"Yeah, Willy cooks much better than you," Ginny informed her solemnly.

The innocent words almost brought tears to her eyes. How many times had the girls gone to bed with only a few bites of boiled potatoes in their bellies? Perhaps Hunter had done them a kindness by bringing them all here.

Kissing them both good-night, she went back to her room to prepare for her talk with him and crossed to the mirror hanging just above the dressing table. It was just as bad as she feared. Her hair was a mess and, despite her nap, there were still dark smudges under her eyes from the lack of sleep she'd had all week. She'd been so afraid that she'd barely slept on the trail.

Plopping onto the chair, she took out the braid

and picked up the brush that had been thought-fully left there for her. After a few minutes of trying to tame the mess, she finally settled on simply tying it back with a ribbon she found in one of the pots on the table. But then she noticed a smudge of dirt on her chin that she'd probably picked up from the stable. Hurrying to the at-tached bathing chamber, she was delighted to find that a bowl of steaming water had been left there for her while she'd been playing with the girls. The room was small and tiled in a mod-est white tile that matched the gleaming, white porcelain of the rest of the fixtures.

But she hardly gave them a second glance as she hurried to clean herself up, briefly debating changing into one of the gowns in the armoire, before deciding against it. She needed to keep her distance. Her sanity depended upon her not becoming too accustomed to this place and its master. In the end, she put on the brown dress she'd carried with her from the brothel, the same one she'd changed into the night at the cabin. It wasn't her best, but she wasn't trying to attract him again. She simply wanted to look present-able for their talk.

Once she had walked downstairs and found it dark, except for a few oil lamps that had been turned low, and realized that no one was around, she knew that she had made the right choice in her dress. She found him tempting enough. She didn't want to encourage his pursuit when she had a hard enough time keeping herself from wanting him. After a few wrong turns that led her through exquisitely decorated parlors and then the servants' quarters, she found her way to his study in the back of the house. The door was open, revealing a room with a wall of windows on one side and a massive stone fireplace on the other, book-lined shelves built into the wall on either side of it. What incredible wealth this man must possess. It was a necessary reminder that any thoughts of pursuing another night with him was out of the question. What was between them couldn't be permanent, so she was only setting herself up for heartache to even consider it.

Catching sight of his head leaned over an oversized desk, his hair perfectly smoothed back and looking more brown than blond in the dim light, she knocked on the opened door. He looked up immediately at her across the ledgers and papers scattered over the gleaming desk and smiled as soon as he saw her. The smile was contagious and she returned it instinctively, her heart catching for a moment before it proceeded with its beating. She noted immediately that he hadn't shaved, then admonished herself for being happy about that.

"Come in." He rose and indicated she take one of the pair of brown leather chairs facing his desk, waiting for her to sit down before he resumed his seat. "I trust you're settled in. Have everything you need?" He noted her brown dress, but didn't say anything about her not wearing one of the gowns Willy had procured for her.

She nodded and found it a little disturbing that while he seemed happy to see her, there was a distance in his eyes. The tiny bit of tenderness she'd seen on his face back at the stables had been replaced by cordiality. It was a good thing. It meant that he'd accepted that what had happened between them last night was over. Maybe that would help her accept that as well. "You really can stand to lose fifty thousand dollars, can't you?" She cast a look at the room to emphasize her point.

He shrugged and managed to look as arrogant as someone should when acknowledging his obscene wealth. He'd bathed and changed clothes since she'd seen him at the stables and now wore a crisp button-up shirt. The top few buttons were undone to reveal enough of his chest that it warmed her to see the tanned skin and light sprinkling of hair. The white shirt was tucked into a pair of dark-colored trousers, emphasizing the hard, flat planes of his stomach as he sat back, his hands folded across his lap.

"You must know that I've come to discuss my—our...captivity."

He raised a brow at her word choice. "That seems harsh."

Perhaps it was. It wasn't as if they were chained in a dungeon, but she wasn't going to give him the satisfaction of her backing down. They both knew it for what it was. She wasn't free to leave. "I'd like you to allow us to leave."

"Not an option."

"I knew you might say that." She held out the folded bank draft, making sure her fingers didn't tremble. When he didn't make a move to reach for it, she unfolded it so that he could see it was the bank draft he'd written out for her and dropped it on his desk. "Fifty thousand dollars for our release."

He smiled again, but to his credit he didn't laugh. "I don't need fifty thousand dollars, as you've pointed out."

What could she say to that bold truth? "Of course," she conceded.

Leaning forward, he picked the draft up only to hold it out to her. "You must also know that

I'd be more likely to allow you to go knowing that you have money with you."

"It's not actual money, though, is it? Do you suppose I could just walk into the bank and have it converted to gold or bills without your permission?" A draft for that much had to be rare, even in Helena. The bank would want to verify with him that it wasn't a forgery before exchanging it.

His smile stayed in place as he gave a nod to concede her point. "I'd be more than happy to have it converted for you if it means you'll take it."

She took it back, folding it into her fist and deciding to ignore his comment. The more she had tried to figure out a way to not take the money, the more she became convinced it was her only real chance of getting away and starting over somewhere. She *could* borrow from Glory, but then she'd have to impose on her yet again and hope the loan didn't run out before she could provide for them.

Instead of responding to that, she tried the only other tactic she had been able to come up with. "How do you expect to get away with this? I know who you are, the children know who you are. You haven't hidden your identity from us. We even know where you live. Ship will question us when we go home and, whether I cooperate or not, the girls are too young to not say anything. They'll tell him your name and all about this place." She waved her hand to indicate the property. "Even if they won't remember how to get here, how long before he figures it out? If he doesn't come for you, he can go to the authorities and tell them what we know. You must realize that you've placed yourself in grave danger."

His smile didn't falter, but it did become more thoughtful and his voice held a slight rasp when he spoke. "Are you trying to convince me that I shouldn't let you go at all? That I should keep you?"

Despite the vision of endless nights in his bed that his words conjured followed by the coil of pleasure unfurling low in her belly, she shook her head. "It's why you shouldn't return us to Ship. You can say we escaped. I'll take the children far away and you'll never hear from us again. I promise I won't ever say anything to anyone. The girls don't even know that we're hostages. They think you're a family friend we're visiting and this is some grand holiday to them. They don't know you're an outlaw, so they won't tell anyone."

"I believe you, Emmy. I think you'll keep my secret." His intense gaze held hers and she believed he spoke the truth. "But you and your sisters are the only way to make sure Miguel isn't needlessly hurt."

Of course. Miguel was the person Ship had taken. She had never really thought that Ship would actually harm an innocent person, so it was time to find out if Miguel was actually innocent. It was past time for her to understand more about this situation she'd been pulled into. "Who is Miguel?"

Hunter took in the woman sitting across from him, in her austere brown dress. Her frame was so small that the chair dwarfed her, making her appear even smaller and younger. But despite her prim mannerisms and the fact that she looked so young and fragile, she'd taken him in her hands as if she knew exactly what she had wanted. He hardened just remembering it. The sounds she'd made had been so soft, feminine, and so damned sweet to his ears that he could still hear them when he closed his eyes. His body wanted to get her to make those sounds again.

Shifting in his chair to find a more comfortable position, he tried to force his thoughts back to the conversation. It would do no good to remember things better left in the past. For now, he'd have to channel his need to take care of her into other things. While she was here he could make sure she got enough to eat so that she could put on some weight before she went home. He'd even made sure Willy included something with apples into the meal that night. His housekeeper had given him an amused glance, but it was the only thing he knew that Emmy liked. Though she could have gobbled the apples he'd given her on that morning nearly a week ago down so fast because she was starving, not necessarily because she had liked them.

Had it been only been days? It seemed like he'd known her longer than that.

Running a hand over his face, he acknowledged that she was quickly becoming an obsession. This was madness. The entire situation had gotten completely out of hand. She was his hostage and, though they could be lovers—he'd accepted that bizarre breach of his values— they could not be anything more permanent. Cas needed him to help save his hacienda and Hunter wouldn't let him down. He couldn't be sidetracked by her.

"Miguel," she repeated. "He's part of your gang?"

"Castillo's little brother." He nodded, answering without calculating how much he should tell her. He was so desperate for any part of her that he *wanted* to tell her anything she wanted to know about him.

"But not *your* brother?"

"Cas was born to my father's first wife. Miguel was born long after my father...moved on. He's a good kid, though. Loyal to Cas. It's what got him in trouble."

She stared at him long and hard before saying, "So they divorced? Your father and his first wife?"

"Not precisely."

"Oh." She chewed her bottom lip as her mind worked over that information. He couldn't stop himself from smiling as he watched her come to the logical conclusion. "But...but that means..."

"It means my father is a sinner bent on eternal damnation," he teased.

Her plump lips dropped open a bit as if she didn't quite know what to make of that. He found himself staring at them, wanting to taste them again. "And you're a bastard," she finally said.

"In the eyes of God, I suppose I am, but not according to the great Territory of Montana. There was a war going on when my father married Marisol. They never made it legal, just said a few words in a church because she was pregnant and I imagine because Cas's grandfather had a loaded rifle he wasn't afraid to use."

He sat forward again, drawn to her in a way he couldn't even comprehend enough to resist. "You see, we're not really all that different, you and I." He'd never spoken truer words. The knowledge made his breath catch for a moment.

She wanted to agree. It was plain to see in her eyes that she wanted to jump that divide between them. Instead, she changed the subject. "I want to know what this whole thing is about. How did your gang become involved with Ship's?"

He rose to hide his smile and walked to the sideboard to pour himself a cognac. He admired how she tried to keep formality between them and a part of him hoped she accomplished the task, but he didn't feel like her captor anymore than she felt like his captive. The formality was a barrier. She didn't know it, but the more she tried to put it between them, the more he wanted to tear it down. "Come have a drink with me."

He poured her a cognac as well and turned to her with both in hand. When she shook her head, he walked over and took a seat on the couch before the fireplace. He'd lit a fire earlier in the evening, but it was burning low now. Setting her snifter on the low table, he sat back into the corner of the cushions so that he could still see her over the low back and took a small sip. Enjoying the first taste as it covered his tongue and warmed its way down to his stomach, he closed his eyes.

"I didn't know I had a brother until Cas showed up here a little more than five years ago. He'd come to tell our father that his mother had just died. It had been her last wish that he see his father again." Glancing down at the dark amber liquid in the snifter, he clenched his jaw. Those hadn't been the words he'd meant to say. He'd meant to tell her about the shooting that had made Campbell angry. There had been no need for her to understand everything that had happened since Miguel and Cas had come into his life, but he had an undeniable need to tell her so that she would understand. So that she would know that there was a reason for all that was happening. That it meant something.

There was a shifting of movement and, without looking up, he knew that she was walking closer. He didn't want to scare her away, though, so he didn't acknowledge her, just kept staring down at the liquor cupped in his hands and continued his story. He'd started it, so he might as well finish it. "Honor is important to Cas. He'd never make a promise without honoring it. So he came here, fulfilled his vow, then turned around and left. Wouldn't stay and get to know the father who'd abandoned him and I can't say I blame him.

"When he left, I followed him and caught up to him just outside of town. You could tell that life hadn't been kind to him. He was angry and didn't trust anyone. It was all I could do to get him to agree to stay in town with me for a couple of days." Hunter grew quiet as he remembered those few days. Cas had been haunted by his mother's passing and angry at the task she'd assigned him. He had never wanted to meet his father and he sure as hell hadn't cared to meet siblings. But over those days they'd discovered they shared more similarities than they'd originally imagined, despite the differences in how they'd been raised. Hunter had returned to university in the fall, but the year he completed his studies he'd ridden down to Texas to meet up with his brother. After a lifetime of only his father, he'd found in Cas and his gang a family that he'd never known.

"Cas's grandfather had come over from Spain years ago with the idea of making his fortune in the cattle business. Looks like he gave it a good try, but the ranch was falling down around them and their calves were getting picked off by rival ranchers hoping to make them sell out. I got there in time to help defend their border, but then other property owners came to us for help. One thing led to another and before you knew it we were the Reyes Brothers or gang or whatever the hell they call us. Then his grandfather was murdered and we can't stop until Cas gets justice."

By this time she'd perched on the other end of the couch and he chanced a look at her. She seemed thoughtful as she listened, her head tilted at a slight angle. "Why wouldn't your father help him?" she asked when he caught her gaze. "He clearly has enough to spare."

"He would, but Cas wouldn't accept." Their father had gifted them both with mining interests, but Cas hadn't touched his. He hadn't even acknowledged it, leaving Hunter to manage it all. "Cas won't acknowledge my father. It's his honor. His life is his hacienda, his family and fulfilling his grandfather's vision. If he can't save his home, he believes he doesn't deserve anything. Not the mines that he should rightfully inherit, especially not from a father he doesn't accept."

"And you feel guilty, as if…maybe, he should be here, own all of this, instead of you?"

He was nodding before he ever even realized it. "Some."

She nodded, a furrow appearing between her brow as she looked down. The light from the fire flickered on the pale skin of her neck and he vividly recalled tasting the sweet flesh and wondered if he'd left a mark. He wanted to mark her all over. Glancing to her profile, he noticed her soft lips, the bottom one plump and pink. Was it his imagination or was it pinker today than yesterday? Shifting, he took a deep breath and forced his attention back to his story.

"We started slipping across the border and bringing back some of his cattle that had been illegally sold off. Because that was so easy, before long we started bringing back other cattle, too." He grinned. "That makes people angry, so they started following us and we had to fight them off. You do that enough, people think you're the one causing trouble. Maybe we were." They'd never caused problems for anyone who hadn't deserved them. "Outlaws are a jealous lot and they lack imagination. Soon, we were fending off all the unsavory types trying to get a piece of our business. That's when we came across Campbell. He approached Cas to partner up, but that's not how we operate. Campbell didn't like that so he started spreading lies about us, tried to get a jump on our jobs, just being a jackass and doing what he could to make things difficult for us. Then one day we were in Crystal City. It's another story, but we'd followed Miguel there. We met up with a man named Hardy who sometimes ran with Campbell. Before we knew it, he was drawing on us. He didn't realize that nobody outdraws Cas. He was dead before he knew what happened.

"Miguel was not at the saloon with us. Campbell found him before we did and took off with him. We tried to follow them, but lost the tracks after a storm. So we tracked down one of his friends and he told us about you. The rest you know."

He paused to meet her gaze. "We have to get him back, Emmy. Miguel is only seventeen, he was just a kid when all this started and didn't have a choice about joining the gang. The gang was his family. If he's hurt because of the choices Cas and I have made, then I don't know if Cas can ever forgive himself. We have to find him."

"Why are you telling me this?"

"Because I hate like hell that you're in the middle of this, but I don't know what else to do. I want you to understand that I wouldn't send you back if there was another choice."

Her deep blue eyes stared into his for so long that he wanted to pull her into his arms and damn the world. His fingers clenched on the snifter to keep him from doing just that.

"I'm sorry that he took Miguel. I know that he won't hurt him."

"I wish I could be so confident."

"I wish for many things." She took a deep breath. "Hunter...if things were different, would you keep me here? With you?"

"Yes." The word came out forceful. Definitive.

Her eyes widened in shock and he knew that she hadn't expected his answer. Neither had he. It just came out, but it was the truth. One night hadn't even been close to enough of her, because her body wasn't all that he wanted. He wanted everything. He wanted to know her: to know her favorite things, to know what she hated, to know everything about her life before him. But dammit all to hell, he couldn't have her. Cas needed him and he'd die before he turned his back on his brother.

She rose and fled the room before he could tell her that.

Chapter Seventeen

Emmy had spent the night tossing and turning. The way he'd looked when he said "yes", as if he could devour her right there, had haunted her dreams and left her feeling aching and unsatisfied when she awoke. It hadn't helped that she had heard him go to his room later and realized that his bedroom adjoined her sitting room. She'd stood at that door separating them for far longer than she should have. Her hand poised just on the knob, not sure if she'd turn it and find it locked or not. What if it wasn't? What if she opened it to go right in and spend another night with him? The warm, languid feeling that had moved through her, softening her very bones at the mere thought, made her turn away. He was too potent to her and too dangerous because of it. She had begun slipping under his spell the moment she saw him. What would happen to her when it was time to leave him?

The next morning when she awoke, she found a satchel full of money in her sitting room. The mixture of paper money and gold coins was a surprise. Gripping the handles and looking inside, she wondered how he'd been able to get his hands on that much in just a few hours. She was so angry she imagined herself throwing it at him, but couldn't deny the strange sense of relief she felt as well. In the end, she'd brought it into her room and hid it under the bed to deal with later. At least it was there…just in case.

Her sisters were already up and dressed when she went to find them in the nursery. They all went down to breakfast together, surprised to find that Hunter was already there at the dining table. Dressed similarly to the night before in a button-up shirt and trousers, though clean-shaven now, he welcomed them and kept the girls chatting throughout the meal by answering their many questions about the horses. Emmy couldn't help but watch him as he became animated, seeming to know every detail about each horse. How old it was, how fast it could run, its favorite treat. The questions were endless, but he didn't seem perplexed even once to answer them and even gave her a wink about halfway through breakfast. She blushed too easily and hastily looked back down at her plate.

"How about a ride after breakfast?" he suggested. "We can go to the river."

The girls immediately chimed in with their agreement.

"They can't ride, Hunter. It's not a good idea."

That didn't deter him and simply made him turn to look at her, his eyes as intense as ever as he smiled. Sometimes he looked at her and she could almost believe that he felt something for her. It was part of his charm. She knew that, but it didn't keep her heart from skipping a beat.

"It's only a couple of miles. They can ride ponies and we'll go slowly. How about we take a picnic?" He looked back to the girls who readily agreed to this updated plan. When he looked back at her, he raised a brow as if to say, *See, they approve of me.*

Her gaze landed on his perfectly formed lips as he smiled again and she couldn't help but remember how those lips had felt on her body. She took a ragged breath and nodded her consent to keep from having to talk. But he knew. As the girls celebrated the victory, his gaze lingered on her, sweeping down to her breasts before meeting her eyes. She pulled her gaze away and avoided him the rest of the meal.

It was even easier to avoid him as they rode to the river just a little later.

He'd been very attentive in helping them all mount and get underway, leading the girls along slowly on their ponies. Emmy lagged behind, not much more experienced than her sisters in riding, though she'd had to learn fast enough on that terrifying ride across the countryside on his horse. It wasn't the horse that made her lag. She'd been given the gentle Cinnamon, who was just as content as her rider to walk slowly, even nibbling a bit of grass along the way. She went slowly because she couldn't stop watching him. The same gentleness that had been evident on the night he'd kidnapped her was on display now as he attended to her sisters. It didn't seem possible that he was the same outlaw who had come into her saloon that night looking so dangerous.

And yet the juxtaposition suited him perfectly. When he wasn't leaning over to answer a question or pointing out a bird in the distance, he was scanning the horizon, alert to anything that could be a threat. He'd strapped his gun to his hip and a rifle was holstered on the back of his saddle, strapped next to the picnic basket. Oc-

casionally his eyes would catch hers and she'd
see the spark of desire that made her wary, just
as it drew her to him.

Later, when the river had transformed from a
silver ribbon to a wide and rushing current before them, he walked over to help her dismount.
She didn't shy away when he gripped her waist
and held her close as she dropped to her feet.
They were obscenely close from chest to hip, his
hard thigh pressed slightly forward against the
indentation between her legs. The contact caused
a warm tingle to travel the length of her body
and she held on to his shoulders when she should
have let go. He took in a harsh breath and she
met his gaze, not surprised to find it deep and
searching. He was confused by her accepting
his touch. So was she. But the more she tried to
ignore all the things he made her feel, the more
she became aware of feeling them.

Rose called them and he slowly, reluctantly let
her go, so she ran over to the river's bank to see
the fish her sister had found swimming in the
shallow water. For the next hour she was extra
aware of his every move. The way his muscles
rippled under his clothing as he jumped the large
rocks at the edge of the river to grab a handful
of smooth pebbles. The way his muscular calves

and bare feet seemed more attractive than they should, when he rolled up his trousers so they wouldn't get wet.

And later, though she had her eyes closed as she lay on the blanket letting the sun warm her face, she knew that it was him coming toward her because butterflies fluttered in her belly just moments before his large body plopped down next to her. He lay down on his back, watching her, the sun glinting off his hair turning it more golden than brown. The girls were wading at the river's edge, Rose calling to her older sister to join her, while Ginny firmly stayed onshore out of the cold water. But she still directed Rose to the location of the next smooth rock they'd skip across the river just like he'd shown them.

"You haven't yelled at me about the money yet. Does that mean you've decided to accept it?"

She hadn't thought he'd mention it, so she could only answer honestly. "I haven't decided."

"What's to decide?" He looked up toward the white clouds in the brilliant blue sky, as if he didn't have a care in the world.

"It's not that easy."

Eyes closed now, he gave a slight shake of his head. "No. The money is yours. That's it."

"You don't understand."

"Then tell me." He didn't look at her as he spoke.

Glancing at the girls to make sure they weren't coming over, she said, "When I decided to do the auction, I knew that someone awful would buy me and, though it wouldn't make it all right, I'd be able to live with myself for what happened. The fact that it was you…makes it more difficult."

He flashed a smile that was pure male satisfaction. "You thought you'd be a martyr and now you're disappointed that you enjoyed yourself."

It wasn't a question, but she wasn't dignifying it with an acknowledgment. "Stop." Rolling her eyes, she looked back to watch the girls in the water. Ginny squealed about how cold the water was as she dipped a toe in.

"The money has nothing to do with what we did together, Emmy." He had moved onto his side to face her and was much closer now as he looked down, blocking the sun from her face. "Even if you had left my room before anything happened, I would have given you the money. I didn't buy you, not that way."

"I think the facts would disagree."

"I don't care. I know what happened that night, Emmy." He tipped her chin up so that she looked at him and the expression of tenderness on his face stole her breath. "You know what happened."

"It's a lot of money. It's made things difficult." The slight weight of his thumb moved across her bottom lip to settle at the corner of her mouth.

"It's not that much money to me. Take it. I want to know you're safe. It doesn't change what happened between us." His eyes were darker now, the pupils reducing the green to a sliver.

"It would make me your whore."

He sighed and then took a long breath, as if coming to some determination before he spoke. "It wouldn't. Emmy, you're not that type of woman."

"You've said that before." She moved to get up, but he caught her shoulder and gently pressed it back down.

"Wait. I know what I'm talking about. My parents' marriage was arranged because my father saw a way to marry into the Hartford family of Boston. My grandfather and his before him were very successful politicians and businessmen. My father wanted that so he bartered himself for it. That's not you. My mother liked the idea of his mining wealth without liking the idea of him. She married him anyway. Emmy, sweetheart, that's not who you are."

She wanted to believe him and, looking up

into his eyes, she came close. But the pain she saw there drew her attention. "This is the second time you've mentioned your mother unfavorably. She hurt you."

When he dropped his head, she pressed her hand to his cheek, surprised when he kissed her palm before nodding. "Isabelle Hartford Jameson stayed with her husband long enough to bear a son, me. Then she hightailed it back to her family in Boston, complaining about the harsh conditions in Helena and her husband's cruelty. She had no qualms about leaving me as well. I believed her lies about my father's cruelty, though I'd never seen it myself."

He took another deep breath and met her gaze, making her own breath stop. "Until I spent some time with her family in Boston and realized the harsh conditions she complained about were the lack of people she considered her social equal. My father's great cruelty had been to insist that she live with him at the ranch instead of in Helena. She could never tolerate it here. Not the barbaric social structure. Anyone could be considered high society with the right bank account. She hates that.

"I didn't realize her hatred included me until I was older. Though I attended Yale, I'm not the son she wanted. Never have been. I prefer herding cattle, tracking elk and raising horses to the high life in Boston. She thinks I'm as barbaric as my father."

Her heart clenched for him and any mother who couldn't value his good heart. "I'm so sorry, Hunter."

"Don't be. She's not a part of my life, because it's her choice."

He went quiet for a moment, just allowing her touch on his cheek. Her sisters were still laughing in the background as they played. She imagined what it might be like to spend many more days like this, just the four of them. Emboldened by the way he had opened himself up to her, she asked, "Last night you said you would keep me if you could. But you're an outlaw."

He nodded, his eyes sad. "I ride with a gang. You deserve more stability than that and I can't offer it to you. My brother needs me and I can't walk away from that."

"Because he's the only family you have?"

The corner of his mouth tipped up in a smile and he nodded once in acknowledgment. "Aside from my father, yeah. Nothing matters more to Cas than his family. When his grandfather was murdered, it almost broke him. He's vowed to have vengeance and I've vowed to support him. If I leave them now, they'll be vulnerable to all the enemies we've made. I won't walk away." He was silent as he took a deep breath and looked off into the mountains in the distance. "This whole place should be his. I'm the illegitimate one."

Pain tightened her throat as she realized that he held the burden of his father's sins on his own very capable shoulders. "You don't have to atone for all of the things your father has done."

"No, I don't. But someone should. Cas deserves it." The fierce intensity in his eyes when he looked back at her went through her like a bolt of lightning.

She loved him in that moment. Every man she had ever known in her entire life had let her down one way or another. Hunter was different, or at least he was when it came to his brother. "What are we doing, Hunter?"

"Hell if I know," he whispered, slowly shaking his head, his gaze tracing her face before lighting on her lips.

Before she could even think of the many reasons she shouldn't, she leaned up just enough to press her lips to his. When they parted, her tongue slipped inside to brush his and it felt so good she didn't think at all anymore. His hand moved to cup the back of her head, holding her close as he deepened the kiss, filling her with his heat and making her ache to be filled in other ways. If she moved just a little, she knew that she'd find him aroused and the knowledge thrilled her.

Another squeal from the water made her jerk back, glancing over to make sure they hadn't been caught. He didn't let her go though, his hand tightened in her hair and a thrill of pleasure shot through her. She loved that he knew what he wanted and wasn't afraid of taking it. Being near him, with him, had made her bolder, too. Like maybe she could take what she wanted as well.

Before she could stop herself, she kissed him again, a quick peck on the mouth before she was sliding out from under him. Too stunned to react, he let her go, eyes narrowing as she backed away. Grinning, she turned and ran, giving him one last glance on her way to the river, but squealed and quickened her pace as he came to his feet to give chase. Her sisters looked up and laughed before they, too, ran along the shallows at the edge of the river.

He closed the distance quickly and a muscled arm wrapped around her waist just as her bare feet touched the icy water, swinging her around. "You're playing with fire," he growled near her ear, and his other arm went around her hips, pulling her back against him so that she could feel his arousal.

"Is that a bad thing?"

He laughed softly and took in a deep breath, his nose buried in her hair. "It is if you don't want to get burned."

"Maybe I do."

He went deathly still at her words as if he couldn't believe they meant what he wanted them to mean. She couldn't blame him for his confusion. She'd been the one putting distance between them, but she was tired of fighting, tired of listening to that rational voice that always made sense but never got her anywhere.

"Emmy…" His breath stroked her ear, making her shiver.

"I do, Hunter. Tonight. Tomorrow. Whatever time we have left, I want you." She closed her eyes because she couldn't say those words with them open.

His breath came out in a low curse and his arms tightened around her so that she savored his hard chest at her back. She wanted this. Him. While she could have it. He turned her in his arms before she could protest, but when he would have covered her mouth with his, she pressed her fingers to his lips.

"The children."

He cursed again and she spared them a glance. They had stopped running and watched them curiously.

"Don't children nap?" he whispered.

"They're too old for naps." She laughed and wiggled away.

"Tonight then." He said it like a warning, making her laugh again. There was no way she could bring herself to stay away from him. No warning required.

After their picnic they had started back for home. It took them over an hour, but despite the fact that he was a vastly better rider than all of them, he had never once seemed impatient. He did fall back once or twice to give her a lingering glance that set her body on fire. Once they reached the stables, a stable hand came out to help her sisters, leaving her to the mercy of her captor. Hunter helped her down much as he had the first time, but boldly cupped her bottom with one hand and held her close as his mouth closed over hers quickly. It wasn't more than a moment, but it left her breathless as she watched him walk away.

They spent the rest of the afternoon touring the property. They played in the loose hay of the barn and then fed corn to the chickens. After dinner, they retired to the nursery to play board games and then Emmy read stories aloud, taking requests from each of them, even Hunter who had apparently memorized every title at their disposal. When she kissed the girls good-night, he met her in the hallway, taking her hand and giving her a wicked smile as he led her to his bedroom.

"I should freshen up." She pulled her hand away, suddenly nervous now that the time had come to be alone with him. She'd washed before dinner and changed back into the blue dress she had borrowed from Glory.

He only shook his head and put his arm around her, pulling her close when they reached his door. "You smell good," he whispered into her hair. "I swear I can still smell you on my skin." His hands settled on her hips and his lips brushed her temple.

"So do you." She knew that she'd never get enough of his smell, that spice that was uniquely him beneath the leather and outdoors scent that clung to him. If she leaned up on her toes, she could press her face into the hollow of his warm neck and breathe him in. So she did, clinging to his shoulders so she wouldn't wobble. Then she pressed a kiss there, allowing the tip of her tongue to taste him before pulling back to meet his gaze.

"Is this what you want?"

She nodded and reached for his doorknob, surprised when his hand covered hers and stopped her.

"If you say yes, this won't be just for a night."

"What do you mean?" Her gaze met his.

"It means that I hope you'll share my bed the entire time you're here."

"Can't we just take one night and see what happens?"

Taking a deep breath, he studied her face for a moment before answering her with a question. "Why are you so afraid of me?"

"I should think it's obvious." Didn't he realize how he could crush her without even meaning to do it?

Her words startled him and he set her back away from him. "Dammit, Emmy, you know that I wouldn't force you. That's not what this is to me. I'm not your captor anymore—"

"No, that's not what I meant." Grabbing his hands, she put them back around her and stepped close in the loose circle of his arms. "You forget that I was given an armoire full of other women's clothing."

He let out a frustrated breath, but he tightened

his arms so that she was against him once more. "That's why you haven't worn them? You're jealous."

"No." She bristled immediately, but couldn't think of a better term for her feelings. "I just don't want that to be the way it is. I don't want to be your mistress. I want things to be more... more equal than that."

"I don't have mistresses, Emmy. Even if I did, you wouldn't be one of them." He smiled.

"But the gowns? The bedroom?"

"Women have stayed here from time to time, but not in that bedroom. My father had it decorated after graduation in the hopes that I would promptly install a wife. The dresses are for various women who have stayed here, yes. My father entertains and, because we're out of town and guests generally stay a night or two, we found it necessary to have extra clothing on hand. There's an armoire of men's clothing, too, if you're interested."

"Why wouldn't I be your mistress?"

"Because mistresses are biddable creatures and you aren't biddable in the least." He kissed her nose and then opened the door and walked forward so that she had no choice but to walk backwards into his room.

A lamp in his bedroom was lit so that enough

light shone through for her to see the sitting room was very similar to her own. But she only got a quick glimpse of golden and cream furniture before he was walking her through the door to his bedroom. The same furniture met her there: a couple of upholstered chairs near the fireplace, two large armoires, but it all faded into the background as her legs pressed against the gold blanket thrown across the oversized bed. He grinned and brought his hands up to begin the buttons between her breasts.

"Do you want me biddable?"

He pressed a quick kiss to her mouth. "Hell, no. I like you just the way you are."

Something about the way he said that, so emphatically, made her happy. He really did seem to accept everything about her. His hands practically shook as he finished the buttons and parted the fabric to pull the dress off her shoulders. Her fingers came up to help, but he shook his head. "Let me do it. I like undressing you. It's like unwrapping a present." When his scorching gaze met hers, all the muscles deep in her body clenched.

Unbidden, she thought of how fleeting this moment was. It would be gone in an instant. True, she planned to spend as much time as she could in his bed, but soon she'd have to leave. He'd take her back to Ship and then she'd never see him again. Before she could stop it the thought made her sad. He must have seen it, because he paused and then he palmed her cheek. "Emmy?"

"What about when it comes time for me to go?"

That stopped him. Only their breaths filled the silence between them before he said, "I don't want to let you go." He spoke so vehemently.

"But how?"

"I don't know." The fierce look on his face made her heart skip a beat and then he was crushing her to him. "I don't know. There has to be a way."

Her hands pulled at the buttons on his shirt, tearing at it before he stepped back just enough to shrug out of it and pull off his boots. She kissed him as her fingers deftly unfastened his belt and then the buttons on his trousers, pushing them down his hips as her hands met his smooth skin. She didn't believe him. Not for one moment did she think he would be able to avoid giving her back to Ship, or that he'd walk away from Cas, but it was lovely to know that he was trying to see a future for them.

For now that was enough.

Free of his clothing, he endeavored to free her

of her own as well, but there was too much. In the end, her dress made it to the floor followed by her drawers. But the chemise, which she *had* borrowed from the armoire in her room, was some fancy contraption that was laced in the back and they couldn't be bothered with that just yet. Instead, he pulled it down in front just enough to free her nipples, and a ribbon ripped, but it didn't matter because he was following her down to the bed. His mouth found her nipple just as his fingers found her ready for him and she cried out at the double sensation of being suckled while being filled. And then he rose over her and his hard manhood replaced his fingers, nudging her before he slipped inside inch by precious inch to make sure she was ready.

"Hunter," she cried in a hoarse whisper when he sank deeper, filling her completely. Gripping his shoulders, she pulled him down to her, unable to get enough of touching him. His mouth covered hers, his tongue stroking deep as he withdrew just to drive home again. It was fast. The entire day had been building up to this moment when they were joined. Her fingers clawed at his hips to bring him back into her when he pulled away. His hands held her so tight she thought she might be bruised tomorrow, but it didn't matter.

It was perfect. For one moment in her life, everything was as it should be. Then she was climaxing around him and he groaned her name as he found his own release within her. To her surprise, the perfect moment continued to last. It was still perfect as he placed small kisses to her chest and neck. It was still perfect as he moved just off of her and pulled her close. Even much later, when they were both naked and spent from their loving, everything was perfect as she closed her eyes and fell asleep. It was like she was living inside a beautiful dream and she never wanted to wake up.

Chapter Eighteen

Just over two weeks later and he still hadn't figured out how to keep her. Hunter stared down at the empty tumbler cupped in his palm, Cas's voice growing dimmer as his mind churned through the various options before he discarded them one by one. The past weeks with her had been idyllic, a word he would never had thought to use before, but there it was. It was the only way to describe their time together. He awoke each morning with her in his arms and from there they'd plan the day. Occasionally, he'd had to spend time in his study or out in the fields when a problem had come up with fencing or the cattle, but most of his days had been spent with Emmy and her sisters. He didn't even mind that Rose and Ginny were around. He liked spending time with them. They were becoming the family he'd never had. The family that he'd never realized he wanted.

More than once he'd almost broached the subject of getting the children a tutor, but with their time so limited it seemed like a moot point. They *would* go back. They weren't his. They had a father and a home somewhere far away from Jameson Ranch, far away from him. Though this felt like their home now. The children had adapted to their circumstances extremely well, settling into a routine of play and learning about horses. Emmy had even begun coming to his study with him in the evenings, picking out books to read through while he worked. He'd noticed that she seemed to like the texts on Ancient Greece and Rome and had even imagined that he could take her to view the ruins. But he never voiced the offer because the future was so uncertain.

"So we head out tomorrow." Cas raised his voice just enough to cut through the haze of Hunter's misery and raised his brow in question.

"Train leaves in the afternoon at four." Hunter shrugged out from under the weight of his morose thoughts and leaned forward to place his tumbler on the desk. "You're sure he still has Miguel?"

Cas had arrived just as Hunter was settling into his study after dinner. He looked haggard and tired, like he'd ridden nonstop, and had brought the news that an arrangement had been made to meet Campbell and make the exchange.

"As sure as we can be." Cas nodded. "He better be alive, Hunter."

"He is," Hunter reassured him, though he wasn't entirely certain of that. Campbell couldn't be that foolish; he'd evaded them for now, but it was only a matter of time before they tracked him down if something happened to the boy. "He'll want his daughters returned."

Two weeks seemed too short. He'd thought they would have had a month together, maybe a bit more. Before he could stop them, the words tore from his chest. "I don't want to give her up, Cas." He ran his hands through his hair and leaned forward, elbows lowered to the desk.

His brother's face went still. "We don't have a choice."

"I know. I know that. I want Miguel back just as much as you do, but I don't want to give her back."

"Maybe just the sisters—"

"No!" Hunter cut his words off. "I don't want any of them to go back. They're not like Campbell." His words trailed off as his mind began to race again. One answer stood out in front of all the others. He hadn't wanted to give voice to it before because it had been so ridiculous, but the more he thought about it, the more he wanted it. "I could marry her. If I married her I wouldn't have to send her back. Campbell couldn't demand it."

"Married. Really?" Cas sat up straight, stunned.

"I know it sounds…"

"Extreme." Cas supplied.

Narrowing his eyes, Hunter continued. "I know that I've known her for less than a month, but out here people marry quicker than that all the time."

"People who have to, people who live secluded lives on ranches. That's not you, brother. You could marry any woman in the territory. I bet some young girl from Boston would be willing to come all the way out here just to marry you."

"Girl." Hunter grimaced. That was just it. He didn't want an immature socialite. He wanted a woman. He wanted Emmy. "I don't want any of those. I've met all of the women in Helena and the socialites my mother threw at me in Boston. They're all—every single one of them—just like my mother or worse. They only care about my bank account. I never wanted a wife because I couldn't see myself shackled to one of them. Emmy is different." So different that he hadn't been careful with her at all. The morning they had left the brothel, Glory had sent along a jar of sponges, perhaps knowing that one night together wouldn't be enough for them. She'd been right. Except for that first time in his bed, they'd been very diligent about using them to prevent a child. A very small, very selfish part of him had begun to hope that their one time of haste had led to a pregnancy, but the hope had been laid to rest just a few days later when her cycle had appeared on schedule.

Getting her with child would have been grossly irresponsible, though it would have solved a problem. Campbell couldn't demand her return if she carried his child. It would have created another problem. He wasn't ready to be a father. Having a child, having a wife, they both meant that he had to give up a part of his life he hadn't thought he was willing to give up. And yet, the idea of a child with her had been so surprisingly pleasant that it had stayed with him. He'd never wanted a child before, never even imagined himself as a father. Until now. Until she had come into his life.

Sitting back in his chair, Cas studied him closely. "It won't matter. Your mother would never let you get away with marrying anyone outside her circle."

Cas was right, but his mother's opinion had

longed ago ceased to matter to him. Even if she disinherited him, his father wouldn't—and he had his own income from the horses and his share of the mines. He and Emmy would be fine. "Her opinion doesn't matter to me. I want Emmy."

"Those are strong words, brother. You're willing to give away a fortune for a woman?"

Cas didn't understand the concept because he was too busy trying to hang on to the Reyes family's crumbling empire. "Yes. She's more important to me than my mother's money or even her approval."

Cas opened his mouth to speak, but closed it again and looked away. "You're fortunate you can feel that way."

"Dammit, Cas, don't. I have money, yes, and you would too if you weren't too damn stubborn to take it. Father offered it to you."

Cas's eyes blazed. "I will never take anything from the man who ruined my mother."

"Fine. Don't take it." Hunter's voice lowered as he regained control of his temper. A strange silence filled the room following the outburst. He finally broke it, saying, "I won't walk away from the gang. I promise you that."

His brother's jaw tightened, but he didn't reply.

"I mean it," Hunter pressed. "I'll stay until we finish what we set out to accomplish."

Shaking his head, Cas said, "I couldn't ask you to do that, especially if you have a family."

The silence grew again, a strange void between them where none had existed before.

"Do you love her?" Cas finally asked, his voice low.

"Yes." Though it mildly surprised him that he'd be so willing to admit that, his answer was immediate. There was no doubt in his mind that he loved her.

"Then you should have her."

Stunned, Hunter took in his brother's impassive features. Cas was loyal to his family, but he wasn't given to bouts of sentimentality. "We'll figure it out, but I won't let you down."

"No, it's my vengeance, not yours. If you love her, I won't let you risk yourself."

"Cas, no. I can figure out how to do both. I can keep her and still keep my vow to you."

His brother leaned forward then, his elbows on the desk, and a strand of black hair falling across his forehead. "There is nothing greater than family. We have that." He motioned between the two of them. "And I saw it with my mother and Miguel's father. There is no greater calling. If what you have with her is real, then it must become your priority."

For a moment, Hunter couldn't speak. He wasn't ready to give up riding with his brothers, but the idea of Emmy being his was so evocative, that he couldn't dismiss it. "It doesn't matter. As you pointed out, without someone to exchange, we won't get Miguel back. So my thoughts don't matter."

"Keep the woman. Send her sisters."

Hunter nodded, though he knew he couldn't do it. "Emmy won't send her sisters unless she goes with them. If I send them back, I can't tell her and we'd have to swoop in again and take them back later."

"We'd have to wait for them to get home. We couldn't risk them, not with Campbell's men around. One of the ignorant bastards could start shooting."

Cas was right, of course. They couldn't risk gunfire. "How do we know that won't happen anyway?" Letting out a harsh breath in response to his own rhetorical question, he pounded a fist on the desk. "I don't like this."

"Do you think Campbell would risk his own flesh and blood? He won't want to shoot anymore than we do, at least while there's a risk to innocent lives."

"Shooting?"

Both men looked up to see Emmy framed in the doorway. She had been upstairs with the girls when Cas had come in, probably waiting for Hunter to join them as had become their routine. Her tiny hands pulled the top of her ivory-colored dressing gown closed, hair flowing free down around her shoulders. She had clearly been expecting to find him alone in his study. Hunter rose and walked around the desk to meet her, taking her hand and drawing her close to him.

"Emmy, you've met Castillo, my brother."

She nodded, but her brow was still furrowed as she walked into the circle of his arms. "Is it time?"

"I'll leave you two alone," Cas said as he rose, but stopped next to her on his way to the door. Hunter bristled, but decided to let him talk. "I apologize that you were pulled into this. Don't fret, *hermanita*." He gave her a wink with a rarely seen smile. "We'll keep you and *las niñas* safe. On my honor." Then he left and Emmy watched until he closed the door behind him, all signs of anger gone from her lovely face. Hunter shook his head and swallowed his laugh. He'd seen his brother's rarely given smile turn even the most righteous woman's head.

But the second he was out of the room, she

turned her attention back to him and he quickly explained the arrangements Cas had made to exchange the hostages in a canyon outside of Billings. Just that very moment, he resolved to not give them up, though he didn't mention it. He'd take a satchel full of cash and try to buy Miguel back first. Anything to keep them from getting hurt. The exchange would take place in a couple of days and they'd take the late-afternoon train tomorrow. He didn't tell her she wasn't going. He'd leave on his own and face her anger when he returned.

"Could there really be shooting? Do you think Ship will put up a fight?"

"It's always a chance, but we'll have men hidden just in case."

"So will he. Ship's not stupid, Hunter. He'll have men to fight back. What if they start shooting after the exchange?" She grabbed the front of his shirt and held tight.

"Shh...it'll be all right." He sounded more confident than he actually was, but she didn't need to know that. If his men were harmed because of Ship Campbell and his band of buffoons, Hunter would make sure they never lived to harm anyone else. Pulling her close to him, he buried his face in the floral scent of her hair and savored the way her tiny body felt against his. It had been just two weeks and already there was more padding on her bones and her generous bottom had filled out nicely from the hearty meals he fed her. He couldn't even think of her going back to how her life had been before. Moving his hands down her body, he cupped her bottom and pulled her up against him, loving her small sigh of pleasure. This wouldn't be their final night together. "I won't let anything happen to you. I promise."

"I'm not worried about me... I'm worried about you." She had pulled back just enough to look at him and the sincerity of that look warmed him from the inside out. She really didn't give a damn about the money he'd given her or how much more she could likely get from him. She cared about *him*. It was a sentiment that had been lacking in his life.

"Don't worry about me either." He managed a half smile and cupped her face in his hand. "Once this is over, we'll have many more days at the ranch ahead of us. You'll see."

"But how? I have to go back."

She wasn't going back. "I took you once. Don't you think I can take you again?" he teased.

Her lips parted in a quick smile and he took advantage by covering her mouth with his, slipping his tongue inside to briefly taste her sweetness before pulling back.

"Do you mean that?" she whispered.

"I do." He wanted to mention marriage, but it was too early, too uncertain to bring that up. Hell, he wasn't even sure how he could wrap his head around the concept just yet, except that he didn't need to. It just fit. Keeping her with him, even if it meant marriage, seemed right. But the gang needed him too.

Smiling, she nibbled lightly on her bottom lip and her eyes darkened. "I don't want this to end, either."

"Then it won't." He met her halfway for another kiss, determined to keep tomorrow at bay for as long as he could.

Emmy didn't go to sleep that night. They had made love three times, consumed with the notion that this could be the last time for a while. A shaft of moonlight spread across the foot of the bed and settled on the mantel across the room where the clock showed it to be almost two o'clock. She knew that a train left most mornings at six and she planned to be on it. She should have left earlier, but Hunter had just gone to sleep.

She rolled over to watch him as he dozed,

his lips parting as he drew a breath. She wanted to kiss them, but dared not risk it. She wondered if this might be the last time she saw him. It seemed impossible that her feelings for him should be so intense after such a short time together, but she couldn't deny the ache growing in her heart. Leaving him was the worst thing she'd ever have to do. With every fiber of her being she wanted to stay with him, to trust him, to create the life with him that teased her in her dreams. The worst part was that she wanted that life even though she knew it couldn't be real. She'd seen her mother's own happiness wither and die in the face of Ship's neglect. No matter how that voice in her soul kept saying that Hunter wasn't like Ship, she couldn't quite believe it.

But she wanted to believe it so badly.

Rising as quietly as she could, she walked to the writing desk and found a pencil. It seemed only right that she leave a note to explain her plan. If she could find Ship and exchange herself for Miguel, then all of the danger could be avoided. She'd appeal to Ship and the little bit of decency she knew he possessed. No matter how she disagreed with him, she knew that he loved the children. He had to know that it was best for them to not return. Surely she could make him understand that.

For insurance, she'd take a little of the money from the satchel in her bedroom and use it to sweeten the deal. The girls' safety was worth a little of her pride. Once she gave it to him, she'd leave and come back to get her sisters. If Hunter still wanted her, then she'd consider staying, if not, then they'd move on. Either way the children would be safe for a while.

Leaving the grossly inadequate note—how could a simple "I love you" at the end possibly explain all she felt?—she tiptoed to her bedroom and dressed. Then she retrieved the satchel from under her bed and made her way to the hallway. Stopping briefly at the children's door, she allowed herself a quick peek inside to quietly tell them goodbye before continuing on. One day, she promised herself, they would have security and she would never have to leave them again.

She made her way outside and took a moment to pause in the shadow of the house. If she allowed herself to stop and realize how many holes were in this plan, she'd get frightened and run back inside. But that wouldn't keep Hunter from getting shot and that wouldn't help Ginny and Rose keep the only bit of security they had ever known. No, she couldn't second-guess the plan. She'd make it onto that train before anyone ever knew she was gone and she'd find Ship and figure out how to get Miguel back. It was the only option.

Taking one last glance toward the house to make sure all the windows were still dark, she ran and didn't stop until she'd reached Cinnamon's stall. She wouldn't saddle her there. The other horses were already sticking their noses out to see who had interrupted their sleep. They'd be too noisy and rouse the two men who slept above the stables. Instead she patted her nose and stroked her mane, talking gently to her as she led her out. She'd take her out into the darkness and return for the saddle.

But she didn't make it that far at all. She was just leading her past the barn, the outbuilding furthest from the house, when Cinnamon snickered a warning. There was no time to react as someone came up behind her and pulled her toward the barn. A large hand covered her mouth before she could even think about screaming and a strong arm came around her waist so tight that it was very nearly painful.

Chapter Nineteen

"Glad to see you sensible as ever, little sis. I'd 'bout convinced myself you'd taken up with Reyes."

"Pete?" She mumbled against her stepbrother's meaty hand still covering her mouth. His soft laugh in her ear confirmed it.

"That's right." He kept his grip firm on both her waist and her mouth as he walked backwards, pulling her into a side door that led into the barn. In the dim moonlight filtering in through a few dusty windows high up under the roof, the place looked deserted. Emmy wished she'd paid better attention the few times she'd run through here with the girls. The bottom floor was mostly open floor and storage, with crates and barrels placed high around the perimeter of the room they were in, a wide door led to another room used for storing tools and there were stalls in the back where a couple of the dairy cows were kept. Because the weather was getting warmer, none of the calves or their mothers were kept inside, so most of the stalls were empty. There was a loft overhead, but she'd never been up there.

Somehow she had managed to keep a tight grip on the handle of her satchel through the entire exchange and the moment he let her go, she swung on him, making sure to keep it hidden behind her skirt as much as she could. "Why did you do that, Pete?" She wiped any grime his hand had left on her face with her sleeve. "I was coming to find you and Ship."

His hat was pulled low over his forehead, almost casting his entire face in shadow, except for his brown beard and the sneer he always seemed to wear. "Lucky me, I found you first."

"What are you doing here?" After a quick glance to verify that she didn't see his horse, she narrowed her eyes. "You're supposed to meet them in two days."

"Well, Reyes there…" he pointed in the direction of the house, looking very proud of himself "…he ain't as smart as he thinks he is. I paid a man to talk to him and set up the meeting, then I just followed the Mexican all the way here. Is this where they've been keeping you? 'Cause I gotta say, I don't feel sorry for you one bit, sis. This barn's nicer than our shack."

Something about the way he looked at her, wearing that sneer and the way she could *feel* his gaze on her, made her skin crawl. Taking a step back, she tightened her grip on the satchel's handle. "Where is Ship?"

"Don't worry about him."

"He's not here with you?"

"We got…separated." He took a step toward her and she instinctively took one back again. Pete generally ignored her and when he wasn't ignoring her, he was teasing her. It had been that way since the very first day she and her mother had arrived at the farm. She'd been a shy seven-year-old looking for a friend, while he'd been a brutish eleven-year-old who'd made it clear he wanted nothing to do with her. He had never liked her and she had always been a little bit afraid of him, but this was different, strange, something was about to happen and she didn't like it. They were so close to the house that one of the girls might come outside if there was any shooting. She had to get Pete away from here.

"Where is everyone else?"

He nodded behind her and she was just about to turn and look when another pair of hands came around her from behind. They held a piece of fabric that looped around her head, sliding tight between her lips. She pushed away from the heavy body behind her, but Pete grabbed her arms and held her steady, blocking her kicks with his knees while the unknown man tied the gag behind her head. The satchel was jerked from her fingers with a force that left them aching. Pete turned her around facing the second assailant and she saw that it was Smith, another man who had ridden with Ship for years. Seeing him might have been comforting if he hadn't just gagged her and if Pete wasn't tying her wrists behind her back.

Giving her a curt nod, Smith knelt to unlatch the satchel, a low whistle sounding from his lips as he saw the money inside. The gold coins clinked together when he dipped his hand in, pulling a few out just to let them rain back inside. "This is a pile of money, Pete."

Pete's gaze jerked to her face, so shocked the sneer was gone. "How the hell'd you get yer hands on that money?"

Emmy took a step backwards, but came up against a wooden crate. Her fingers at her back searched for anything to grab, but there was nothing. She tried to talk through the gag, but it came out muffled, causing Pete to curse as he closed the distance between them. He reached for the tie at the back of her head, but fixed her with a cold stare before he loosened it.

"If you scream I'm gonna hit you hard. Got it?"

Her stomach knotted as she nodded. He'd never hit her before, but she wouldn't put it past him. Still, when the gag fell free, she couldn't resist taunting him. "Go to hell, Pete." She would never tell him that Hunter had given that money to her. He'd find some way to use that against them.

He slapped her. Just hard enough to leave her ears ringing faintly, before he gripped her chin with enough force to leave bruises and pushed the back of her head against the side of the crate. "No more sass! Tell me or it'll be my fist next time."

Knowing that she had to tell him something, she said, "What do you think? I stole it." She didn't know how much Pete knew, if he knew this was the Jameson Ranch or if he even knew who Hunter was, so she decided not to tell him any names. Just in case. "Reyes kept some cash stashed under his bed, so I stole it before I ran."

He still looked as if he didn't believe her. "How much is in there?" he called over his shoulder.

Smith rummaged through the bag, but shook his head and shrugged.

"How much, dammit?" Pete growled, causing a chill to chase down her spine.

Scratching his head, the older man who was probably having trouble counting in the semi-darkness—if he even *could* count to fifty thousand—shrugged again and said, "Looks like ten thousand dollars."

Pete laughed and finally released her chin. "Guess we wasted our time all these years robbing banks and outlaws. We should've found Reyes sooner." Swinging back to her, he sneered as his gaze ran lasciviously down her body. "Under his bed, huh. D'you spend a lot of time there? How many of his men had you, or did he just keep you for himself?"

Smith was on his feet again and had joined in the laughter. With them both looking at her, her stomach revolted at the expressions of interest on their faces. "Don't look at me like that. I'm your sister." Despite her best intentions, her voice trembled a little.

"We're not blood, little sis." His hand accompanied his eyes and he palmed a breast through the coarse, brown wool of her dress. "You filled out while you were gone."

"I had decent meals because someone wasn't drinking all the money. Get off me!" She jerked away as best she could with her wrists bound behind her and kicked out at him. "Where is Ship? Is he okay?" She wanted to distract him, but she was also genuinely worried that something had happened to her stepfather. Pete had never been so bold before and she wondered if his sudden change in demeanor was because something had happened to Ship.

"I'm right here, girl, I'm okay." All three of them turned to see Ship walking in from the other end of the barn, the reins of his horse in one hand and a gun pointed at them in the other.

Hunter shoved open the door of Castillo's bedroom so hard that it knocked against the wall. He'd already dressed and was checking the bullets in the guns strapped to his hips as his brother sat up in bed.

"She's gone, Cas!" Not more than five minutes ago, he'd rolled over to find her side of the bed empty. He'd known right away that something was wrong and it hadn't taken him long to find her note and then to see that the money under her bed was gone. She'd ended the note with "I love you". They'd never said that to each other and he regretted now that he hadn't let her know how he felt. He'd been afraid, but now that she was gone, he realized the truth in those words. He loved her and if he lost her, he'd lose a part of himself.

"What?" His brother wiped at his eyes and peered at him through the light streaming in from the hallway. "What time is it?"

"Half past two. Get up. Emmy knows the plan and, according to her note, she's going to get to Campbell before us and try to negotiate the exchange herself. We have to make sure she doesn't get on that train. It leaves in just over three hours."

Cas was cursing as he slipped into the trousers he'd left lying across the end of the bed. *"Las niñas?"*

"She didn't take them. They're sleeping."

After he'd stepped into his boots, Cas shrugged on his shirt and was fastening the buttons as he approached Hunter. "She's a handful of a woman. Are you sure she's worth the trouble?"

"Yes. I'm going to marry her." If he'd had any doubt before, finding her gone had solidified that for him.

Cas paused, eyes frozen on Hunter as he realized what that meant.

"I won't desert the gang. I made a vow to you and I'll honor it."

"I already told you, it's my vengeance, not yours."

"And I don't give a damn. We're brothers."

Cas grinned and reached for his gun belt lying across the footboard. "Seems like a lot of trouble. A woman with fire in her, like that one, can be good for some things, but not for a wife. A wife should be obedient, biddable."

His gun fully loaded, Hunter slid his second revolver into the holster. "Sounds boring as hell."

"That's why they invented mistresses," Cas called from behind him as he started for the stairs.

Now that they were dressed and on their way, Hunter had no worries about overtaking her before she reached town. Even if they didn't, with hard riding they could be at the station in under two hours. They had plenty of time before the train left. He'd find her and bring her back home before leaving in the afternoon. "One day," Hunter promised and clapped Cas on the shoulder as his brother came abreast of him. "One day you'll find a woman you'll want to be both."

"The only woman I'm interested in is one with a fortune at her disposal."

"The Susanne Harrises of the world? Finally taking my advice? A wealthy bride could restore your hacienda."

Cas grimaced. "Not her."

"Not any of them. They're all the same,"

Hunter reminded him. They'd had this conversation many times before.

"Perhaps. But it'll be worth it to have my home back."

"All the years you've worked have made you too cynical." Hunter smiled.

"Perhaps you're right, but at least I'm not losing my head over a—"

They were just descending the main staircase when the front door crashed open. Angel, one of the men who'd ridden back with Cas, stood framed in the doorway. "Eduardo just saw Campbell head into the barn. Looked like he had Miguel strapped to the back of a horse."

For a moment his mind couldn't accept what he had heard. The idea that Campbell could have found them *and* ridden right into his barn was impossible to accept. "Tell me what happened."

"It's Eduardo's night to do the rounds. He was just riding back in from the East Field near the river when he saw a horse. Thought maybe one had gotten out, but he followed and realized a man on foot was leading a horse. Someone was strapped to the back. He didn't get close enough to see for sure before they walked into the barn and barred the doors shut behind them. The horse looked like that dapple Campbell rides."

Hunter's heart paused for a beat as he imagined Emmy out there alone. "Has anyone seen Emmy? She left. About a half hour ago is my best guess."

Angel shook his head. "No."

"Damn. Go check the stables. See if a horse is missing. Then get all the men together."

They watched Angel run back across the yard, Cas managing to wait until he'd disappeared into the stable before turning to Hunter to ask, "You don't think she planned this with—?"

"No!" His brother was cynical enough to believe that Emmy might have somehow conspired with Ship and was meeting with him now. Hunter might have believed that at one time as well. But not anymore. He knew her. She wouldn't do anything that would put them in danger. She loved him. "If she's with them it's because they've taken her."

"Did she take the fifty thousand dollars with her?"

Hunter didn't bother to answer the question. She had taken it to negotiate for Miguel and no one would make him believe differently. "Give it up, Cas."

Cas was smart enough to raise his hands in surrender. Both men made their way in the dark to the stables, keeping a wary eye on the barn which was roughly two hundred yards further out across a black expanse of pasture. It came as no surprise when Angel told them moments later that Cinnamon was missing, though all the saddles were accounted for.

"Send Jim along the road to town to see if he can find her." The stable hand should be able to overtake her as easily as Hunter could.

But, only moments later, he knew that wouldn't be necessary. Jim came into the stable, leading a spooked Cinnamon. Her bridle had been put in place, but not the saddle. His gaze once again went back over to the barn and a cold chill swept down his spine. If she was hurt because of those brainless cowards, he'd kill every single one of them.

"Let's get a man at every door of the barn. We can only assume Campbell came with his men and we can't risk any of them getting out," Cas ordered.

"We have to get in there." Hunter muttered, staring toward the cart that rested just outside the stables. They used it to carry seed and occasionally water barrels out into the fields. It was heavy and, if they loaded it down even more, it just might break open the barn doors.

"What are you thinking?" Cas asked.

Hunter nodded toward the cart. "The feed should load it down. We get it heavy enough, we can push it right into the barn doors, splinter the boards."

Cas nodded his agreement and they quickly set about getting it filled with the bags of feed. It wasn't a perfect plan, but he couldn't sit around while Emmy's life was on the line. The longer they waited, the more time it gave the Campbells to come up with a plan. Or to at least take high positions in the loft in an attempt to start picking them off with shots so they couldn't approach the barn. They had to get in there fast.

Before Emmy could reason out why Ship was there with a gun pointed at them, Pete wrapped an arm around her shoulders, positioning her in front of him as a shield, and then pulled out his own gun, ramming it into her ribs. She shrieked in protest and struggled until he pushed the muzzle against her even harder and barked a warning in her ear. Ship didn't say a word as he wrapped the reins of his horse around a hook, pulled the door closed behind him and latched it. Smith made a move as Ship was throwing the board leaned against the wall into the block, but Ship yelled for him to stand still, then drew his other gun once his hand was free.

A shaft of moonlight came in through windows tucked in just under the roof and glinted off the barrels of the guns he held in each hand: one aimed at Smith and the other aimed at her and Pete. As he walked toward them, she noticed that he looked haggard, as if he hadn't bathed in weeks. His normally well-groomed, salt-and-pepper hair was in disarray and there was a gray beard on his usually clean-shaven face. A body was tied across the back of his horse. It was a young man with dark hair whom she assumed to be Miguel, but if he was alive or dead, she couldn't tell.

"Ship! You're alive." Too relieved to see him to heed Pete's warning, she pushed at her stepbrother with her elbows. "I was so afraid Pete had done something awful."

"Shut up, Em!" Pete tightened his grip and glared back at Ship. "How'd you get here?" He glanced to the closed door behind them, the one they had just come through, as if to make sure it was still latched. "What'd you do to Rowly, old man? You kill him so you could take that boy from me?"

"I followed you. Rowly outlived his usefulness the second he ran off with you, so I thought I'd put him out of his misery. What you're doing ain't smart, Petey. Nobody takes over my gang. Nobody."

Pete laughed in her ear. "You ran 'em off yer-self, you yellow coward, when you wanted to trade that Mexican for the girls and give up that money."

"They're your sisters."

"Who gives a damn? You know how much we could get for that boy? Reyes has money. Maybe we would, too, if you weren't so chickenshit. You ain't in charge no more."

"Not your choice, Petey."

"The hell it ain't. We don't listen to you. Not now. Rowly and Smith left with me because they know I can get us where we want to be." He jabbed the gun into her ribs again, making her wince. "I hoped you'd come to your senses, but get the hell out if yer here to cause trouble."

"Not gonna do that. Reyes has Ginny and Rose. We're giving Miguel back to him."

"Yer a stupid coward, Ship. Take the money. Let him have those brats."

"They're family. That's important, something I guess you know nothing about. I failed with you, boy."

Pete cursed and tightened his grip on her. "Last chance, Ship."

"I ain't letting you do this," Ship warned.

Pete laughed, but it was nervous laughter. Smith hadn't drawn his gun and from what she could remember, he wasn't a very good shot.

There was no way out for Pete. Ship would kill them both before she even hit the ground and then the whole place would be swarming with Hunter's men, alerted by the shooting. The very thought made her close her eyes, her mind racing for a solution.

"The difference between us, old man, is that you think family is worth something. You won't shoot me, but I'll sure as hell shoot you. Now put down yer guns and get the hell out of here. Smith warned me you'd try to mess this up. Put down the guns and I might even share some of the ransom. Hell, I'm feeling generous. This bitch brought money of her own. You can have some of that."

"Ten thousand dollars!" Smith chimed in, as if proud to have something to add to the conversation, but he kept his arms out wide, away from his gun.

"Yep." She could hear the smile in Pete's voice. "Stole it like a good little whore. Just like her mother."

A look of pain crossed Ship's face. He glanced at her for a moment as if to determine for himself if that were true, but didn't comment on it. Instead, he said, "We already lost Hardy to Reyes's bullet. Rowly's dead. You've only got Smith left and we both know he's smart as a rock. This ain't worth it. The gang's gone."

"It ain't gone, you just ran most of 'em off years ago. I'll round 'em up, get us going again. *Yer* gang is dead. Mine is just starting," Pete spouted back.

"You think you can outsmart Reyes? He was running the border towns while you were still pissing your britches. Even if you ransom the kid back, Reyes won't let you get away. You expect to get out of here alive? Even if you do, he'll hunt you down just to make an example out of you. You took that kid back in Crystal City and wouldn't listen to me when I said to turn him loose, but this ends now. The kid goes back and we take our girls and walk away. That's it."

"See, this talk is why you lost yer gang."

Before Ship could reply, the sound of a pair of boots running by outside reached them. "God-dammit, they already know we're here." His voice lowered.

Emmy hastily did a count in her head to figure out how many men Hunter might have with him. Besides Hunter and Castillo, there were the men who worked the ranch. She wasn't sure how many men, at least ten, but she'd seen most of them wearing guns. Castillo had probably brought some of the gang back with him as well. It was impossible odds. This wouldn't work out well for Pete.

"There are at least fifteen men out there, all with guns." She turned her head to look at Pete, because clearly he was the irrational one here who needed to be made to see reason. "You won't be able to outfight that many."

"Shut up, Em. He don't know we're here."

"Listen to her, boy. She's been with him, she knows how many men he has," Ship advised.

"Yeah? If he has so many men, how'd you manage to get away?" All three of them looked at her when Pete asked that.

How could she tell him the truth? He'd never understand what she had with Hunter. "It was easy. They don't really need me since they have the children, so I wasn't tied up. I ran as soon as I could after I heard the details about the exchange."

The fact that Pete could so easily believe she'd abandon the children was more a testament to his character than her own. He gave her a nod of respect and glanced back to the door. Ship still studied her closely and she wasn't entirely sure if he didn't believe her or if he was simply disgusted that she'd leave the girls.

"Draw yer gun, Smith. Get to the door in case somebody decides to open it," Pete ordered.

"Don't you dare move, either one of you," Ship warned, still holding a gun on Pete and a gun on Smith.

"Dammit, old man, yer going to get us killed."

"No, you're going to get us killed. You never think before you act!"

They never got to finish that argument. Before either of them could say another word, the barn doors nearest them crashed open, wood splintering from the weight of a wagon barreling through it.

Chapter Twenty

Hunter would never forget the sight of Emmy standing there with the muzzle of Pete's gun pressed against her temple. It was a memory that would haunt his nightmares for years to come. He never wanted to see her sweet face so pale with fear again and he vowed that as long as he lived he'd do everything he could to make sure it never was. The problem with that vow was that it depended solely on the outcome of the next few minutes for it to mean anything.

When the wagon crashed through the doors, Angel and Eduardo both moved ahead to take cover behind the stack of crates that flanked the entrance. Hunter stayed so that he had the most direct view from behind the wagon, though it had tipped forward, spilling some feed bags onto the floor. He held his gun aimed straight at Pete, while Cas had his on Campbell. The moment

Pete saw them, he tightened his grip around her shoulders and tucked her tight in front of him. He backed up so they were partially hidden by a stack of crates, but the angle didn't hide them completely. Hunter could still shoot the bastard if he wasn't so damned worried about hitting Emmy by mistake.

"Don't shoot!" Hunter yelled the order to his men.

Campbell didn't know who to hold his guns on. He kept one firmly on Pete, but the other wavered among the group, going from Hunter to Cas and back again. Smith had moved so quickly he'd managed to draw his own gun, but Angel and Eduardo had him in their sights. Hunter hoped no other men from Campbell's gang were hiding, but he couldn't take his eyes from Pete and his gun to look for them.

"That's right. You shoot and she's dead," Pete yelled back. "Don't even try and pretend you don't care. If you didn't, we'd all be dead by now."

"Even if we don't want her dead, you won't get out of here alive," Cas growled the words.

"I will. You'll let me walk out or she's dead."

"She gets hurt, you die." Hunter's voice was strangely calm, even to his own ears.

"Is that how you found that money, sis? D'you

make 'em like you? Which one, Reyes or his brother? Or both?"

"Stop, Pete." She wiggled against him, twisting to try to get away. "It's over. Give up now while you're still alive."

"Don't move, Emmy!" Hunter yelled in alarm. He could just imagine Pete overreacting and pulling the trigger. "He's desperate and stupid. Don't push him to react."

"Listen to Emmaline, son." Campbell broke his silence and spoke to Pete, though he didn't move his eyes from the men staring them down. "It's over."

"Like hell," Pete spat. "I ain't giving her up. I give her up and they kill me. This is what's going to happen. I'm walking out of here with her and that satchel on the floor and nobody follows us."

"You won't get two steps out that door, boy." Campbell shook his head in warning.

Without moving his head, Hunter glanced to the crates and then the loft, looking for some way to make this turn out in their favor. About a hundred different scenarios played out in his head, but none of them could guarantee that Emmy wouldn't be hurt so he discarded them as quickly as they came to him. If there was just some way to get her out of the way so he could have a clear shot. A movement toward the other end of the barn caught his eye. It was one of the stable hands walking around the outside, his boots visible just under the locked doors. It meant they'd found the ladder and would now be climbing up to the loft. If that were the case, it'd be best to keep Pete talking so he wouldn't notice them.

But as soon as he looked back down, his eyes met Emmy's and he knew she was planning something. She tried to gesture as gently as possible so as not to arouse Pete's suspicion and Hunter shook his head once, hoping she could read on his face that he didn't want her to do whatever it was she was planning. If Pete got spooked and shot her, he knew that he'd lose his mind.

Dammit! Her eyes became solemn and determined and he knew she was going to act. Hunter took a few steps to his right to work his way closer to her, but Campbell noticed the movement and moved his gun from Cas to Hunter, so he paused. At that exact moment, Emmy jerked on her bonds, but they held tight on her wrists. The struggle made Pete loosen his grip, just enough to move his hand intending to get a firmer grasp on her shoulder. She took the opening and leaned her head forward as far as she could, then whacked it backwards, catching Pete in the nose. He yelped in pain as she fell to her knees and then her belly.

Hunter was moving the second after she did. As soon as she fell he was on top of her. And just in time, because the world exploded in gunfire. Cas shot Pete before he'd even raised his hand to his bloody nose. At the same time, Angel and Eduardo both shot Smith. He wasn't sure where Campbell had gone, because he'd been too busy shielding her head, with his own head, shoulders and arms. But as soon as the gunfire stopped, he looked up to find out.

Angel had already found him cowering behind a barrel and had his gun aimed right at him. "Hand over the guns."

After a moment of hesitation, Campbell complied and just like that Hunter's heart settled back into his chest. He took a moment to relax against her as he caught his breath, breathing in her precious scent.

It was over and she was safe. He was never letting her go.

As quickly as it had started, the shooting stopped. It hadn't even been that many shots. Three or four, she couldn't be sure because of the ringing in her ears. The ties on her wrists fell away after Hunter cut them free and then he was turning her over and hauling her into his arms. She melted into him. She couldn't help it. As Pete held the gun on her she'd been so sure that she'd never feel Hunter's arms again that she couldn't let him go. Her arms went around him, holding him so tight that she shook.

"Jesus, Emmy, I was so afraid. Are you hurt at all?"

She kept her eyes closed for a little longer to savor how good he felt. "I'm not hurt." Then she pulled away just enough to look for Pete, but Hunter stopped her by cupping the back of her head.

"Best not to look. Pete and Smith are both dead. Do you know if there were any others?"

"No, Rowly was killed and that was the last one I knew. Castillo already got Hardy back in Crystal City. I'm not sure who he sent after you back at the cavern."

Hunter nodded and she could see the tension drain out of him.

"What about Ship?" He probably deserved punishment, but she didn't want him dead. He hadn't been the best father in the world, but he had kept a roof over their heads. She couldn't hate him, no matter how she disagreed with the way he lived.

"He's alive. Over there."

She looked where he indicated to see Angel helping her stepfather to his feet. Eduardo was picking up the two guns Ship had been holding before he had dashed for cover behind the barrel. "Please don't let them hurt Ship. He didn't take Miguel. It was all Pete's idea. That's what they were arguing about when you came in. He wanted to give Miguel back in exchange for us, but Pete just wanted the money."

Hunter looked horrified at the suggestion, so she pressed. "Please. He's a horrible person, I know, but he isn't all bad. He did his best to take care of us. I know he never would've taken Miguel without Pete. It was all Pete's idea and he's dead now. Killing Ship won't help anything. It'll just be revenge, but the wrong kind because none of this is his fault."

"It's all his fault, Emmy. Do you think Pete could've done any of this if his father hadn't raised him to do it?"

"I don't know, Hunter. But it's not right. He can't hurt us...now." She hesitated to even say the word because she wasn't sure there was an *us* anymore. Part of her expected him to walk away from her now that this was over.

Castillo, who had run past them to Ship's mount at the other end of the barn, called Miguel's name, drawing their attention. The horse was accustomed to gunfire and had managed to keep relatively calm throughout the shooting, but Castillo still had to calm him down before the horse would let him get close. As soon as he could, he cut the ties holding Miguel down and pulled him onto the ground. She breathed a sigh of relief when the man immediately roused, rolling into a ball on his side and groaning as he regained consciousness.

"What the hell did you do to him?" Hunter demanded.

Ship actually managed to look a bit sheepish and shrugged. "He put up a fight after I took him from Rowly."

They all watched silently as Miguel roused. His skin looked pale and wan, but soon he was sitting up on his own and rubbing what was probably a knot on the back of his head. Castillo rose and stormed back over to them toward Ship. She was so worried that he might just pull his gun and shoot her stepfather right then that she actually tried to intercept him. Hunter tightened his arms around her waist to make her stay by his side.

"Please, Castillo. Please let him go." He paused just as he strode even with them and looked over at her. "Pete had taken over the gang. Ship had nothing to do with him taking Miguel. He was trying to convince Pete to give him back. Please don't hurt him, he won't bother you anymore."

"You don't know that," Cas scoffed.

"It's over," Ship said. He looked defeated, his shoulders slumped forward and his eyes downcast. "My men are all dead. My s-son…" He paused and took a deep breath. "My son is dead. Charlotte is dead. My girls were taken because of the things I've done. I've nothing left. Not a damn thing. I can't do this anymore."

Reaching out to touch Castillo's arm, she implored him one last time. "Please." His sharp gaze came back to her, striking her with their intensity and how similar they were to Hunter's. He really was a very handsome man with his high cheekbones and granite jaw, but there was a danger that lurked beneath the surface, a ruthlessness that made a shiver run down her spine. "He can't hurt you now."

Only once his gaze finally released hers to move on to Hunter, his brow raised in question, did she think that she might have gotten through to him. Hunter nodded his agreement and then Castillo relaxed, his gun going back into its holster.

The moment the gun disappeared, Ship looked up to meet her gaze. "Em, I want you to know that I never meant for you to be in harm's way. I never wanted you to be taken. I should've done better by you. I know that. I only ever wanted to give you and the girls a good life."

"I can do that." Hunter's voice surprised her. "I can take care of them and give them a good life."

She looked up at him in surprise and he met her gaze.

"If you'll let me." His voice lowered. "Please let me take care of you."

Her lips parted but she had no idea what to say. Ship didn't give her time, because he spoke first. "Is that what you want, girl?"

To be with Hunter for the rest of her life? Yes, but not as his obligation. She didn't say that, because now wasn't the time. "Yes, I love him." That much was true at least. Hunter's arm tightened around her waist in response.

"Then you won't have to worry about me." Ship turned his words back to Castillo. "All I wanted is for the girls to have some security."

"I'll give them that. More than that. They'll be educated and find good marriages later, if that's what they want." Hunter promised.

Castillo nodded toward the dapple horse that Eduardo had led over. "Your mount's waiting. Get the hell on it before I change my mind."

Then he turned on his heel and walked back toward Miguel.

"Where will you go?" she asked Ship just as he was mounting.

"Back to the farm."

Hunter released her long enough to retrieve the satchel and pull out a bound roll of bills. Once Ship was mounted, he pushed the roll into Ship's hands and then stepped back to put an arm around her shoulders.

"I won't take your money," Ship argued.

"Consider it a bride price."

Emmy was stunned, but she didn't take the time to consider what exactly Hunter was saying. She just wanted to see Ship safely gone. "Please take it, Ship. I want to know you'll be okay." She ran forward and pressed her hand to his.

He didn't take her hand, but he didn't pull away either. After a moment he nodded and spurred his mount forward. "We'll both be okay, girl."

Hunter was at her back as they watched him go. She felt sad for Ship, but she wasn't sorry to see her old life go. Once he'd ridden into the night, Hunter moved to her side, keeping his arm at her waist.

"Let's get you inside."

Chewing her bottom lip, she nodded, uncertain of how to talk to him after everything that had happened…after all that he had said. There was tension in the arm curled around her waist and she wasn't entirely certain if it was simply leftover from the confrontation or if it was because of her. She nodded and let him lead her back to the house, keeping a watchful eye on his stony profile.

They paused near Miguel and Hunter walked over to talk to the boy. Once he was sure he was okay, he came back to her and took her hand, walking toward the house. He didn't look at her once. Not until he'd walked them to his bedroom and let her go to close the door behind him. Only then did he turn to face her, his back pressed to the door as he studied her. A lamp that he must have lit to read her note still burned low on the desk, giving the room intimacy.

"You scared the hell out of me. You know that?" His face was stern.

"I know and I won't say I'm sorry for what I did, but I'm sorry you were afraid." Clenching her hands into fists, she leaned against the bed, uncertain of how this conversation would go.

He let out a breath and all of his tension seemed to leave with it as he walked toward her, coming to a stop just inches away. "I meant that, you know." His voice was low and deep, rumbling through her.

"The bride price?"

He nodded and tilted her chin up when she couldn't meet his gaze. "Will you marry me?"

"It's too soon. We barely know each other." *And good things like this don't happen to me.* She didn't add in that last part, but it was the rational voice in her head coming through. This time she could hear it clearly.

"It's not too soon. I love you, Emmaline Drake. I love you so much I can't think of facing a day without you. Seeing you at Pete's mercy, knowing your life hung in the hands of that imbecile, that was torture. I want you in my life, Emmy. I want to be a part of your life. I need you with me. I want you to marry me."

It almost killed her to hear him say the words she wanted to hear so badly, but then to have to turn him down. "But don't you understand? That's just what I mean. You don't want to marry me. My father is Ship Campbell, for heaven's sake. You don't want that. A lot happened tonight and we're all too wound up."

He exhaled on a harsh laugh and sank to his knees before her, taking her hands in his. "You're too damned stubborn. Give me some credit for knowing my own mind. I love you. I've known that for a while. I made up my mind about marrying you last night. Ask my brother if you don't believe me."

She didn't want to believe him, but she did. It scared her how easily she trusted everything he said. "What of the children?"

"What of them? They seem happy here. I love them, too."

"But I'm the closest thing to a mother they have. Though they do have Ship, he's never been around. It doesn't seem fair that you would have to be their…" She stuttered over the word.

"To be their father? This isn't something I decided on a whim, Emmy. I love you and all that comes with you. That includes Ginny and Rose. They'll still have their father, but I'll be there for them, too."

"What of your parents?"

"It doesn't matter. My mother isn't part of my life and my father will love you."

"Your father… I haven't even met him and the ranch is his home." She tried to pull her hands free, but he held tight and brought her palm to his mouth.

After he kissed her, Hunter nodded, looking slightly amused. "He'll love you. But he's rarely here. He has a house in town. We can get our own house, if that's what you prefer."

"But your life with the gang, with Castillo. I know how important they are to you. I can't ask you to leave that, but I can't marry an outlaw, Hunter. I just can't live that life again and I can't put the girls through that."

"I know. I don't want that either. I've spoken with Cas and I'll work out another way to help, one that doesn't take me from home as often." His expression became solemn again. "I can't promise that I'll never have to go, but I can promise it won't be often. I can promise to be by your side far more than I'm away. Can that be good enough to start? You're important to me. The family we make will be important to me. I won't risk that."

She wanted to say yes. She wanted it so badly she couldn't even imagine her life if she said no. "I want to believe you, Hunter." And she did believe him, but it was so hard to give in to that belief.

He laughed and she sank down to sit in his lap where he pulled her against him. His hands roved up and down her back as his forehead pressed to hers. "Then say yes. What's stopping you?"

"I don't know how to say yes. My life… I just never get what I want. That's not how things work for me."

"Then take what you want. Make things work that way."

She stared up into his green eyes, sure that she'd never seen a more beautiful sight in her life than the love she saw staring back at her. "I love you. I love you so much it scares me."

"I know. When I read your letter, I knew that I'd been so blind to not tell you how I needed you, how I'd do anything to keep you with me. I love you," he said. "Don't be afraid. I know that you've never been able to rely on anyone, but I promise you can rely on me. I promise you I won't let you get hurt."

She laughed, but it got caught on the tears threatening to clog her throat. He was always making sure she didn't get hurt and he'd risked his life more than once for her. The least she could do was risk her heart. Just this once. "Yes. Yes, I'll marry you." And just that easily, she took what she wanted and made it hers.

Epilogue

E̲mmy couldn't look away from the band of
gold encircling the finger on Hunter's left hand.
On *her husband's* left hand. It was a perfect
match for her own slightly smaller one. Even
the thought made her breath catch. They had
exchanged vows mere hours ago and her mind
still hadn't caught up to the fact that this magnificent man was hers.

She stared at that hand, fingers clasped with
hers, and couldn't resist reaching out to caress
the strength there. He looked down at her and
gave her that half smile she adored before bringing her hand to his lips.

"It's right in here." His eyes twinkled with
mischief as he led her into the stables and let her
go to pull the door closed behind them.

Music from the wedding celebration still
going on in the house followed them outside,

but it was softer here. A large group of people had spilled out onto the lawn to enjoy the warm summer night. One of them laughed, but it barely reached them in their cocoon. It was the first time since they'd taken their vows that they'd had a moment alone. For some reason she felt nervous—possibly because he'd enforced a two-week period of celibacy on them before the wedding—and fidgeted with the lace of the short train she'd draped over her arm.

The lantern caught, the blaze lighting his face as he hung it back on its post. He was so handsome in his formal wear that she'd had trouble keeping her hands to herself all night. But she'd tried to maintain some propriety. She knew there was talk about how improper it was that she had lived at the Jameson Ranch before the wedding. Though Hunter hadn't cared in the least, she had wanted to prove to his father's friends that she wasn't some loose woman using Hunter for his money. She thought it had worked, either that or no one from town really cared while imbibing the champagne, escargots, and all the other exotic and wildly expensive food his father had brought in for the reception.

Hunter had concocted some story about how their families were distant acquaintances and that he'd lost his heart the moment he saw her.

She'd laughed at that part when he'd told her the story while wearing that devilish grin on his face. But he'd maintained that it was true.

She finally believed him. She'd spent countless hours over the past months replaying the night they'd met and the day that followed. There had been something drawing them together even then. Something inexplicable had happened and he had felt it as much as she had. It was why he'd followed her to Helena, and it was why he'd asked her to marry him. The past months had been like some enchanted fairy tale, but she finally believed that it was real.

Hunter walked the few feet separating them and smiled, arms going around her waist to hold her close. His eyes were positively glowing with the love he felt for her.

"I don't need another wedding present from you." She'd been telling him this for weeks, when he'd first starting hinting at a surprise. Touching the sapphire necklace he'd given her that morning, she said, "This is more than enough."

"That's not a wedding present."

"What is it then?" Her hands moved up the strong length of his arms, settling on his broad shoulders. The train slipped down between them, but she couldn't help touching him.

"That's because it was pretty and made me think of you. It matches your eyes."

Of course. He was so generous with her and the children. It didn't surprise her at all that he'd buy something so expensive for such a frivolous reason as that. "I only need you. You're enough for me."

Moving a hand up her body to cup her cheek, he said, "And that's exactly why I want to give you everything."

She laughed at that, her nerves flitting away at his touch. "You already have. I have everything I could possibly want." It was true. A new wardrobe that she was sure rivaled the best-dressed woman in town, any book she could ever want to read, and he'd even opened an account for her with fifty thousand dollars at the bank. Though she never planned to touch it—or step foot near his banker, Mr. Westlake, since he was one of the men at the brothel that night—it had been a nice gesture. Hunter had even hired tutors for the children. It amazed her how good he was with them and how concerned he was with their happiness.

Even Tanner Jameson had surprised her. An older, near duplicate of Hunter, he was more care-free than she'd anticipated for a man of his wealth and influence. If there had been any hesitation on his part to accept her as his son's choice, she hadn't seen a glimmer of it. He'd welcomed the news of their engagement with open arms and had more fun than she had planning the ceremony, even insisting on a gown that cost more than she'd even known gowns could cost. She had talked him down to something simpler, something the modiste said would work well with her small frame. Something she actually liked, all the while knowing that what she wore didn't matter. She'd have married Hunter in the coarse, brown dress she'd been wearing the first time he'd kissed her as long as it meant he was hers.

"No." Shaking his head, he kissed her gently. "There's one more thing you need." Then he took her hand and led her past the stalls lining each side.

Hurrying to save the length of lace from the stable floor, she followed him. As he turned the corner at the end to the large stall in back, her breath caught, already suspecting what he planned. Using his free hand, he unlatched the door to show the mare and foal she knew lived inside. The mother snickered a soft greeting while the foal, who had been born soon after Emmy had arrived, slept at her feet in the straw, their golden coats just barely catching the light from the lantern left behind.

"The foal is yours. We'll raise her, train her, and when she's older you'll ride her." His arm tucked around her waist drawing her to his side. "I think if we do this together, it'll help you conquer your fear."

Squeezing her eyes shut, she turned her face into his shoulder. "This is too much."

He turned and brought his hands up to her face to tilt it back. "What's wrong? What do you mean?"

The concern in his eyes brought an ache to her throat so that she had to swallow several times before she could talk. "You've run out of tangible things to give me so you've moved on to the intangibles. Love, security, hope, now this. What's next?"

"Everything. Emmy, this is only a small part of what you've given me. You realize that, right?" He searched her face for the answer and must not have seen certainty, because he continued. "I love you. You've given me a life I never realized was possible."

"I love you, too. Come on." Grabbing his hand, she pulled him from the stall, pausing only long enough for him to latch the door.

"Where are we going?" But his tone was light again, he knew exactly what she wanted.

"The public wedding celebration is over as

far as I'm concerned. You've kept me waiting for two weeks—"

"I just wanted to make you miss me." He pulled her up short and dragged her close for a searing kiss.

Smiling, she slipped out of his grip and ran to the stable door, pausing to grab a length of rope looped on a hook. "Time to consummate your marriage, Mr. Jameson."

"What's the rope for?" He grinned as he stalked her. "I can assure you, you won't need it to drag me to bed." He grabbed her hips before she could dart away and pulled her flush against his body.

"You tied me up once, it's only fair that I get to return the favor."

He growled as he grabbed her hand and pulled her out the door. They ran all the way back to the house. No one approached them and they were able to slip upstairs without the ribbing she had feared. Once in the safety of his bedroom, their bedroom now, he kissed her with all the pent-up fears and longings of the past months. He was hers now, just as she was his. The way it was meant to be. The way it always would be.

* * * * *

MILLS & BOON®

& HISTORICAL

AWAKEN THE ROMANCE OF THE PAST